Monongahela Blood

By

Robert Lee Bailey

Monongahela Blood by Robert Lee Bailey

Published by Anatomy Press at Amazon

First Edition, 2013
Cover Design: Robert Lee Bailey

ISBN-13: 978-0615851389 (Anatomy Press)
ISBN-10: 061585138X

I am myself indifferent honest; but yet I could accuse me of such things that it were better my mother had not borne me: I am very proud, revengeful, ambitious, with more offences at my beck than I have thoughts to put them in, imagination to give them shape, or time to act them in. What should such fellows as I do crawling between earth and heaven?

William Shakespeare, *Hamlet*, Act 3, Scene 1

One

Byrnes had the weight of a mountain on his back. The seam had pinched down to just about thirty-six inches and it was like working under a kitchen table all day, always bumping your head and scraping your back. He'd spent all morning crawling around in the muck on his sore knees, breathing coal dust and stale air. But the company knew that the seam was thick again on the other side, and he had to work through the pinch until he got there.

He'd loaded his second ton and was drilling for his third, boring holes with a six-foot breast-auger at the coal face for his black powder shots. He leaned into the U-shaped plate and turned the hand-crank clockwise. He had just gotten the auger sharpened by the company blacksmith, and the bit twisted into the begrudging strata of bituminous coal. His loader, Butch Blizzard, lay on his side like a slug in the muck, undercutting the seam, working his pick at the base of the coal in that awkward position as far as his arms could reach. As he cut in deeper, he crawled under farther. Blizzard had propped up a sprag to prevent the seam from collapsing on him, and all that Byrnes could see of him were his legs in his damp trousers. The burning wicks on his teapot headlamp flickered in the dark chamber and cast quivering shadows on the lacquered craggy walls. The chamber was silent as a tomb save for the sound of the pickaxe hacking at coal and the unoiled squeak of the auger. They worked like that for hours, until the sputtering lamplight of an approaching miner lit up the crosscut.

Byrnes turned and used his filthy shirtsleeve to mop the skin of sweat off his brow. Blizzard wiggled his way out from under the seam and crouched and put on his soft cap and lit his headlamp. The whites of their eyes and their teeth shone like bleached bone.

"Who's there?" Byrnes called out.

"It's me," a gruff voice answered. "O'Brien."

"What do you say, Charlie?" Blizzard asked.

"Oh nothing," he said. He was down on one knee and his eyes swung around uneasily in the darkness of the chamber as though he'd never been underground before. "Is the meeting still on for tonight?"

Blizzard looked to Byrnes for his answer.

He spat dryly on the floor and smiled at him. "You bet."

O'Brien shook his head gravely. He had been gnawing at his fingernail. "A lot of the boys are worried about what's gonna happen, Byrnes," he said. "There's a lot a talk going around."

"What about?"

"Look, I've been here longer than you. And it's been peaceful. And you don't want to stir up trouble. Call the meeting off tonight."

"It's been peaceful?" Byrnes snorted incredulously. "I saw a mine-guard knock Zelinski's teeth out for complaining about how thin the butcher sliced his meat in the company store."

"There's no need for you to be a martyr…" O'Brien chewed at his fingernail again and looked to Blizzard for support, but he had taken up a rusty file and was sharpening the pickaxe, refusing to look up from his task at hand.

Byrnes spat into the corner. "Will you be there tonight or not?"

"What about your boy?" O'Brien asked. "What'll happen to him without you?"

"Are you telling me how to raise my own son?"

"I just wanted to tell you myself I'm out," O'Brien said. "I got a family to feed, and I'm not getting blacklisted."

"Why am I not surprised?" Byrnes said.

"I'll see you later, Butch."

When the light of O'Brien's headlamp had faded into the darkness, Byrnes returned to the breast auger and resumed drilling his last hole. "You can't expect any help from such a goddamn dirty coward," he said. He cranked the auger and it jammed against a piece of slate. He struggled against it, grunting and gritting his teeth. He spun it back and cranked it in again, the whiteness of his clenched teeth showing against his coal-black face. Finally he gave up and withdrew the auger. "To hell with it," he said. "That's good enough. Let's bring her down."

*

The miners emerged from the shaft at Elsinore just as the red sun faded like a slash of blood behind the Appalachians. Their leather caps sagged over their coal black faces as they walked, carrying their tin lunch buckets past the breaker down the guttered dirt road. Byrnes's damp clothes clung to the skin, and when the wind gusted he shivered and pinched his coat collar tight around his neck. He was not yet at the bottom of the hill when his boy Daniel came running past, dusted coal-black from head to toe, wearing an oversized black cap. Byrnes snatched him by the arm and held him there.

"Aren't you going to say hello to your father?"

Daniel seemed incapable of looking his father in the eye. "Are you coming home?"

"Not just now. The Union is meeting tonight."

"And then you'll come home?"

"Yes, after," he said. "You'd better be in bed by the time I get home. I don't want to find you waiting for me outside the tavern again like last time."

"I don't want you to go. Please. Everyone's saying... "

Byrnes stopped got down on one knee so that he was eyelevel with his son. "Hey, look at me. Don't you ever beg, you hear? Not me, not anyone."

Daniel looked down. One of his shoes was untied.

"And don't worry about what everyone's saying," his father told him. "Sometimes there are things a man has to do, even when everyone tells him he's wrong. When they tell him he can't do it. But in his heart of hearts he knows it's the right thing to do. So he does it. Even if he's afraid. You'll learn that someday. You understand?"

"Yes," Daniel muttered without looking up.

"Good boy." Byrnes stood up, ruffling his hair. "Now go home. I'll be there soon."

*

The tavern took on an odor of the mine as they came in from the cold with their clothes sagging and sopping wet, a hard-bitten lot who drank and fought and gambled and whored. The oldest among them wheezed and coughed with lungs full of dust. They could scarcely keep their sunken eyes open after slopping around all day in chambers flooded with sulfurous water, bent double swinging picks with six inches of clearance all day, the slate roof scraping at their backs, the endless drudgery of the pick and shovel. Old timers fumbled with crooked arthritic fingers, stuffing their tobacco pipes. By now, the evening was well advanced and a light snow had begun to fall. Byrnes stood at the bottom of the staircase with his elbow propped on the banister. He sipped slowly at a frothy beer, and if he had any apprehension about addressing that rough crowd his face showed no indication of it.

Adam Burke, the company doctor who moonlighted as the camp bartender, filled pint glasses with straw-colored beer and poured amber shots of bad whiskey. He always kept two glass specimen jars prominently displayed in front of the barroom mirror, both filled with an eerie, yellow formaldehyde solution. The first was the liver of a healthy young miner who had died in a flood, and it was unpleasant enough to behold when you were trying to unwind after digging coal all day, but it was nothing compared to its companion, the swollen liver of an old miner who had died of delirium tremens. They were a kind of memento mori, and Burke had hoped the boys would cut back on their drinking, but instead they all just drank more to forget what they probably looked like on the inside.

An ash gray mutt lay curled on the floor by the bar, wagging her tail erratically, sweeping it across the dusty floor, watching Byrnes with her sad-looking eyes. Butch Blizzard pounded his fist on a table top, rattling the half empty glasses. The crowd went silent with anticipation. "Everybody quiet down," he bellowed. "Byrnes's got the floor."

"There's a cold wind blowing through the camp tonight," Byrnes began. "It'll be another hard winter for us. Working ten hour days. Getting cheated by the company. The check weighman will knock our pay because he says there's a couple a pieces of slate in the car. We'll get that same sick feeling in the gut when pay day comes. They'll tell us we owe them for a can of black powder or for getting a pick sharpened at the smithy, or for our bills at the company store where they charge us twice what we could be paying down in Monongahela."

"None of that's going to change if we don't organize. I can tell you that." His eyes wandered across the crowd. "How many of us came from the old country, thinking we'd make a decent living for our honest work, only to find out we were denied our God given rights. Where is the liberty we are told we have? The company makes it so a miner is a miner from the day he's born. It's all most of us have ever known. Our school was the breaker, the tipple, the shaft, and the chamber. Your dad's a miner. Your brother's a miner. And they make damn sure you can't do anything else. Is that freedom? We work in *his* mine. We live in *his* house. On Sunday we go to hear *his* preacher. And when we die we are buried in *his* cemetery…"

His eyes raked across the room and he shook his head with grave deliberation.

"And still we do nothing to stop the injustices we suffer every day of our lives," he said. "Some of you say it's a battle that can't be won. Some of you say the strikers in the anthracite fields were all defeated and things will be no different here if we strike." He paused and studied their tired-looking faces. "But I'm here to tell you we cannot be defeated. Our time has come. Our time is now!

"I know you're all brave men. But when the time comes, will you fight as well as you work? Are you done letting him and his thugs push us around? Are you done living in fear? Are you done suffering so that Jack Carver…"

He stopped midsentence when he heard the scratch of the dog's claws on the floorboards as she rose up on her haunches and her hackles went up. She bared her teeth and had begun to snarl viciously at something across the room. Heads turned, a murmur passing through the begrimed crowd.

"He done did it now," someone said ruefully.

The dark figure looming in the doorway shifted. And then he stepped forward into the lamplight. Jack Carver was followed by two deputies armed with carbine rifles. The miners fell silent. No sound save for the snarling dog. Carver took off his hat and brushed away the dust of snow and then dipped his head slightly to replace the hat. He was packing a huge .45 Schofield in his holster and had a glare that was dangerous enough to unnerve the boldest, poker-faced gambler in the worst kind of riverside saloon.

In the quavering lamplight, you could just make out the scar, stretching from ear to ear, that showed where his throat had been slit. People said he had come to Monongahela from the Colorado coal fields to evade the warrants out for his arrest. They said he had started the Elsinore Coal Company with nothing but a rusty pick, a borrowed harness, and a mule. Now he was one of the richest men in Washington County, though you wouldn't know it by looking at him in his mud-spattered boots and rugged denims. And if he had been running from the law, now he was the law.

He approached the bar with his thumb hooked behind his belt buckle, the room silent, heavy boot falls thudding on the wooden floorboards. The snarling mutt stood her ground until Carver's gaze fell upon her and she quieted and slunk off behind the bar, her tail tucked between her hind legs.

"Suffering?" he asked. "These men don't suffer. Hell, half of them don't even speak English." He turned to the bar and poured himself a shot of whiskey and rifled it down his throat. "And what's this about God-given rights? What do you know about God? You supposed to be some kind of prophet, Byrnes? Does God talk to drunken Irish louts?" He poured and drank another whiskey. His back had been turned to the room, but now he turned to address them. "I been listening and I think what you got—what all of you got—is exactly what God wants you to have." He leaned and spat on the floor and then looked up again. "Or maybe God just don't give a damn."

"You think everyone's afraid of you." Byrnes tapped his finger to his chest. "I'm not afraid."

Jack Carver laughed with delight. He sniffed around and inspected the bottoms of his boots. "Jesus Christ, boys, it's getting deep in here. It stinks like someone dumped a fresh load of manure on my boots." He looked at Byrnes. "If you say one more goddamned word, I'll asphyxiate from the bullshit."

The deputies behind him erupted with paroxysms of laughter.

"I speak for those who are afraid to speak for themselves," Byrnes said. "And there's a lot that remains to be said..."

"You've said enough for tonight," Carver observed. Then turning to the miners: "If you all want to keep your jobs, then I suggest you get the hell out of here."

Gradually, shamefacedly, the miners abandoned their seats and shambled out of the tavern. The deputies lowered their carbines and let them rest in the crooks of their arms. Behind the bar, Burke polished the same glass endlessly with a white towel. More miners stood up and walked out, shaking their heads disappointedly.

The tavern was empty now save for Byrnes and Jack Carver and his deputies. Burke poured their whiskies. Byrnes stood at his end of the bar holding the empty pint glass, looking straight ahead at himself in the long mirror behind the bar, brooding. "Give me a whiskey," he called out.

The bartender went to him. "Byrnes, I think you should just get the hell out of here."

"Give me a whiskey and then I'm going home."

Burke sighed and found the bottle he wanted and fetched a tumbler and poured it full. Byrnes swirled it, sniffing the faint aroma of vanilla and honey under his nose, taking that first sip, then another, a long slow pull. He glanced down the bar to where Carver stood sideways against the bar with his thumb tucked in his ammunition belt, his holstered revolver hanging at his hip.

Byrnes downed what was left of the whiskey with a swift gulp. He stood up, counting out a handful of the scrip coins that were stamped with the Elsinore Coal Company name. He slapped the coins down on the bar and thanked the bartender. He moved down the bar slowly, approaching Carver, who was laughing with his deputies as he raised another shot. But when he turned around to meet Byrnes, the jaunty smirk drained swiftly from his face.

"You look like you got something on your mind?"

"The Union's here to stay, Carver. And if it comes to blood then it comes to blood."

"Is that right?"

"That's right."

"Well, all right then."

The gunshot left Byrnes's ears ringing. The two of them came close together in an ill-shapen embrace. Byrnes staggered back a few steps, holding his gut with a look of complete astonishment, and then he bumped into the bar. A bone-handled knife dropped to the floor. He seemed to be in the act of sitting, but instead he fell heavily on the floor and there he remained with his back propped up against the bar, a puddle of blood spreading out across the hardwood floor.

"You saw him," Carver said. "He pulled a knife."

"I didn't see no knife," Burke said. He moved forward towards the bar and one of the deputies leveled his rifle at his chest and the bartender stopped suddenly and held his hands up.

"I know what you got under that bar," the deputy said. "Now, you just keep yer ass against that wall."

"I'm a doctor," Burke pleaded. "Lemme see if I can help him."

"That's all right, doc, we'll see to him," the deputy warned.

Byrnes squirmed on the floor. His boot-heels, kicking slashes across the floor, toppled a ladder-back chair at the poker table. He gritted his teeth and then he looked at the blood soaked shirt clinging to his gut and his face went pale white. "Oh god," he muttered, his eyes rolling about. "Daniel... *Daniel*..."

"You see, boys, when you lose all that blood you start talking nonsense." The sheriff squatted on his haunches so he was eye-level with Byrnes. "Do you understand why I'm doing this, Byrnes? I've been waiting for this. You've been pissing in my ears about this Union of yours for so damn long." He sheriff drew his revolver again and drew back the hammer. He leaned in closer and whispered hoarsely in his ear, "Now it's my turn. Now I'm puttin' a bullet in your ear."

Byrnes never heard the second gunshot. He saw a white hot flash just as the bullet entered his ear, mushroomed through his brain, and exploded through the bone on the other side of his head. He stared vacantly up at the ceiling. Carver wiped his nose with his knuckle and turned to the bar, leaving nickels and dimes for the whiskey he drank.

"I didn't mean to make a mess on your floor," he said to Burke. He took a billfold from his shirt pocket and unclipped it and flipped through the bills. He tossed it on the bar nonchalantly and the money scattered. "If I hear people talking about this," he said. "I'm going to know it was you."

"Jack, I won't say nothing. That's the gospel truth on that."

"Anyone asks, you say Byrnes got on the last train out of town. Said he was lighting out for the territories."

"I can do that," Burke stuttered. "But—well—what about his little boy, Jack?"

"What about him?"

"People are going to ask questions if they hear Byrnes left without…"

"I'll take care of it."

"Jack, it weighs on my conscience, knowing…"

"Why, now, what kind of monster do you think I am?" he interrupted.

Burke laughed nervously. "For a second there, I thought you meant…"

"Yeah, yeah, yeah, go get your scrub brush." Then he looked at the deputies and wagged his finger at the body. "This son-of-a-bitch needs to disappear."

"What do you want us to do with him?"

"Make him disappear."

*

Daniel was there waiting for his father on the portico when Carver emerged, pulling on his riding gloves. Few and far between were the

13

men who looked Carver in the eye and yet here was a child whose gaze he refused to meet. He looked out into the night. His breath clouded in the cold and he saw the windows in the miners' shanties glowing yellow with coal-oil lamps through the wind-crippled tree limbs. His deputies had begun to unhitch their horses and climb into their saddles and tuck their rifles in their saddle scabbards. Carver tried to find words. He could tell Daniel was a breaker boy by looking at his coal-dirty hands.

"You all alone now?"

He waited but Daniel never answered him.

"Yeah, you're all alone," he decided. His deputies were watching and waiting. He looked out again into the thick darkness and could hear the misery in the sound of the wind. He leaned and spat off the porch. "If it don't kill you, it'll make you one mean assed son of a bitch." He looked into the boy's eyes. "You don't look like you kill easy."

Two

Daniel looked like his father now. But if he was a man, he was scarcely older than a boy. He'd long since left the orphanage behind, but his mind stayed shackled to the past. Days of iniquity, days of supplication and lamentable destitution. Nights of self-poisoned misery and ceaseless inebriation. He worked as a blacksmith's apprentice along the banks of the Little Schuylkill River south of Broad Mountain, finding fleeting solace in the dark shop, a clean fire spitting from the black caldera of coal. The old smith admired his prodigious craftsmanship. The molten iron wrought with the blows of his hammer. Releasing his innate hostilities through pounding the iron. Sweat shining on soiled skin. His drinking began when the work ended and continued without respite until he was sick and delirious.

He lived like that, finding work, losing it, fighting, gambling, and getting arrested. He did whatever he needed to do to get from one wretched day to the next. And then he began to hear voices in his sleep, often his father's, never actually seeing his face because he couldn't remember it, and he would wake in the predawn dark from the half-remembered dream, expecting to see him sitting there on the edge of his bed. But the moon-dappled room would always be empty. He would sit up in a cold sweat, always remembering Elsinore, something always calling him, drawing him inexplicably back—it was his home, the only one he had ever known.

He drifted across Pennsylvania in a fog of alcohol, his existence desultory and doleful, alternating through intervals of madness and sanity. His thinking turned on issues of drink, namely how to procure more of it with the least effort and minimal consequences. Foul taverns that stank of unwashed vagrants, cheap perfume, spilled liquor, and overflowing spittoons were his familiar. In the soot-black streets of Pittsburgh, churlish whores called to him from recessed doorways like amorous birds of prey, luring him towards their flats and furnished rooms. He passed a young woman, wasted by tuberculosis, lying across a doorstep, gasping for air, choking down a sip of water from

15

time to time and spitting blood into the gutter. He stopped and put a silver dollar in her palm and closed her limp fingers around it. Delusional, through her thin lips she muttered, "My father was twenty-seven years a yard master on the B. and O." Days later he saw her on the same street, dead with horseflies on her face.

Manure dotted the unpaved streets. A deliveryman passed with his thin and bony horse, calling out his wares, peddling dry goods, joining the ranks of fruit, vegetable, and dairy vendors. Wandering onward, Daniel blinked incredulously at the smoke rising up out of the dark satanic mills all along the Monongahela River. His clothes were heavy and damp, for it had been raining seven days straight. He'd been drunk for the last three of those days and had only choppy flashes of memory. Second Avenue by the river, then Liberty Avenue, a nest of alleys lined with squalid dwellings, homes barren of all affection, tenement quarters where Jewish, Italian, and black millworkers stood smoking cigarettes, watching him suspiciously. He walked among the drifters, yeggs, and pickpockets, and found cocaine and vile liquor in the slums of the city.

A barkeep slapped his hand on the bar to wake him from his drooling openmouthed sleep. "You're a young man," the barkeep said. "You got your whole life ahead of you."

Daniel lifted his head up a little and swirled his finger sarcastically in the air by his head. Then he suddenly became aware of the beer glass he clasped with the other hand even in sleep and he raised it to his lips, his throat pumping gulps of beer until it was gone.

"Why are you drinking yourself into an early grave?"

Daniel looked around blearily and didn't say anything at first. "I'm older than a lot of people who have died," he said after a while.

The bartender just shook his head and left him alone.

Later, Daniel went out into the back alley to piss in the gutter. He spent his last dollar on a half-empty bottle of whiskey which he clutched about the neck as he staggered miserably down the street, sloshing through puddles in the rain. For a while when he drank, he was quiet and composed. But each drink deepened his loneliness, his

16

contempt for humanity. He grew erratic. Half-crazy. You couldn't tell what would set him off. He returned to the bar and put his head down on the bar.

When he woke up again, there was an old drunk with an aquiline nose on the barstool beside him, his fly unbuttoned, grinning fiendishly at Daniel's boyish face, stroking himself under the bar. Immediately, Daniel jumped up and throttled him. He threw him out into the street where he got on top of him and began beating him with increasing fury, cursing and motherfucking him through his teeth. He cut his knuckles on the old man's teeth and smashed his nose.

It was broad daylight, around one in the afternoon, and a police officer patrolling Liberty Avenue heard the commotion and blew his whistle. By the time he got there, the blood had spread out across the wet street around the old man's face. The officer got his nightstick under Daniel's chin and hauled him off. Whether from excessive drink or the nightstick choking him or the sheer exertion of his outburst, he went unconscious. The old man rolled this way and that on his back, groaning, his bloody tongue worming behind his broken teeth.

Hours later at Western Penitentiary, the guards threw a bucket of cold water over Daniel's head to wake him. He stripped out of his clothes and stood pale and naked in the dark under the guard's supervision. His head felt like it was being crushed in a vise. He looked up at the guard who was waiting to take him to his cell. "What did I ever do to deserve this?"

"They said you nearly killed an old man."

Daniel mumbled drunkenly.

"That's what they said."

"Why?"

"That's what I was just wondering."

"He gonna die?"

"No," the guard said. "He's in the infirmary getting stitched up. You just happened to do what you done right in front of a police officer."

"Well," Daniel said, "sounds like my luck."

Once he sobered up and his stomach settled, he was hungry, having eaten little or no solid food in the past three days. But there wasn't enough food to go around in the penitentiary. They only gave the men enough food to keep them alive. For as long as he was there, three months, he was always hungry. He was never warm. He learned to steal what food he needed to survive and to fight for what he couldn't steal. He had always been meager, but now he was frail and sickly looking, with dark circles under his wild eyes, living like a rat in a sewer. He hardly ever slept because he was too paranoid, and so he was always tired. He passed the time by reading an old torn King James Bible, the only book available to him. When it rained, water dripped from the splintering fissured ceiling and fell on the thin pages. *Every way of a man is right in his own eyes: but the Lord pondereth the hearts.*

*

Then the snow came and they sent him back out into the world. Though by then, he had long been in a mind of winter. The only constant in his life was isolation, and the thought of suicide surfaced perpetually in the bubbling cauldron of his mind. Before he left Pittsburgh, he encountered an old peddler, selling his odd wares out of a wagon by the river. Daniel perused the little brown glass bottles, tinctures of herbs in alcohol, various cure-alls, laudanum and other opiates. He found one tiny vial of white powder, thinking it was cocaine.

"What's this?" he asked.

"Poison."

"Will it kill a man?"

"It's for killing rats," the peddler said, shrugging.

"What's the difference between a man and a rat?"

"I don't know," the peddler answered.

"Neither do I."

*

When Daniel got off the train in Monongahela City he was utterly destitute and he had a cold and snuffled loudly. He was shocked to see how it had grown. What had once been a rural community with dirt roads was now a bustling town with the Anton Brewing Company on one end and the Catsburg Mine on the other. In between there were hotels, brothels, saloons, a bank, six churches, a public school, a glass company, a saw mill, a lumber company, and a foundry. The *Daily Independent* was the local paper. Fresh killed deer hung from meat hooks outside the butcher's shop. Invalids panhandled at the train station. People came looking for work, usually found it in the mines, or if not, moved on towards Pittsburgh.

If he had merely been looking for work, Daniel could have found it there in town. But he was going home. He had old scores to settle. The Elsinore mining camp was up in the hills, about three miles away from the river. It was below the Van Voohris dam that had been built in 1836. It sprung leaks after every hard rain, and they patched it with mud and straw. Folks went there to fish in the summers on Amleth Lake. But other than that it was just miners and their families, the odd moonshiner, a few scattered farms. There was a railroad that snaked up along Pigeon Creek to the camp, but Daniel didn't have enough money for the fare so he had to walk.

For some time now the tracks had been silent and swept with snow. The air had a winter's edge to it. The skin of his knuckles had cracked and bled. Daniel walked on, guided by the manacles and chains of fate. He came upon a turkey vulture perched on the open ribcage of a deer carcass. The vivid memories he cherished from childhood of the valley's ceaseless springtime verdure were now at variance with the world in which he walked as a young man, a rotten world in constant decay.

He was weary and fatigued from traveling through the bleak barren rolling hills of Pennsylvania, carrying only his Bible, which he kept from the penitentiary, its thin pages dog-eared, torn, and stained with blood. As he walked through the snow, lightheaded with hunger, strange feverish thoughts gave him pause. He hadn't slept for three days and he rarely slept more than a few hours each night. From time

19

to time, he stopped to rest. The sky was tempered steel, cold and hard-looking, a murky stratum of clouds.

The swollen brown creek below the embankment gushed around ice-glazed rocks and steam rose off the eddying water. He produced from his coat pocket a half pint of rye whisky, all but empty, and cocked his head back to get at the dregs. He wiped his lips on the back of his hand and cast the empty bottle into the thicket. On the hillside across Pigeon Creek, fretful deer looked up silently from their foraging and suddenly fled, taking long, graceful leaps over the fallen logs, their hooves stirring up the detritus and rustling the dead leaves. He turned again to the railroad tracks. He wasn't far now. A glossy-feathered blackbird cawed from its bare ruined choir of tree limbs. The blackened wood of the tipple peaked above the treetops, and he heard the droning of the crusher rolls, the lowing of cows at Beazell's farm. His childhood at Elsinore he remembered as if it were a vanishing dream.

Daniel figured it must have been going on five o'clock as the horizon was bruised with twilight. When he saw the loading dock behind the Elsinore company store, he made his way through the thick chokecherry bushes and negotiated a narrow path down the railroad embankment. He was finally home for the first time in twelve years.

The mine was on the eastern side of the creek. The seven-story black tipple loomed over the land, a towering structure of blackened wood with an abundance of grimy windows at unusual points. It stood above the mouth of the slope mine from which car after car came dragging and creaking up an inclined cable. The coal was cleaned and sorted here before being loaded on a train of begrimed coal cars waiting below the breaker. Nearby a mighty hill of culm, heaps of waste from the mine, smoked silently. Adjacent to the breaker was the engine-house with its four tall black chimneys, surrounded by clusters of sheds and machine-shops.

Below the colliery were the company store, the tavern, and the train depot. There was a red oxide covered bridge that took you across Pigeon Creek to the patch, where the miners lived in identical rows of company double-houses, a few raw-board shacks, and a boarding house. Daniel dug his pale bloodless hands into his pockets to find warmth as he walked on, hunched like a beggar burdened by heavy thoughts on such a cold and grim day.

He went into the company store, which doubled as the small town's post office. Browsing the aisles of canned goods, Daniel realized he couldn't remember when he had last eaten a decent cooked meal. He perused the bottles of cough syrup, wine tonic and dyspeptic medicine, anything to alleviate his perpetual nausea.

The mousy, bucktoothed clerk, Cyrus Swank, a living specimen of human mold who was known to open and read the miners' mail on a regular basis, looked up from a dog-eared Sears Roebuck catalogue on the countertop. He had sweaty palms and urine-colored sweat stains around the armpits of his white cotton shirt. There was a wall of stacked canned goods and mason jars on the shelves behind him.

"How can I be of assistance?" Swank asked.

"I'm looking for work. I'm a blacksmith."

"An *American* accent—how increasingly rare these days—and here I took you for another degenerate squarehead." Swank rubbed his knuckle back and forth under his nose, scratching an itch. Then raising an eyebrow skeptically, "How many years of experience have you got?"

"About six years," Daniel said.

The snarky merchant snorted doubtfully. "Of course you do. Do you have any papers?"

"Got robbed at the train station in Monongahela. Lost everything I had but the clothes I was wearing."

"How unfortunate…" He returned to his Sears-Roebuck catalogue. "I'm sorry. I can't help you."

"I'm a damn good blacksmith."

"But you're not a good liar," Swank said without looking up.

Daniel dug his hand into his pocket and produced a bill fold. Tenaciously, he slapped down every last dollar he had, right in the middle of the catalogue. Swank pinched his brow and looked up. "What's this, sir?"

"My papers... I guess I didn't lose them after all."

Swank raised his eyebrows, bit his lower lip with his buckteeth, and hurriedly, like a rodent, tucked the bribe in his pocket. "What a fortuitous turn of events," he said. "Name, please?"

"Daniel."

"Would you happen to have a last name kid?"

"Yeah…"

"Well, what is it?"

"Cavanaugh."

"Daniel Cavanaugh," Swank repeated. "Can you read?"

"Well, the big words tend to throw me," Daniel snapped back, "But I know how to make my fucking mark if that's what the fuck you're worried about."

"A mere formality, let's not let matters take a contentious turn." He reached under the counter and produced an official company contract. He pushed it across the countertop and offered his pen. "Sign the bottom. Read it if you desire."

Daniel gave him a look and then took the pen, dipped it in the inkwell, and signed the contract. It said *Elsinore Coal Company* in an elaborate bold font across the top. He signed it, pushed it back. Swank stamped, initialed, and filed the sheet of paper.

"I'll pass this on to Mr. O'Brien."

From there Daniel went straight to the tavern. His boot soles clapped up the three wooden steps to the portico where floorboards warped with moisture curved their backs, exposing rusty nails like serpent's fangs. Stepping into the lamp-lit warmth, the coal stove fogging the windows, he smelled sawdust on the floor and the reek of stale booze.

Not since the nights of his youth had he been to this tavern and yet he remembered well its golden hued lamplight, the rough-sawed maple wood wallboards. The tavern was empty save for a lone white-bearded old man snoring in his chair, a pair of crutches propped against the table where he sat. Then he noticed the old man's left leg was gone from the knee down. Daniel walked quietly over to the iron-black potbelly furnace and put his palms up to thaw out his frozen hands. He opened his palms and closed his bony fists repeatedly. The flesh of his hands and his boyish bearded face thawed and reddened. He went over to the bar and called out hello, but no one answered and his eyes wandered to the human livers, as vile as ever, still on display in the dusty specimen jars.

Looking down at the floor, he saw that he was standing in a dried rust-colored bloodstain, his father's blood. His memory flashed back to that winter now outside this selfsame tavern when the sheriff confronted him on the porch. He felt the bloodbeat of revenge slamming his heart against his chest. Daniel moved a few paces down to the corner of the bar, where he didn't have to confront his own miserable reflection in the barroom mirror.

Adam Burke staggered out of the backroom, his horseshoe moustache twitching under his bulbous whiskey nose. He opened his eyes widely, then closed them tightly shut, pinched his nose between the eyes, and stood there for a moment. "Mother of God," he said. And then he rubbed his drink-galled eyes and poured himself a shot and raised it crudely to his lips with trembling hands. He poured another shot of whiskey and tossed it down his gullet and afterwards slapped the side of his head repeatedly. Then he set about studying the young man before him.

"I judge by the fact that I ain't seen you before and you ain't in the mine that you're new to this pukehole?"

"I'm the new blacksmith."

"Blacksmith, huh?" He set a shot glass on the glistening bar and poured a whiskey. "This one's on me. Welcome to Elsinore."

"Thanks."

"Looks like you need it."

They drank their shots, and Burke said, "That's a whiskey that'll cure the devil's thirst. Pickles your brain, too."

"You've got one hell of a nice bloodstain on your floor," Daniel said. "I'd hate to have been that poor bastard."

"That's old blood."

"Looks like it happened yesterday."

"I tell you what," the barkeep said, propping himself up against the bar on his elbows. "I scrubbed and scrubbed at that for days. Sends the wrong message, you know? I got down on my hands and knees with a scrub brush and soap bucket working at it and for a minute it'd look like it was gone." The bartender raised his right hand up and shook his head. "I swear to Christ I'd come in the next morning, and there it was, just like it was new."

"The past just keeps coming back," Daniel said.

The barkeep poured a shot for himself and another for Daniel and he raised it up. "To hell with the past," he said.

They downed their shots and clapped the glasses down on the bar. He poured another round and they drank and it was warm inside the bar and, beyond the window glass in the fading daylight, there was the tranquil quietude of slowly falling snowflakes.

"Here comes the snow," the bartender observed.

Daniel simply nodded and turned the empty shot glass in his fingertips.

The shrill cry of the breaker whistle sounded from the hill. Only then did the drunkard asleep at his table slowly awaken, oblivious to his surroundings. He sneezed into his hand and when he opened his fingers they were slimed with snot. He got up and staggered drunkenly out the door into the unforgiving cold. Burke began to pour pint after pint of beer, though the place was empty, and arrange the frothy overflowing glasses in a neat line along the bar.

Shortly after, the first of the tired-looking miners entered the tavern wearing their heavy work-soiled boots and grimed scowling faces. Each of them carried a tin lunch bucket and they all smoked and drank. The tavern soon smelled like the mine and it filled with tobacco smoke as they lit their cigarettes. They spoke in short staccato sentences, whiskey or beer on every breath exhaled. Some sat to games of five card stud, wages lost at the turn of a card, cursing, blaspheming, the scuffle of chairs pushed back when they went to replenish their glasses, a haze of smoke hanging in the air. Daniel drank his whiskey slowly and spoke to no one and no one spoke to him. Growing very tired, he felt a drowsy numbness.

From out of the clamorous crowd, a stray hand clasped Daniel's shoulder. He spun wildly and swatted the arm and cocked a fist. His eyes softened when he saw him. A young miner stepped back and held out his grimy palms benevolently. He had a slightly crooked nose that had been broken and never healed properly, a cowlick in his sandy blonde hair, his face all black.

"Take it easy," he stammered. "Thought I knew you."

"You don't know me."

"You ain't from around here?"

"I said you don't fucking know me."

The young miner looked him over quickly. Their eyes met. "All right," he said. "I don't know you. I ain't looking for trouble. Let me buy you a drink."

"I ain't much in the habit of letting strangers buy me my drinks."

"And what if we weren't strangers? Would you have a drink?"

"Maybe."

"You remember what happened to my nose?"

"What?"

"I said you know what happened to my nose?"

"Probably wouldn't shut up, so someone shut you up."

"That's not how I remember it," Michael said. "The way I remember it, we worked together in the breaker, and we all thought you were a mute, so I didn't think nothin' of it when I started calling you a no good weasely piss-ant behind your back. See, I used to stutter real bad, and I figured the other kids wouldn't bother me so much if I got 'em started on you. Turned out you could hear just fine. Had ears like a fox. Figured that out when you chased me outside the breaker and broke my nose."

"So it's just like I said... You wouldn't shut up."

25

Michael grinned. "What are you drinking?"

Daniel found his glass and raised it to his lips. "Whatever I can get my hands on."

"Well, stranger," he said. "We got that in common."

They waited while the bartender refilled their drinks and for a minute neither one said anything. Then Michael broke the silence again. "I never thought I'd see you in this pukehole again," Michael said.

"I guess you thought wrong."

As Michael drank his beer, he scrutinized the ravages of time in Daniel's hardened visage. The bone-white strands of hair showing in his thick dark hair, the bags sagging under his eyes. He would have recognized those same mad-looking eyes anywhere. "I'll tell you what, friend. We're getting old fast," he said. "I come home so tired some nights I can't pull my damn boots off. Some days I'd rather put a bullet in my head than go down in the pit another day."

Daniel's eyes were fixated on the floor boards, staring at the old traces of his father's gore as the miners stepped on it without even seeming to notice it. He was hardly listening to Michael, lost in his own thoughts when another miner approached them.

Big and broad-shouldered with hands like bear paws, Butch Blizzard wore an eye patch ever since he lost an eye in a blasting accident. He had lit his squib and hollered fire in the hole, but when the shots didn't go off he went back into the chamber to investigate and they went off. Now he considered himself uncommonly lucky.

"Blizzard, I want to introduce you to someone," Michael said, reaching his arm around the miner's shoulder.

"We've been expecting you," Blizzard said to Daniel.

"The hell you talking about?" Daniel asked.

Michael cleared his throat. "This ain't our Union guy, Blizzard."

"Who the hell is this then?" Blizzard picked up a shot from the bar and tossed it down his gullet.

Michael gave the room a quick once over and spoke so low you could hardly hear him. "This is Davie Byrnes's son." He said the name

26

Byrnes with profound reverence as if he was speaking of a saint who had once walked among them.

"Bullshit."

Daniel snorted and shook his head. "Why don't you just tell everyone in the place."

Blizzard looked at Michael. "You're serious, aren't you?"

"Let's go have a smoke on the porch," Blizzard said. "Take the air."

Outside, the coal-black firmament glittered with the pointillism of a thousand selfsame stars. The air was crisp and chilly. In the eaves of the building, old brittle wasp nests still hung from the summer. Michael cupped his hand around his cigarette as he lit it with a match. Daniel leaned and spat over the banister and then stooped over and produced an old bone-handled knife he'd kept concealed in his boot. It was his father's knife. The blade had a mirror shine to it.

"You know what I came back for, don't you?"

"I have a pretty damn good idea."

"The sheriff… I aim to kill him."

Blizzard scratched a match on the banister and lit his cigarette. His eyes narrowed, his interest piqued. But Michael just crossed his arms and shook his head, trying not to sound condescending. "Do you even know what you're saying, bud?"

"You're going to try to talk me out of it?"

"Listen," Michael said, "I don't want to tell you what to do, but I will tell you this right now. If you have at that man, I guarantee you'll get your throat cut. And that's the gospel truth on that. You goddamn don't know what you're up against."

"You don't think I've thought about that? Well, let me tell you something. That man took the only family I ever had. And you don't even know. Don't come talking to me about getting my throat cut. I can't tell you how many times I had a pistol to my temple. I didn't have the guts to do it. Well I'm going to do this. I don't care if Carver is Satan walking the earth: I aim to kill him."

27

Michael took the cigarette out of his mouth. "Well, you might as well be Jesus Christ, because he'll nail you to the cross."

"Maybe he will," Daniel said. He fished a cigarette out of his shirt pocket and lit it with a match. "At least I have the guts to try."

"You're not going to try to do it tonight, are you?"

"Whenever it happens, it happens."

"You need some sort of a plan," Blizzard said. The smoke of his cigarette swirled in front of his black eye patch. "Come with us to Belladonna's Saloon over in Monongahela."

"What the hell would I want to go there for?"

"You need to get your head cleared. Here, look. I got these." Michael produced from his pocket two brass tokens, each stamped with a slogan: Good for one screw at Belladonna's Saloon. "One for me and one for you."

Daniel made a sound of disgust in his throat. "I'm not interested."

Michael shot him a glance with one eyebrow cocked. "You been with a girl before, haven't you?"

"Fuck you."

"You might be a little less edgy if you got your joint worked on," Michael speculated.

Daniel took a drag on his cigarette, his eyes narrowing.

"Look here," Michael said, "the sheriff, he's always there. Hell, he owns the place. I'll loan you the money to go if you just promise not to do anything tonight. Just watch him. See what you're up against. But don't go doing anything crazy, you hear?"

Daniel kicked his boot toe at the roughsawed banister of the porch. "You're sure he'll be there?"

"Like I said, he owns the place."

"Supposing I was to borrow a couple bucks. You won't care if I don't pay you back until next week?"

Without even answering, Michael grabbed Daniel by the arm and tugged him along. "Come on, boys. We got a train to catch."

*

Back in Monongahela City, they stood at the bar at Belladonna's Saloon sipping whiskey with the lion-headed Irish drinkers carousing in the brothel, a pall of tobacco smoke hanging in the parlor room's stagnant air. There were colored glass doors in the vestibule, a light shining through the scarlet glass panels, an Oriental rug on the floor. The ember on the end of Daniel's cigarette glowed as he pulled on it, his eyes narrowing in the smoke. The iniquity in the room was almost palpable. There was not enough lamplight and the bedizened whores peered out of the darkness. Some of the whores hung on the arms of unkempt miners and others lounged on davenports and heavy Victorian furniture with their stocking legs spread wide apart. In the back of the parlor, desperate gambling men, who would later explain their losses to their incredulous wives with various forms of illogic and half-truths, lost wages at rigged faro games. When Daniel glanced over his shoulder, a girl who looked to be about fifteen, with a black eye in the yellow stage of healing, held his gaze with a salacious, daring wink and a coquettish smile. He blushed and turned back to his drink, noticing that he was drunk, the music harsh in his ears. Seated at the parlor piano, which was badly out of tune, a drunken pianist played his rags too loud, grinning and red-faced with inebriated abandon, melodies clinking along the keys, his drunken fingers stumbling on the wrong notes, the chords swinging in thrilled syncopation.

They clapped their empty glasses down on the bar and the barman wiped his wet hands with a white towel, raising his chin in anticipation. Blizzard made a circling gesture with his coal-dirty finger over the glasses and the barman poured them full to the brim with the brownish red whiskey. Daniel hunched over the bar and rotated the glass in his hands, eventually raising it to his lips to take a sip. Michael turned around to face the room, leaning his back against the bar, brazenly eyeing the whores, pushing the brim of his soft cap back with his knuckle so that his sandy blonde hair fell across his forehead.

"I won twenty dollars on the wheel one night here," Michael bragged. "Must've lost twice as much trying to do it again."

"I wouldn't mind getting in on a game of poker," Daniel said.

Then Michael turned around abruptly so that he was facing the barroom mirror. He elbowed Daniel in the ribs. He gave the room a quick once over and lowered his voice so as to be scarcely audible. "Don't look now, but there he is."

Daniel glanced up at the mirror, scanning the myriad faces in the dark crowded room. "I don't see him. Where is he?"

"Sitting at that table in the back with the two whores."

And Daniel saw the sheriff's face reflected in the wide mirror, his eyes gleaming under the shadow of his hat brim, diabolically staring in their direction from across the crowded parlor. "I see him." He felt the quickening bloodbeat of revenge. "Yeah, I see him. Son of a bitch looks like he hasn't aged a day since we were kids."

"Yeah, well don't do anything stupid," Blizzard warned. "This ain't the time or place. Just about everyone in here works for him in one way or another."

Then one of the plump and rosy whores came sashaying towards them. She slapped Michael on the ass. "Michael McKeeta, what's this I hear about you getting married this summer?"

"Boy, word gets around fast in a town like this. Where'd you hear something like that?"

"A little birdie told me." When she smiled, Daniel could see that a couple of her teeth were missing. The heavy influence of opium was apparent in her voice and glassy eyes.

"It's true—I'm marrying the prettiest little girl in Monongahela valley."

"Does this poor girl know what kind of trouble she's getting herself into?"

"Not yet!"

"I sure hope I don't end up losing my favorite gentleman caller," she pouted.

"Well, don't worry, I ain't married yet. And hell," he elbowed Daniel on the side of the arm, "even if I was… Shoot, where are my manners? This here is Dirty Delilah." He drank from his whiskey, grimacing as he swallowed. Then he threw his arm around her ample

30

figure and squeezed. "She's got a clock on her nightstand upstairs, and if you don't finish in less than two minutes, she doesn't charge you."

Daniel responded with a vague murmur.

"Never made it two minutes yet," Michael continued. "But I'm working up to it."

Dirty Delilah cackled and threw her hair back flirtatiously with a flick of her wrist. Michael shifted and tugged at his crotch to accommodate an increasingly conspicuous erection. Daniel shook his head and looked off into the distance.

"Well are you coming upstairs, or what, Michael?"

Michael, staring with such hunger at her brimming cleavage, might not have heard her at all by now, but as she turned and walked towards the staircase, he slapped Daniel on the shoulder, and winked, smiling slyly as if they carried a secret between them. "I'm gonna go put the dick to Dirty Delilah."

"So I'll see you in about two minutes?"

"You bet, Cowboy."

Beyond the reach of the lamplight, a dark-haired woman surveyed the parlor. She went by many names, she came from many places. She was in charge of the girls, making sure they kept themselves presentable and weren't getting hooked on dope. Whenever there was a clash among the hard-drinking miners, she could usually diffuse the situation with her cleavage, but when they were beyond the realm of reason, she kept a Derringer tucked in her brazier. There were bullet holes in the ceiling around the brass chandelier. Tonight she was watching the scarce-bearded stranger who was in turn being watched by the lethal-looking gamblers at the card table, unsubtle in their intentions. The stranger, a brooding enigma, seemed to be having a conversation inaudible to anyone save himself. She came and took Daniel by the arm, smiling at him eye to eye, her sweet perfume wafting around him. She looked at Blizzard, who took the hint.

Blizzard squeezed Daniel's shoulder. "Bud, it's payday, and I've got some socializing to do tonight."

"Why don't you have a drink with me?" the girl asked.

Daniel tossed his chin to catch the bartender's attention. "I'm not looking for company."

"You're in the wrong place if you want to be alone."

"What's your name?" she said.

"Daniel."

"Is that your real name?"

"One of them. What's yours?"

"Katherine."

"That *your* real name?"

"One of them," she said.

"Still wanna have that drink, Katherine?"

"Thought you weren't looking for company."

"I'm real fickle like that."

The bartender poured them drinks. Daniel looked over his shoulder just in time to see Delilah leading Michael by the hand towards the stairs. He risked a glance in the sheriff's direction, but found that he was gone. He craned his neck, searching the room, unable to spot him again. There was a loud-mouthed drunk at the end of the bar swaying on his feet, sipping his drink, scowling at Daniel. Katherine leaned in closer and whispered in his ear, her warm breath on his neck, sending a tingle down his spine. "Why don't you come upstairs and let me give you a hot bath?"

Daniel raised his whiskey and drank it down.

A strabismal gambler at the card table pushed a chair with his boot heel towards Daniel. His gold canine winked in the lamplight. "Interested in a run of the cards?"

He tilted his head towards the gamblers. "Looks like they're in need of a third."

"Forget about them," she said. "They'll find someone."

"They just did." Daniel took his glass and sat down with the card players, a group of lethal-looking drunks, their eyes like knives. "What are we playing?"

"It's nickel poker, dime on the pair."

An hour later, Daniel was down five dollars. "Tens," said one of the players.

"Beats me," said the other.

"It's mine," Daniel said, laying down his cards: suicide kings. "Won the dime."

"Shit, boys—that's one in a row for the kid." The strabismal man across the table spoke to him. "You ain't from around here," he said.

Daniel did not respond, no flicker in his cold eyes.

"What shithole did you crawl out of?" the card player persisted.

"Where'd you learn how to deal off the bottom of the deck like that?"

"What'd you say to me?"

"I said you've been dealing off the bottom of the deck since I sat down."

The gambler nudged the man next to him. "Tell Bobby this turd's had enough. He's drunk himself blind."

Daniel shuffled his chips, the artery thumping in his neck. "Do you have some sort of problem with me? You've been eyeballing me since I got here. You've been talking to me like I don't know how to play a game of poker, and I haven't said a word about it, but if you keep dealing off the bottom of the deck, I swear to Christ you're going to leave here tonight short of a significant quantity of blood."

The strabismal gambler's lips twisted with restrained outrage. "The hell you say."

The chairs scraped against the floor as the two stood up. The gambler flipped over the poker table with one backhanded swipe, spilling chips and scattering the deck of cards on the floor, fallen glasses shattering in pools of whiskey. As soon as the bedlam broke out, the barkeep looked to the doorman and tugged his ear and the doorman responded with a nod and went out the door. The dealer and prostitutes had backed out of the melee and were swamped by the grim-visaged miners crowding around the circling fighters, hooting and jockeying for position at the front of the crowd.

33

The fighters knuckled up and the cross-eyed man swung a fast upper cut, connecting under Daniel's chin, knocking his head back. Daniel saw a white flash when the blow landed. He regained himself and punched back, hitting him in the nose, but drawing no blood. The man's face clouded and he drew his hand across his mouth and spat. "You're gonna have to hit me a lot harder than that."

The gambler lurched and threw a left hook, then a fast right, knocking Daniel's scarce-bearded face this way and that. He staggered back one unsteady step, two. The gambler drew back and hit him below the eye. Daniel went pedaling backwards a few steps until he tumbled over.

"That's one country ass-whooping, boys," someone yelled.

Daniel tasted his own blood in his teeth. Hot stinging where a flap of skin had peeled off his bony elbow. He touched a hand gently to the back of his skull. His hair felt sticky. When he looked at the hand, it was painted blood-red. Daniel got up with a smirk, a bloody-headed half-smiling miscreant, one eye purpling, his teeth bloody behind his split lip. He put his knuckles up and they started circling again.

The miners yelled louder. Daniel sidestepped the next punch and returned with a blow to his jaw. It dazed him just enough. Daniel grabbed him by the arm and whipsawed him around, sending him crashing into a tabletop. He toppled the table and crashed to the floor amid shards of glass and spilled liquor. Daniel straddled him and plunged his thumbs into the man's clenched-shut eyes, trying to pry them out of their sockets, the gambler's hands manacled to Daniel's wrists, bared yellow teeth gnashing.

"I may have misjudged the kid," someone admitted aloud.

The shouting suddenly died down and the miners parted and the sheriff passed through them with a few heavy-booted swift strides. He grabbed Daniel by the collar and hauled him up to his feet. The sheriff stood four inches over six feet tall, towering over Daniel like a looming thunderhead.

"Get the fuck off me," Daniel shouted.

The sheriff simply flung him down to the floor. He was kneeling overtop him before Daniel even knew what was happening. He snatched a fistful of his shirt and lifted him up off his back with one tug. He jammed the cold barrel of his Schofield in Daniel's cheek.

The crowd had fallen dead silent.

The sheriff leaned in very close and whispered hoarsely in Daniel's ear. "Do you know who I am?"

Daniel was looking at the gun and then he looked up at him. "No," he said. "I don't know who you are."

The sheriff cocked the revolver and the cylinder turned and clicked into place. "The lord thy fucking god."

"Well, you've got your little tin star on your tit," Daniel said. "So you must think you are."

The sheriff's face clouded and without the slightest hesitation he pistol-whipped Daniel once across the temple with his Schofield. It knocked him out cold and he bled tremendously as head wounds are wont to do. The sheriff wiped the blood off the gunmetal on his thigh. He jammed the gun in his belt, then turned and looked at his deputies standing over the squirming, bloodied body on the floor. "How's the cross-eye doing?"

"He ain't any easier to look at, that's for sure."

"You," the sheriff said, pointing directly at Michael. Then he reached down and grabbed Daniel by the collar, still unconscious and bleeding badly from the head, and lifted him up like a pup by the scruff so that his arms dangled before him and his knees just touched the floorboards. "You know this cocksucker?"

"I-I-I..." Michael stammered. "I don't really kn-kn-know him..."

"Th-th-that ain't what I fuh-fuh-fucking heard," the sheriff mocked.

"He ain't no friend of mine," Michael said, holding his hands up in front of him as if he had a gun pointed at him.

The sheriff released Daniel, dropping him to the floor, and looked over the miners encircling him. "Is there anyone here who will claim this scrawny cocksucker?"

They turned and scattered away, each murmuring with drink in hand. Blizzard was there on the edge of the crowd, watching the scene unfold, but he kept his distance.

Then Katherine came forward from the crowd. "I'll take him upstairs, see to it that the doc comes and stiches him up."

"Since when the fuck did you become the tenderhearted type?"

"He's just a kid, Jack."

"So what do you want with him?"

"Don't you want to find out who he is? Make sure he's not with the Union?"

"Florence fucking Nightingale," the sheriff said, shaking his head. He looked at Daniel who was out cold on the floor. "He's your responsibility. If he stirs up any more shit in my joint, I won't be so fucking nice next time. And I better not find out any of these whores are giving out any free pussy while he's on the mend."

The deputies carried away the gambler as he coughed and choked on his own blood, groaning miserably. They had him by the arms and legs, his body sagging like a sack of grain between them. The sheriff walked over to the bar where the bartender chatted with one of the French prostitutes, her hair in a chignon. She got up off the stool and left when she saw the sheriff coming.

"You got something for me, Bobby?"

"Sure, Jack, just a second."

The bartender went over to the cash register and opened the drawer. He counted out a considerable sum and then closed the drawer again and held out the money. The sheriff thumbed through the bills and then tucked them in his coat pocket.

"How's your old man?" the sheriff said.

"He died two years ago, Jack."

"Lucky fucking bastard."

*

Before dawn the company doctor came to stich Daniel's scalp. He gave him a dose of laudanum. Daniel opened his eyes and found Burke sitting at his bedside with intense eyes, holding two fingers to Daniel's bone-thin wrist, watching the seconds tick by on a silver pocket watch, his horseshoe moustache twitching slightly under his nose. Burke touched a hand to Daniel's bloody forehead. Daniel's eyes slowly opened and closed as he felt the numb sensation of the needle penetrating his flesh. "We meet again," Burke said, as he pulled the needle and thread.

"Mother of God," Daniel mumbled.

Three

It snowed in the early morning. Flakes drifted slantwise in the dark beyond the warped windowpane. Even with a small fire burning in the potbelly furnace, Sheriff Carver's office was frigid. He liked it that way. Even though he felt the cold in his rheumatism when he opened and closed his fist, he liked the winters. The cold slowed the blood and he was sure that it was that brutal unforgiving Pennsylvania winter so many years ago that had saved him from bleeding out and helped him survive a wound that by all rights should have killed him dead. Maybe in a way the cold slowed time too. He let his pocket-watch dangle on its short fob as he watched the second hand moving quickly, hearing each second tick away, barely audible over the gusts of wind and crackling fire. Time was the one thing he feared. The one thing he couldn't control. Every second brought everything that lives and has blood flowing in its veins closer to its inexorable end. No matter how much power he had, no matter how many men he controlled, he didn't have power over time, and in the end death would own them all. He looked across his desk at Charlie O'Brien and his son Logan. Coffee in a tin cup steamed on his desk. The lamps sconced on the wall were all lit in the dim office, their glass flues charcoal black. He had the *Daily Independent* on the desktop folded neatly.

"All right," Carver said, "what have you got for me?"

"I gotta tell you, Jack, work was down this week. We had more drunks than usual. The price of coal is dropping. The working face is just about under Beazell's farm right now, and it's getting tight. It's barely four feet. And we're pumping out a lot of water. We're probably going to need another pump, especially when spring comes."

"Are you done?" the sheriff asked. "Are you done pissing in my ear? You know what I want to hear about."

O'Brien held out his palms and shrugged. "I haven't heard any talk about organizing, Jack. That's the god's honest truth. You do a damn good job of putting the fear of god in them boys."

"Nothing at all?"

"Not a word."

Carver glanced out the window at the breaker up on the hill. "You had a chance to talk to that new blacksmith who showed up this week?"

"What's his name—uh, Cavanaugh? Not yet."

"I gave him a little attitude adjustment last night."

"I heard about that."

"Tough one to figure, that kid… I want you to keep an eye on him. Something about him… he stares at me funny."

"I'll see what I can dig up on him."

The sheriff leaned forward over his desk. "Well, that's what I'm fucking paying you for, ain't it?"

O'Brien said nothing, but only chewed his thumbnail.

"Now…" The sheriff sighed and leaned back in his chair. "They're organizing on both sides of the county. You expect me to believe that out of three-hundred fifty miners, not one of them is talking about bringing in the Union? And for Christ's sake, take your thumb away from your goddamn mouth. You're like a child."

"I did overhear the Glemba brothers talking the other day," O'Brien said.

Charlie and Logan exchanged a sheepish glance in their arrow-back chairs.

"For God's sake, what did you overhear?"

"It was at the end of our shift, and we were riding the cars out of the mine. When we got out, it was starting to snow and so the older brother started complaining about how his pants usually froze solid by the time he got home, and he said that they would be so stiff he could prop them up in the corner until the ice melted. Then the younger one, he said that the company ought to build a wash house like they got over in Marianna so they could change out of their wet work clothes and clean up before going home."

The sheriff gestured dismissively with his hand in the air. "That's it?"

"That's all I heard them say, but I can't be certain that more wasn't said."

"This is what you bring me? Two kids bitching about a wash house? Christ, they could be rolling out a socialist newspaper right under your nose..." He turned to Logan and pointed. "And why haven't you said a goddamn word?"

"I'm their boss's son," he said. "They watch what they say around me."

The sheriff turned back to Charlie O'Brien. "A man of few words," he said. "You sure he's yours?" He poured himself a second cup of coffee. "You're an O'Brien, huh? Well, you're not much use around here, then, are you?"

He tossed his chin in the direction of his folded newspaper.

"Those goddamn *Daily Independent* bastards are still going on about the explosions down in Monongah and Jacob's Creek. People see that many dead bodies and they start pointing fingers at the operators. They start organizing.

"Now, I know for a fact," he continued, "that all up and down Pigeon Creek, the UMWA is looking for a foothold. Well, they ain't getting it here. What I need is a pair of eyes and ears in the other camps. I need to know what's coming down the line, so when it gets here I can take care of it. If you got any sense left in you, you know the last thing we need is for the all-mighty Baldwin-Felts to come to town."

O'Brien chewed at his fingernails, his eyes focusing on a point on the desktop from which they would not deviate. In the chair beside him, Logan had endured the meeting thus far with stoic composure. Then the sheriff drank the last of his coffee and went to the window, opened it, and pitched the grinds outside. He turned and looked directly at Logan.

"And since you're deadweight at Elsinore, maybe I can at least get some use out of you in Marianna. I want you to listen to who's talking Union up there, get in good with them, you understand? When you come across an organizer, and believe you me, you will, you latch onto him like a leech. I want to know everything. If he breaks wind, you better remember which way the wind was blowing. I'll be expecting a letter from you to me every other week."

The sheriff sat back in his chair and sighed, looking at Charlie. "I can see you're fucking champing at the bit Charlie, spit it out..."

"Well, Jack, a little notice in advance would be nice."

"What the fuck did I just give you?"

"I mean Logan's my eyes and ears underground. Hell, I depend on him for information."

"And what a fine fucking job the two of you were doing." The sheriff leaned forward to open the cigar box on his table, selected one, struck a match and rolled the cigar, puffing until it was lit. He blew a cloud of smoke across the table. "I got my own guy on the inside."

"You have a spy down in the pit?"

"You don't think I'd rely on you alone for that kind of business."

"Are you going to tell me who it is?"

"If there's a need for me to tell you, I'll tell you. But right now, there ain't no fucking need Charlie."

"I have to say, Jack, as the superintendent, I feel a little..."

"What?"

"Haven't I earned my keep around here? I've been giving Union scum to you for twelve years now, Jack."

"And your fucking loyalty is the only reason you're still sitting in that chair with all of your organs intact, Charlie," the sheriff barked. "You ain't exactly irreplaceable. I made you what you are today. Don't ever forget that. Don't ever forget where you fucking came from. And don't ever forget you can just as easily go back to being a two-bit nothing piece of shit."

O'Brien squirmed in his chair. He was afraid to look up. He consciously wanted to chew his thumbnail, but he was afraid to even do that. The sheriff leaned back in his chair, flicked the cigar ash off the edge of the table. He looked away and made a low guttural sound in his throat, about as close as he ever came to making an apology when he knew he had gone too far.

"And you being the superintendent and all," he added less severely, "ought to know that Liam O'Loughlin's knees are so shot he can hardly walk up the hill to his goddamn house. I don't even want to think what a pitiful sight he is underground."

"What do you want me to do about it?" O'Brien asked.

"Give him an easy job at the breaker or something, huh? Something where he can sit down all day. Christ. I don't even go down into the pit and I know more about what's going on down there than you do."

The sheriff looked out the window. More and more miners left their home, making their daily pilgrimage to the pit. He was a man seeing, unseen. His brown eyes had a glistening, dark melancholia in them. He looked back at Logan O'Brien, giving him a wave of his hand.

"Go on, you're done. Get out of here."

Charlie got up to leave, too, but Carver pointed at him. "I wasn't talking to you."

O'Brien sat back down and rubbed his hands on the edge of the armrests. The sheriff offered a cigar from the box to O'Brien. He took one, lit it, and took a puff. The silence in the room was palpable until O'Brien couldn't stand it anymore. "Damn good cigars you got, Jack."

The sheriff folded his hands on the top of his desk. He was looking intently at Charlie.

Charlie laughed uneasily. "Are we celebrating something?"

"That daughter of yours…"

"Mary Beth?"

"It's about time she got married, don't you think?"

*

Waiting for the coal cars at the mouth of the mine, O'Brien lingered outside the engine room, chewing his grimy thumbnails which now reeked of tobacco smoke, silently processing the meeting with Carver, the kind of meeting that left him feeling muddled and drained even before the workday began. There were a few Slovakian and Polish miners standing around them, smoking cigarettes, nodding off, all but sleeping on their feet. Logan struck a match to light his hand-rolled cigarette in the light of early dawn, and he said: "All in all, I think that went pretty well."

"Don't be a smartass," Charlie snapped back.

"Hey, I'm all right with going to Marianna…"

"While you're there, don't forget that they have their Coal and Iron Police, too. And they aren't going to be doing you any favors. They won't know who you are. So don't screw around while you're there. You keep your nose clean."

"I'm nineteen," Logan said. "I know how to take care of myself."

"Nineteen. What do you know?" Charlie shook his head. "Carver's lost his mind, sending you to Marianna. Thinks just because he owns this damn company he owns my whole damn family."

"You're starting to sound like one of them, you know that?"

"Like who?"

Logan nodded in the direction of the enervated miners lining up to go down into the mine. "Them."

"They don't have to put up with half of what I put up with. They wouldn't last a day in my shoes."

"Anyways, he's got a point," Logan said. "Union's got strongholds up and down the valley."

"What do you think we have to worry about? The Union? Hell, we have all the county officials in our pockets. Mark my words: as long as Carver has a breath in his body, there won't be a Union in Elsinore."

"What did he want to talk to you about after I left?"

"You weren't eavesdropping outside the door?"

"No."

"Well, then don't worry about it. It wasn't about you."

The long chain, pulled taut, disappeared into the dark mouth of the mine. And then the engine kicked in, jerking the chain, slowly retracting the iron links, and then the coal cars materialized out of the darkness.

*

Her name was Mary Beth O'Brien. Her hair the color of an autumn leaf fell around her apple-cheeks, her face lightly freckled. Her fraternal twin, Logan, had his black glistening hair slicked against his skull with pomade. He carried his black portmanteau at his side as they walked together to the train station. They were both tall and lanky, but he was a fast walker, eager to leave Elsinore, and he was continually stopping and waiting for her to catch up as she drifted along like a brittle leaf blown along by a gentle breeze. As they went under the covered bridge across Pigeon Creek, they passed Michael McKeeta walking with two other miners on their way down to the pit. He smiled at Mary Beth and touched the brim of his canvas miner's hat. After they passed one another, she glanced back over her shoulder and saw him looking back at her, smiling still, and she blushed and tucked her stray hairs behind her ears and looked down at her black lace-up boots as they walked to the station.

The conductor called out for the passengers to board the train. When they were at the platform, Logan put down the portmanteau and wrapped his arms around Mary Beth. "I want to hear from you at least once a week," he explained hurriedly, sounding as though he had drunk far too much coffee that morning. "Spend every last dollar on ink and paper and live a life of destitution, so long as you remember to write to me."

"You sound like a little breaker boy, worried to leave home..."

"Your coffee was too strong this morning. Don't make it so strong for our father while I'm gone. Our father's walking on eggshells as it is with Carver always breathing down his neck. He doesn't need you making him jittery with your coffee."

She yawned, covering her mouth with her hand. "Any more commandments for me to live by while you're gone?"

"I'll leave you with just one more." He looked at her intently. "Now that I won't be around to look out for you, a lot of these roughnecks will start coming out of the woodwork. They'll be falling all over themselves for you. So I should warn you when it comes to getting what they want—and they only want one thing—a man will say or do whatever it takes to manipulate you and convince you he's devoted entirely to you. Men my age are nothing but trouble. Don't believe any of us."

"Would you like me to live in a convent?"

"Take this seriously, Mary Beth. Men can get away with that sort of thing," he said. "But a woman, once her reputation is stained, it's stained for good. But enough of that. Here comes our father."

"Now it's your turn for a lecture," she said.

"Haven't you gotten aboard yet?" O'Brien asked. "Hurry up. They'll leave without you. Do you have your papers?"

"Of course," Logan said.

"And the money?"

He patted his coat pocket. "Every dollar."

"What about your Bible?"

"In the luggage."

"Remember," his father said, "keep your ears open there, and your mouth shut. If anyone asks you where you're from, tell them you worked out in the anthracite fields."

"I know, I know."

"Go to the tavern with everyone else after work, but only stay for one drink. You don't want your tongue loosened with liquor when you've got lies to tell."

Logan looked at his sister and rolled his eyes.

"What goes around comes around," she said.

"All right, then," O'Brien said, patting his hand on his son's shoulder. "But remember, you're my only son. You'll be the only one to carry on the family name when I'm gone. Above all else, come back alive and in one piece."

The train whistle blew. The conductor gave one last call for passengers to board. They embraced and said their final goodbyes. O'Brien and Mary Beth stood waving as he left. The train slowly rolled away, the black coal-smoke clouding up out of the smokestack, the steam whistle blowing.

They walked homeward, and for a long time there was silence between them.

"Mary Beth," he said, "what's wrong with you lately?"

"What do you mean?"

"You used to be full of confidence."

"Was I?"

"What's different?"

"I just don't feel well. You know how I get without…"

"Yes, I know, without your medicine. You're starting to sound just like your mother did. It's all in your mind is what is it is," he said. "You don't need that damn medicine. What you need is to start thinking about getting married."

"Daddy, please. Not now."

"It's always 'not now' with you." O'Brien stopped walking and took her hand. "What if something were to happen to me in the mine? What if something were to happen to your brother? Who would take care of you?"

"I can work," she said, freeing her hand and resuming their walk home.

"Listen to you," he said. "You sound like a green girl. You need only look at a young woman's body to see that it is not meant for rough work. It will be your husband's business to earn money, and yours to spend it."

"There are more important things in life than money."

"Of course there are," O'Brien agreed, "but you won't get any of them without it."

"You have it all figured out don't you?"

"You know, when your mother and I came to this valley, we had nothing but the clothes on our back and you and your brother in her womb…" Mary Beth rolled her eyes. She had easily heard the story a dozen times, his slow ascent to a position of minor authority and wealth, both of which were greatly exaggerated in his appraisal. "And I went from working for pennies in the pit with the hunkies to being their superintendent. Now I make more money in a year than twenty

46

miners. We have a nice house, our own house, which we don't have to share with another family or rent out rooms to boarders. Now I..."

"Now you want to arrange a marriage for me," she interrupted.

"Well, yes..." They had reached their home, a three-story brick house, well distanced from the pine-board shacks and shanties, the company houses, and they paused at the steps leading up to the front porch. He removed his hat and smiled. "You have captured the fancy of an honorable young man—a Catholic, needless to say—with your fragile charm, and I have given him my consent to ask your hand in marriage..."

"Who is this young man?"

"He's a miner, whom you have known since you were a child, and although he comes from a modest background, I will have him, along with your brother upon his return, promoted to bosses in the company, positions in which they will be paid respectable salaries."

"And will you tell me his name?"

"Michael McKeeta."

*

When she came into her room, she closed the door behind her and sat before the mirror of her vanity set. A great hoarder of books like her brother, she had towering stacks of them everywhere against the splintered plaster of the walls and her bookcases were all crammed full. Nightly, after the housework was done, the sweeping of coal dust from the kitchen floor, the scrubbing of Sunday clothes in the galvanized tubs, too tired even for sleeping, she would read away her insomnia until the early hours of the morning, learning by heart the great soliloquies of Shakespearean theater, of Sophocles and Aeschylus. As a doe-eyed girl in awe of the illusion of this world, self-schooled in the thespian arts, she had nurtured wild ambitions of performing on a stage before the bated breath of an audience of aesthetes somewhere, anywhere, far beyond the confines of this backwards coal town that was all she ever really knew, though by now those dreams would never come to pass. She studied herself a moment in the mirror, as if she was caught in a lover's gaze, her tight chest rising and falling with constricted and shallow quickening of her breath.

Her fingers found the two-pronged silver pin that held her hair, and she pulled it out. It was her mother's pin, and she always wore it as a token of remembrance. She brushed her hair, slowly and carefully, and when she thought about Michael, how she had turned around to look back at him and he had turned around to look back at her, she couldn't help but smile.

She opened the drawer where she kept the bottle of laudanum with its dropper and filled the bottom of a glass with the amber liquid. She swallowed it down, closed her eyes. When she opened them again, she was smiling still. She put the dark brown bottle back in its drawer and went over to her bed to lie down but not to sleep.

Four

When he woke again it was daylight, blinding and dazzling. The room was empty. He smelled cheap perfume. His heavy eyelids drowsed and shut. When he opened his eyes again he was lying in bed somewhere by candlelight and Katherine dressed in gray and black was sitting at his bedside with a damp cloth on his forehead. Another day passed as he slipped in and out of opiate sleep.

On the third day, he got out of bed in the dead hour before dawn, his head wrapped in blood-crusted bandages, and he lit a tallow candle and waited for the sunrise. He had a kind of doomed indifference in the eye that wasn't swollen shut, and watching from his second floor window above the tavern, he waited for the company doctor to come back. As he sat by the window, this malcontent of endless winter, gazing out at the thoroughfare below, he noted the way the coal miners carried themselves, their pace and posture, calculating the quiet desperation of each. Memories of the night at the brothel foggy in his mind: sudden accusations over a poker game, sudden violence. He lit a cigarette and leaned back in his chair, his eyes narrowing, his brow pinched. *If only I can be patient and calm enough*, he thought, *I could get him to let his guard down. From now on there'll be no more drinking whiskey and beer. I've done too much damage to myself for too long. I need my senses to be as sharp as my blade.. For the first time, my life has a meaning and the meaning is revenge.*

Soon, he heard the sound of knuckles lightly tapping on the door. He turned to the door.

"Come in," he said aloud.

She was beautiful but with an ugly scar on her chin, and she covered it with her hand and didn't look him in the eye. She set her bag down. "You're the one who got in a fight at the tavern last night," she said. She had a languid, honey-voiced way of speaking.

"I'm not the one who started it."

"That's not what I heard."

"Well you heard wrong," he said.

"Who are you?" she said.

"No one."

"And you came here alone?"

"Yes, alone."

"Without any family?"

"None."

"None?"

"Without any family."

"And you're here all alone?"

"Yes, alone."

"Who are you?" she persisted.

"No one," he said, a hint of a smile visible at the corners of his mouth.

"Do you remember what happened to you?"

"More than I care to."

"Do you know how you got that cut on your temple?"

"That'd have been from the butt end of the sheriff's Schofield."

"He's not someone you want to be causing trouble for."

"Well, maybe he's the one who ought to be worrying about me."

He coughed and held his fist to his lips. His tongue was parched after two days of sleep. And without needing to ask, Katherine went to the dry sink and poured from the pitcher a glass of clear water that she took to him. He drank thirstily and she watched him.

"I think I need to lie back down."

"The laudanum will do that to you." She pulled the wooden chair up to his bedside and sat down, soaking a washcloth in a basin of water and wringing it out. She dabbed at his sweaty forehead with the washcloth. "Just about every girl who comes through gets hooked on it sooner or later."

"I can see why. I could drink that stuff all day and die a happy man."

"Do you need anything else?"

"Did the doc mention whether or not I was allowed to have a little whiskey?"

"No," she said. "No whiskey."

"Good," he said. "I'm giving it up anyhow."

*

After six o'clock the miners emerged up into the twilight, riding the jerky bumpy chain of cars up out of the mineshaft from darkness to darkness, the fast fading glow of the sunset beyond the valley hills. They shuffled out of the cars, coal-black in the face, their shoulders slumped in exhaustion, heads hanging down, simian shapes carrying their empty lunch buckets. The coal came out of the mine and was weighed and recorded at the tipple. Every miner went there. There was a blackboard with his number and the tonnage of his cars scrawled in chalk.

Only a week ago, one of the Slavic miners had sent up his cars to the tipple, but when he went to the check-weighman, he was told his number wasn't on any cars that came out of the mine on that shift. Each miner had brass checks with his number on them, and he hung these checks on a hook on his loaded coal-cars before sending them up to the tipple. The check-weighman was known to take weight off cars of miners he disliked and add the weight to the cars of miners who bought him drinks and curried favor with him. Sometimes the checks would be switched by other miners. After arguing with the weighman over the weight of his cars, the miner went off cursing. Someone said they saw him drink a quart of gin straight down. They found him two hours later dead in the outhouse by the tavern.

When Blizzard saw the boisterous crowd assembled outside the raw-board office of the superintendent, he knew it could only mean bad news. As he approached the multitude, he read looks of boredom, suspicion, and agitation in their sooty faces. He produced a pouch of tobacco from his pocket and rolled a thin cigarette and licked it. He stood beside Kelvin Ekvie, the oldest of the mule drivers, the one with the most seniority. He was a jug-eared eighteen-year-old, newly married with a pregnant wife. He was prone to silliness at work in their somber underworld, known to break into dance whenever the seam was tall enough to stand, clapping and stamping and crooning tunes.

51

He made them all forget the weight of the world bearing down upon them.

"What's going on?" Blizzard asked. "Doesn't look good."

"Price of coal's down… we're doing more work for less money."

A murmur passed through the small crowd. Other miners confirmed that in addition to the wage decrease, the workday would be extended from ten to twelve hours. "It just ain't never enough," said Ekvie, shaking his head. "I'm already giving them ten hours a day. Now they want to take twelve."

*

The first paychecks with deductions were to be distributed on their next payday. The sheriff posted a proclamation at the company store and the company office reminding the miners that the homes they lived in were company property and that seditious activities would result in eviction. But the next morning at the mine, thirty or so workers, most of them mule drivers, nippers, and spraggers—under the *ad hoc* leadership of Kelvin Ekvie—stood interlocked at the arms, forming a human chain, preventing anyone or anything from entering the mine. Heated disputes broke out among the miners. The Slavs, Italians, Polish, Greeks, and other foreigners couldn't communicate with the English-speaking miners. The Slavic miners in particular were disliked for their apparent willingness to work under any conditions and for any pay.

It was a bitterly cold morning for such uncertainty. The wind felt like it was peeling the flesh off, leaving their cheeks red and numb. Though small in numbers, the wildcat strike began effectively enough. The bosses argued over the situation as snowfall accumulated on strikers' shoulders.

O'Brien stopped in his tracks when he saw them. "What in the *hell* is going on here?"

"What's it look like, boss?" Ekvie hissed.

One of the miners tried to duck under their locked arms and walk into the mine but he was met with an onslaught of kicking boots. One of the Slavs who couldn't speak English, perhaps still drunk from the night before, walked up to a driver and spat in his face. The spittle hung from his nose, a slimy glob of dangling mucous. Agitation abounded. Scuffles broke out. It was only a matter of time before he came.

*

The sheriff heard a loud knock at the door. He looked up from his *Daily Independent*, peering through a pair of wire-rimmed spectacles. He removed the glasses and placed them in the top drawer. "Yeah," he called out. The door swung open. Deputies Pearce and Spearman stood in the doorway.

"Jack, we got a situation."

"What in God's name is it now?"

"Those mule drivers started a wildcat strike going. Got all their arms locked up in a chain."

"Yeah," Spearman added. "They got their arms all like this."

The sheriff took a long drink, finishing his cup of coffee, then donned his hat. "I told them there were gonna be consequences. And now I have to fucking deal with this. Christ." He gazed out the window, the breaker distant in the snowy panorama. "Are any of them armed?"

"No, boss," said Pearce.

"Let's make this quick. It's too cold for this shit."

They rode out under the urine-colored sunlight, the deputies flanking the sheriff on either side, the three of them riding at a steady canter, stopping when they reached a certain distance from the mine.

"What's the plan?"

"The plan," the sheriff said, "is to break the fucking chain."

Pearce dismounted his horse and approached the line of strikers, the muscles in his legs bulging out of the tops of his black boots, his beard dark and thick, his eyes full of violence. The bull-necked deputy cradled a Winchester in the crook of his arm.

"How many times do we have to go through this little song and dance?" the sheriff yelled from his saddle. "Do I look like a man of infinite patience? Does your pay not come regularly enough? I don't

53

intend to freeze my ass off out here all morning. You know how this is going to end. These little fires of rebellion start up, but it'll all be forgotten in a week or two. I'm giving you one chance to disperse peacefully, to do this the easy way. And by God every one of you little pricks ought to be grateful for that chance."

Someone in the line snickered. It was one of the sardonic Glemba brothers.

Pearce stopped suddenly and turned. Brawny and well over six feet tall, he had to lean down so he was nose to nose with Glemba. "Did Mr. Carver say something funny?"

Glemba tried to look serious, resolute.

Pearce brought back the Winchester and thrust the butt end at Glemba's nose, crushing cartilage and bone. The boy's head fell back, his legs gave out beneath him and his body went slack. He would have fallen if the arms of the other boys weren't still locked with his own. He remained conscious, or at least his eyes remained open. The dark blood coursed in rivulets from his nose, staining the peach-fuzz on his upper lip.

"Any of you other piss-ants wanna laugh at what Mr. Carver's got to say?"

You could hear the crows cawing in the distance.

Pearce fired the rifle into the air, the report echoing throughout the valley. The crows lighted from the snow-crusted tree limbs. The young workers startled, the muscles in their throats pulled taut. They let the boy with the bloody broken nose fall to the hard caked dirt and dust of snow. The chain was broken. One of the Slavic miners seized the opportunity and stepped over Glemba. A few others followed him into the mine.

"We got grievances," Ekvie finally blurted. "We just want to be treated fairly."

Pearce looked down the line, following the voice.

Now the sheriff clicked his tongue twice and rode his horse forward, the hooves plodding slowly in the hard dirt. The head of the

54

horse came within inches of the speaker, the earthy smell of the beast and its mouthful of yellow horse teeth.

"This is an unlawful assembly on company property," the sheriff announced. "And as for your grievances, you can start wishing in one hand and shitting in the other and see which gets filled first. Now I'm only saying this one more time. If you don't disperse, and get your skinny asses down in that pit right now, I'll have no choice but to remove you from the property by any means necessary."

A few of the boys looked at one another.

"You won't be walking your mules anywhere with a couple broken legs," Pearce added.

"You see," the sheriff said. "Think of your bones snapping."

"To hell with this," someone said. "It ain't worth it, boys."

The sheriff clicked his tongue again and turned the horse around, riding slowly towards the engine room.

"They can't just beat us like that," Ekvie said. "It ain't right."

"Look who's wearing the badge," one of the miners warned as he stepped over the unconscious Glemba. "There is no law in Elsinore except the law of the company."

Some of the mule drivers had already abandoned the chain. Others followed. Soon they were all skulking through the portal into the pit. The sheriff sat watching from his saddle. Behind him, the engines started, the chains clanked. The first coal cars jerked forward, beginning the first slow descent into the cavernous mine.

*

Daniel forced himself to get up and walk weakly about the austere room. He struggled out of bed and lurched unsteadily to the window where he sat in the chair and waited to watch the sunrise. His temple pulsed painfully where the revolver had knocked him unconscious. He looked malnourished and in all likelihood he had survived the last few weeks on little more than cigarettes and bad whiskey that left him snorting and coughing, the blood in his veins feeling hot and thick as oil. But now he was three days sober and diseased thoughts tormented him without respite. *Therefore does my Father love me, because I lay*

55

down my life. No man taketh it from me, but I lay it down of myself. He looked beyond the window glass and the murky reflection of himself to the dissolving predawn darkness and the promise of a new day.

He heard the door open gently on its hinges, and he turned around with difficulty. Katherine walked into the room, bringing with her a clean sweet smell. He realized he had not bathed since he had been injured and had spent too much time alone with his own unclean odor reeking out of his shirt collar and on the pillowcases. Now that he had no cigarettes to smoke his sense of smell seemed strangely acute.

"You're up," she said. "You must be feeling better."

"I don't know if better's the right word."

"I'm going to have to change your bandages today," she said.

She approached and carefully unwound the bandages from his head. He clenched his teeth and shut his eyes. "Hold still, we're almost done. There."

"I hate being stuck in here all the time," he said. "I'm restless."

"I can heat some water for a bath. That will make you feel better."

"Is that a nice way of saying you're about to asphyxiate from smelling me?"

She laughed aloud and covered her mouth. "No," she said.

Downstairs in the kitchen a black pot of water simmered on the coal stove. An empty galvanized tub sat in the center of the room on the hardwood floor. Spoons, cups, ladles, pots, and a colander hung from nails by the dry sink. Empty milk bottles on the roughhewn shelves. She took the pot by the handles, a small towel in each hand and poured the water into the tub, releasing a haze of steam. He pulled off his shirt with some difficulty and peeled off his rank socks, leaving on only his denims. He knelt before the tub as if in worship, cupping the hot water in his hands and ladling over his lank hair, the warmth sending pleasant chills down the flesh of his back. Already the water was grimed, so completely filthy he was with coal-smoke and dust.

She draped a towel over the back of a chair and came closer. He was busy scrubbing at his face with the washcloth. "Would you like me to wash your back?"

"All right."

He rubbed his eyes and gave her the cloth. She dipped it in the water and wrung it out and began cleaning his back, dipping the washcloth in the water occasionally, slowly cleaning his neck and upper shoulders, the long crevice of his spine. His muscles were tight and knotted and he began to relax, the tension loosening, his mind at ease in a way he could scarcely comprehend.

"What are these scars below your neck?" Her fingertips glided across the pale slashes down his back.

"Nothing," he said. "They're old."

"These were deep cuts. Did somebody do this to you?"

"They're just scars."

"Every scar's got a story behind it," she said. He stood up and the water cascaded off his body into the filthy tub below. She gave him a towel and he set about drying his face and hair. "You don't like to talk, do you?"

"I don't talk when I don't have anything worth saying."

"Is that your way of telling me to shut up?"

"I didn't mean it like that..." He folded the damp towel, draped it over the back of the chair, and held her delicate smooth hands in his rough calloused hands. He touched the scar on her chin and tilted her head up so that she was looking at him. "You see, anyone who spends enough time around me finds out I'm just an asshole."

"It's almost seven," she said. "I have to go make sure the girls are getting ready."

"Is that your way of telling me to get the hell out of here?"

"You can go whenever you like."

"I think I'm going to go have a little whiskey."

"I thought you said you were giving it up?"

"I think that was just the laudanum talking."

*

Mary Beth knew exactly what his intentions were when he asked her to go for a walk in the middle of January. She wasn't stupid. It was, in Michael's defense, an unseasonably warm afternoon—well

57

above freezing—but cold enough to remind you that springtime was still a ways off. And yet the whole thing felt completely contrived. Why couldn't they just stay in the house by the fire? For the privacy a walk afforded without any impropriety—that was why it was necessary. Why couldn't he wait until spring to propose then? She had long ago given up on pondering the brash and inscrutable ways of men, but the truth was the young miners going down into the pit were not unlike soldiers going off to war. You didn't know if you were going to survive your shift. And so they wanted to have someone to come home to, or someone to mourn them if they didn't. Anyways, at least now she would have something to keep Cyrus Swank, that groping oily clerk at the company store, from pestering her.

"How come you're not married?" Michael asked before they had even reached the bottom of the hill. He walked with his hands in his pockets.

Without making eye contact, she said, "Am I supposed to be?"

"Well, I just thought a pretty girl like you..."

"My brother's real protective of me I guess. Scares most boys off."

"Logan'd probably break my neck if he saw you out here with me."

"How come you're not?" she asked.

"Well, it's funny you should ask... " Michael laughed uneasily. They had reached the covered bridge and he stopped walking.

"I know that's why you brought me out here."

"You do?"

"I can't say I love you."

Michael took his hands out of his pockets, held up his palms innocently, chin dropping a little.

"Knowing what I know about you, I can't say I trust you either."

"Whatever you've heard about me, it ain't true."

"Them girls in Monongahela ain't true?"

"Mary Beth, I'll change I swear..."

"And as the poet says..."

"What poet?"

"Men are April when they woo, December when they wed."

She seemed to be staring at something far off in the distance, and Michael turned to look over his shoulder to see what she was looking at, but he saw nothing. "Are you feeling okay, Mary Beth?"

"I have a strange infirmity," she said breathlessly, "which is nothing…"

Before he could say a word, she had pulled him into the shadows of the covered bridge and kissed him hard on the mouth. Night was newly fallen. His mouth hung open, back pressing against the boards of the bridge as she kissed his ear and down his neck. His face turned bright red with carnal desire. "Lively little girl," was all he could say.

*

When Daniel woke the next morning, there was daylight coming through the dusty windowpanes, and the sheriff was seated at Daniel's bedside, his hands clasped around a tin coffee cup in his lap, a cunning smile across his clean-shaven face. His hat was on the nightstand near the lamp. Daniel startled and sat up in the bed, pulling the bed linens close to his sweaty chest, glaring at the sheriff with bloodshot eyes.

"You're a troubled sleeper," the sheriff said.

"I have all kinds of troubles."

"You talk in your sleep."

"Am I under arrest or something?"

"A man starts talking like that and I'm inclined towards suspicion? You got something you want to tell me, son?"

"How much time have you got?"

The sheriff laughed and sipped his coffee, shaking his head. "Not enough," he said. "That's the one thing there ain't never enough of."

"Do you mind if I get dressed?"

"Not at all."

"It's cold as hell in here," Daniel said. He dropped his bare feet to the cold floor and fished his socks up off the floor. He stepped into his trousers and fetched his shirt off the back of the chair and pulled it over his head. He looked across the bed at the sheriff. "Shit," he said. "I was having a bad nightmare."

"You were talking to someone."

"Who?"

"Don't you know?"

"I never remember my dreams."

"How are you healing up?"

"I'll live."

"You want a cup of coffee, son?"

"No," Daniel said. "Do you want a shot of whiskey?"

"I forgo libations before noon."

"I don't," Daniel said.

Daniel sat on the edge of his bed, looking curiously at the sheriff.

"So look, kid, you got two choices. You can either get the hell out of Elsinore or you can start answering my questions. And I can smell bullshit a mile away. It's my fucking gift and it's kept me alive this long. Now, you want to tell me who you think you are that you'll start a fight in my joint without my fucking permission?"

"I didn't start anything. That goofy-looking fuck was eyeballing me all night. Then he called me a cheat at the table."

"Were you fucking cheating?"

"I'm not a fucking cheat. I was just on a lucky run."

"You better believe you're on a lucky run. What's your fucking business in Elsinore?"

"I'm just a blacksmith. I came looking for work."

"You got one hell of a way of looking for work."

"Well, I found a fucking poker game first."

"You see, I don't just let any cocksucker who walks into the camp have a job. Why don't you have any papers?"

"I was robbed at the Mission House in Pittsburgh. They stole my duffel bag while I was sleeping on a bench. Lost everything but the clothes I was wearing."

"And the knife you got in your boot there."

"Yeah," he said. "I still got the knife. And if I'd have woken while they were robbing me I would have used it."

"So would I," the sheriff said. "I would have gutted them right there." He shook his head as if reflecting on a mounting problem. "No. I don't tolerate criminals around here. Unless they're working for me. And I don't put up with organizers either. You ain't with them Union boys are you?"

"I've done most things that don't pay and lead to trouble, but I ain't never been an organizer."

"I only ask, because—well, you show up—then next thing I know, I have these fucking hunkies organizing a wildcat strike. It just doesn't sit right with me," he said. "I had an undercover Union man materialize out of thin air once."

"What happened to him?"

"He's at the bottom of the fucking slate dump." He looked up at Daniel and smiled. "But you're not a Union man."

"I don't care about what's going on in the mine. I work in the smithy and that's it. If I got a little whiskey to look forward to at the end of an honest day's work, I'm all right. The rest of my life, if you don't mind, I prefer keeping to myself."

"You look me in the eye when you're talking," the sheriff said. "I like that. You can't get a damn hunky to look you in the eye to save his life." He finished the cold dregs of his coffee and donned his hat. The sheriff started for the door and then stopped and turned as if remembering the last question he meant to ask. "Whatever happened to your father?"

Daniel felt his blood rush. "My father?"

"That's who you were talking to in your sleep."

"That's strange—I barely remember the son of a bitch. He died in the mines over in Schuylkill when I was a kid."

"Orphanage get you?"

"Yeah."

The sheriff nodded slowly. "I lost my old man when I was a boy. He got all shot up to hell in Gettysburg. Anyhow..." The sheriff touched the brim of his hat. "I'll be seeing you around."

"Does that mean I got the job at the smithy?"

"Yeah, kid. You got it."

Five

Dark in the morning hours when Daniel came to the blacksmith shop. The odor of coal-smoke and man-sweat lingered inside. He removed his hat and brushed off the snow before hanging it on an exposed nail. There was a tear-off calendar on the wall boards: it was the twenty-first of January. The gritty little shop was soundless save for the occasional hiss and pop of the forge fire whose blood-orange flames, flickering in the caldera of bituminous coal, gave the only light. He shut the smithy door behind him and stepped into the dirt floor workspace. The worktable was littered with chisels and punches, mangled scraps of rusty steel, little mounds of white flux. There was a wooden crate filled with animal bones. The familiar tools, all handmade: cross peen and ball peen hammers, a menagerie of tongs. A two hundred and fifty pound anvil was clamped down to the top of a mammoth tree stump. A quench bucket made from a whiskey barrel and horseshoes hung about the rim. He took up a cross peen hammer in his right hand, tilted it and tapped it on the anvil face. It made a sound like the ringing of a bell.

An ill-shapen figure appeared in the threshold, chiaroscuro in the flickering firelight. Wiping his hands clean in a greasy towel. "It's a good hunk of metal," he said. He limped forward into the dim light. He was slightly hunched. A crippled blacksmith.

Daniel laid the hammer on the face.

"So you're my new help?" He looked Daniel over with his red-lipped eyes, the old smith's skin as dry and dark as boot leather

"I am," Daniel said.

"They call me Badger." He pinched a wad of tobacco chew and tucked it in his cheek and tongued it, offering then the pouch to Daniel who didn't use the stuff. "So how long have you been forging?"

"Seven years," Daniel said. "That was over in anthracite country. I was apprenticed to a smith in Schuylkill."

Badger regarded him with a dubious eye. "How old are you?"

"Nineteen."

"You okay with shoeing mules?"

"As long as they're not out to kick me."

"Most of them probably will be. The rest of them definitely will be."

"Then I guess I'll learn to deal with it."

"How about welding?"

"I can weld any two pieces of steel you give me."

"Well, don't go breaking your damn arm patting yourself on the back. We got a lot to do today."

The sun had begun to blush over the valley treetops and the apricot morning light filtered through the dusty windows. Daniel pumped the bellows a few times. It worked smoothly and the flames licked high. Badger took a sprinkler can and watered around the edge of the flames. The water sizzled and spat in the bright glowing embers and the fresh coal smoked profusely. Black smoke disappeared up the brick chimney. The blacksmith said he wanted the coal to clump together and he shoveled on fresh coal and watered it so that the coal took the shape of a bread oven that encased the fire.

Daniel worked the squealing suspended bellows, the leather expanding and collapsing, the air tunneling through the tuyere, feeding the fire at its heart, the flames growing smaller as the fire grew hotter. Badger went to his work table and rummaged around a moment before he returned with the head of a pickaxe clasped in his black tongs. The clumped coal was like a cave now in which the fire burned. Intense heat gusted out of the mouth of the coal caldera. He carefully placed the steel deep into the heart of the fire.

"Okay now," Badger said. "Give me some air. Slow now. Real slow now. Want her to get hot real slow. She's burning hot now. Yes sir," he said. "She's burning hot. Baking her like bread in the oven."

Daniel gazed into the forge fire, the steel glowing dull red, then brighter cherry red. Badger waited with the tongs in his left hand and a cross peen hammer in his right. When the steel turned transparent yellow, he clasped it with the tongs and turned quickly to the anvil and laid one point of the pickaxe over the edge of the anvil. His hammer

64

blows fell and yellow sparks showered all around him and the malleable steel flattened noticeably. The hammer pinged steadily, and he quickly turned the steel ninety degrees and hammered the tip into a fine point. The pickaxe tip had cooled to a dull red color and he put it back in the fire to take another heat.

"Never gets old," Badger said. "Never gets old."

"No it doesn't," Daniel said.

"Why do I get the feeling that you're hiding something?"

"I never met a man that wasn't hiding something."

The blacksmith smiled and shook his head. "You don't say much, but you make your point."

They waited in silence. The blacksmith hovered over the fire, shifted on his feet, his right leg completely bowlegged. When the steel was nearly white hot in the fire, Badger tonged the pickaxe and took it to the anvil and gradually the vigorous pounding grew softer and he began tapping gingerly at the piece. He straightened the small delicate lines that made a sharp four-sided point designed so a miner could stab and break apart the coal. When the steel had cooled to a dull red, he replaced it in the forge. He winced painfully and let the hammer down on the floor. He opened and closed the arthritic fingers of his right hand.

"Goddamn it," Badger murmured to himself while shaking his head. He bent down and clutched the hammer and stood again waiting and watching the colors of the metal change. He looked across the fire at Daniel. "The flesh is weak."

In the following heats, the chisel end of the pickaxe was tapered. When all the forging was done for that particular piece, it was set aside to slowly anneal throughout the morning, until it could be tempered in the afternoon. Then they started with the next one. Daniel controlled the blower and held the tongs and Badger did the hammering and told Daniel when and how to rotate the piece on the anvil with the tongs. They worked in near silence, sharpening a dozen pickaxes. The two of them stood drenched in sweat under their greasy leather aprons in the sweltering little shop while outside fresh snowflakes fell all about the bleak colliery landscape.

After lunch, Daniel opened the ash gate on the forge and let the weightless white ashes fall to the heap of ash below. He fished out from the bottom of the forge the heavy, metallic clinkers, little amorphous masses of impurities burned out of the coal. Then he was ready to rebuild the fire from the hot coals. He worked the bellows gingerly and stoked the embers until the flames ignited again and the embers pulsated luminously. When the fire was strong again, they heat-treated the pickaxes, then cooled them with a rapid quench, first in a bucket of oil and then in water. With each quench the transparent yellow steel set fire to the lacquered surface of the black viscous oil. The flames shot up and licked across the opaque surface and he swished the pickaxe around in the thick liquid. And after a few seconds, the searing hot steel was bathed in the quench bucket where the metal and water hissed violently upon meeting, and plumes of warm steam wafted up around his face.

Long hours of the winter afternoon were spent over the blacksmith's vice, polishing the ends of the twelve pickaxes to a shine with a diamond tipped file. This was the last step before tempering them. He worked the files back and forth, back and forth, his body beaded with sweat, leaning forward with all his weight, his dorsal muscles tightened into a crippling fist. A harsh zipping whiz each time he sawed the file across the steel, scraping away the black firescale, revealing the steel's shine.

They returned to the forge and held the steel over the fire. Without ever letting the pickaxe out of the tongs, they watched the colors change rapidly, first straw, then brown in the smokeless fire. Daniel turned quickly with it and plunged the tempered pickaxe into the wooden quench bucket. The water smoked and hissed. When he held up each pickaxe for Badger's inspection, the pickaxe smoked and glistened wetly in the grip of the tongs. The old white-haired blacksmith nodded approvingly and they went ahead with the next piece.

66

Marianna, PA.
January 29, 1889

Dear Mr. Carver,

You wish to know what kind of place this is. And here let me remark that I have discovered things to be just as you had imagined them to be. Things are far more uncertain than at Elsinore. It is miserable, dangerous, and frozen. The mine guards will shoot you as soon as look at you, and the miners will spit on you as soon as talk to you. But it is amusing to overhear the camp rumors, the certainty with which they speak of securing a contract. It is easy to see that the public sentiment here is rotten to the core with resentment of the iron heel of power, as the socialist calls it. And although there is no immediate danger of any fighting here, I suspect the operators will soon crush this matter and put an end to it. I have yet to meet any Union agitators, but I hear rumors whispered everywhere of their presence, organizing secret meetings and so forth. Will write again in two weeks' time.

Your humble and obedient servant,

Logan O'Brien

P.S. I now realize what it is to be away from home and the surroundings of familiar faces. Give my love to my sister and tell her I should like to see her very much.

*

The sheriff sat with O'Brien that morning over coffee and then later cigars for their weekly meeting to go over general matters of the camp's management. There was nothing Carver hated more. It was always just one damn headache after another. He paid as little attention as he could to O'Brien, instead focusing his attention on reading "Wealth" by Andrew Carnegie. He had come across Cyrus Swank, that sniveling little rat, leaning over the counter and reading it in the company store earlier that day, when Swank damn well knew he wasn't getting paid to edify himself. So the sheriff swiped it right out from under his nose without any intention of reading it himself. But now, because he could hardly stand to hear another word come out of Charlie's mouth, he was skimming it. The gist of it was this: the man who dies rich dies disgraced. Carnegie was saying that a man ought to divide his life into two parts: the first for acquisition, the second for distribution. Carver knew that his life was to be entirely concerned with acquisition. He wasn't interested in the ornate mansions, the extravagant luxuries, or the collections of European art that men like Carnegie and Frick amassed. But money was power in America. He wanted as much as he could get.

The sheriff got up, shaking his head, went over to the potbelly furnace, and threw the magazine into the fire. Just now, O'Brien was elaborating on plans for installing several new privies throughout the camp and colliery. "The honey-dippers just aren't getting around to cleaning out the few we got often enough, Jack," he explained with a meaningless gesture of his cigar hand. "Overflow's getting to be a real problem. Every week, I'm telling you, they're overflowing. And the smell…"

Back in his chair, the sheriff had his head in his hands, his elbows propped on his knees.. "Yeah, yeah, yeah, I get it, Charlie. The squareheads shit a lot. Fine. Invest in some new fucking shithouses. What do I care. Just get it done."

"As for the cost of labor…?"

Carver rubbed his forehead and pinched the bridge of his nose "If the squareheads want to dig a hole to shit in, I'm not paying them to do it. It's dead work. Christ, Charlie. It's bad enough the way I'm getting bent over by the lumberyard."

"Everything all right, Jack?"

"I'm fine. You're just giving me a fucking headache like always."

"Maybe you ought to take a day off. Get some rest."

"What, and leave you in charge?" He sat up and rolled his neck. "Not on your fucking life."

"Sure enough." O'Brien gnawed at his worn-down nub of thumbnail.

"You got anything else for me?"

"Well…" He took a few compulsory nibbles at his thumbnail. "Any word from my boy?"

"As a matter of fact, yes. Says he misses his fucking sister. Some fine fucking penmanship that kid's got."

*

The days passed without drunken rage or harrowing blackout as Daniel worked regularly with Badger in the smithy. The embers sizzled violently in the forge as he tilted the quench can, the water sprinkling and showering down on the flames, the flames desperately flaring up, wafts of steam billowing and vanishing, and then slowly the flames extinguished and the embers turned to a mound of gray ashes. He raked through the coals with the fire poker and dug the heavy metallic clinkers out of the base of the forge, discarding them on the dirt floor.

At the worktable Badger sat hunched over his account ledger with his perpetual scowl on his face, racked with violent fits of coughing, cursing and shaking his head. He produced a grime-stained handkerchief from his pocket and wiped his lips with it. He turned to look over his shoulder at Daniel, his frost-white eyebrows scrunched in agitation. "When did we upset that ax for O'Brien? Yesterday or the day before?"

"The day before," Daniel said. He seated himself on a wobbly stool and he popped and milked a big blood-filled blister on the web of his hand between his thumb and index finger. "He still hasn't picked it up yet."

Badger leaned in his chair and pressed a knobby finger to one of his nostrils and shot a clot of yellow snot onto the dirt floor before he turned back to his ledger, scratching out what he'd just written, scribbling something in its place. "I hate that son of a bitch," he said. "You know what he said to me the other day?"

"Who?"

"O'Brien. Said my yard was an eyesore and my vegetable garden was all dying. Said I couldn't keep two pigs penned up in the yard. I says, Charlie the whole goddamn patch is an eyesore. Nothing grows

69

here. Anything you plant just withers and gets covered in coal dust. The houses are all falling apart. Hell, the whole camp smells like an overflowing privy on a hot day. And Charlie, he's worried about my goddamn pigs, just because he wants me buying pork from the company store. I told him just worry about the mine, not my pigs and vegetable garden."

"What'd he say to that?"

"Oh he just started gnawing on his fingernails the way he does. Then he just shook his head and said it's an eyesore. Guess what I told him?"

"I don't know. What?"

"Told him the sheriff was the one who sold me the hogs, and that's the god honest truth. So if he wants to complain he can go complain to the sheriff about something the sheriff done himself."

"Is that true?"

"Hell no, it's not true. The only thing that man ever gave me was a black eye."

"You got in a fistfight with the sheriff?"

"I didn't say we fought. You don't fight a man like that. How could you anyways? No, he locked me up one night for behaving in a frontier fashion, as the company likes to put it. I don't remember a thing except him hitting me and me hitting the ground. I woke up in the lockup with a black eye and a headache like you wouldn't believe."

Daniel untied the leather apron from around his waist and pulled it over his head and hung it on a nail. He squatted on his haunches. "I thought you didn't drink?"

"I was drunk all the time back then." Badger nodded gravely a moment. "My wife cured me of that though. I put that poor woman through hell. May she rest in peace."

"Sometimes I wish I could give it up," Daniel said. He went over to the stool by the work table and sat down, working the toe of his boot back and forth into the dirt floor. "I tell myself that's it. The last time. But I always pick it right back up."

Badger nodded sagaciously. "I swore off it many times. I broke many promises. Then one day about twelve years ago I gave it up and I haven't had a drink since."

"How? What'd you do differently?"

"I couldn't tell you. Couldn't put it into words. I guess one day I just made my peace with God. I woke up and realized I don't even know what God is. What I hated was some damn fool's opinion about God."

"What's your opinion on God?"

"In a nutshell?"

"Sure."

"I guess I'd say... God loves you when you can't love yourself. That's my opinion."

"Well, that sounds all right," Daniel said, shrugging. "But I just can't see why God makes bad things happen to innocent people. Seems kind of downright mean-spirited sometimes, don't you think?"

"Kid, this is the most I've heard you talk since you came in here and started working."

"I guess it's just something I spend a lot of time thinking about."

"Well, maybe those innocent people aren't as innocent as they think."

"Little children, they're not innocent?"

"What, you mean like those little foul-mouthed imps picking slate over there in the breaker?"

"Some of them, yeah... Some of them are."

"Well, they probably don't love their mother and father all the time. Don't always like what their mother and father make them do. If they got any schooling, they probably didn't like going, but they had to learn. They sure as hell don't like going to work, but they got to pull their own weight and help out the rest of the family. They don't always like eating their dinner, but they got to grow. Just because they got to do things they don't really understand, it doesn't mean their mother and father don't love them. And if their mother and father just let them do whatever the hell they want, well then they'd just turn into selfish little shits… like most of them are anyhow."

Daniel laughed a little bit. "I guess what I'm trying to say is that I believe in God," he said, lifting his head to look at Badger. "I just don't think I have it in me to love him. And I don't really care what he thinks about me. The things I've been through… I won't ever forgive him. I know I won't."

"Don't say never," Badger said, closing the ledger book and rising from his chair. As he hobbled past Daniel he patted him on the shoulder. He was almost at the door when Daniel spoke.

"He killed my father…" His head was hanging down as he sat hunched forward, fingers interlocked, legs spread apart.

Badger stopped and looked over his shoulder. "Who did?"

"Who do you think?"

Badger turned around, his brow pinched. "Carver…?"

"Truth be told, he's the one I won't forgive."

"Who are you?"

"Who am I?" Daniel said, pausing reflectively. "I'm Daniel Byrnes."

Badger's eyes lit up briefly with clarity. He came closer. "You came back?"

"I didn't know in my head why. Why I came back… I don't know why I do half the things I do. But I think now I always knew it in my heart."

"To kill him…"

"Yes."

Badger sat down on the stool next to Daniel. "I was there the night it happened…"

"So was I."

*

After Badger left the shop, Daniel was alone. The evening was well advanced, the last iron of the day hissing in the slack tub. The colliery whistle screamed in the coming darkness, and still he worked, a laborer of indefatigable blood. His begrimed face and his dusty beard

72

bore the evidence of his trade, the stains of the foul black coal-smoke. He took up the ax and set standing a piece of hickory wood, his calloused hand gripping tightly below the heavy axe head, raising it back over his shoulder, his hand gliding down the long smooth handle as he swung in a swift arc, his hands finally meeting one atop the other, the tempered axe blade chopping into the fresh wood, splitting the log dead center. The two halves fell and lay on their sides. He propped each again in turn and quartered them for kindling. He swung the axe down again, the hickory wood cracking open, and he could smell the fresh wood. Afterwards, when the wood was split and stacked, when the embers of the coal and coke in the forge were cool, and the steel therein lay slowly annealing, when the work was done, he found he had no desire to get drunk, no desire for that first sip of whiskey that warmed his blood on those bleak winter nights, no yearning to fall into the dark and deep oblivion.

Charlie O'Brien had come straight from the mine. He did not knock before entering. He closed the door behind him, a cold draft of air whistled through the smithy. He was a stranger to Daniel and he stood looking about, his face soiled with coal, the carbide lamp sagging on his soft cap. His hair was speckled with gray and he worked a wad of tobacco in his cheek. He leaned and spat juice on the dirt floor.

"I'm done forging for the day," Daniel said. "You can leave your pickaxe and I'll sharpen it first thing tomorrow."

O'Brien disregarded this and ambled over to the worktable where he stood studying the assortment of rusty tongs, taking up the wolf-jaw tongs for inspection and then replacing them on the table. "I always wanted to be a blacksmith when I was a boy," he said. "I used to go to the smithy and watch the old blacksmith work every chance I got."

"Is that right?" Daniel said.

"All the boys did. All we ever wanted to do was hammer that hot iron over the anvil, but the blacksmith, he didn't speak nothing but German, and he'd just scowl and stomp his foot at us."

"And what, you're here because you want to play blacksmith or something?"

O'Brien smoothed his moustache with his thumb and forefinger, sizing Daniel up a moment. "I'm here because you're not who you say you are."

Daniel's eyes glanced at the hammer resting on the anvil. "What business is it of yours, who I am?"

"I make it my business," O'Brien said. He walked around the smithy casually, inspecting the tools. "Now I know you're a fool, but just what kind of fool are you going to be?"

"If you're looking for trouble," Daniel said, "you're about to find it."

"I think you're the one who's looking for trouble, and I'm here to tell you to get the hell out of Elsinore. You're lucky to be alive as it is. You're lucky you only got stitches in your head and not a bullet."

"You think I'm with the Union." Daniel scoffed. "That's what this is about isn't it?"

"No," O'Brien said. "I don't think you want anything to do with the Union. But I know you. I know your father was with the Union. And you see where it got him."

Daniel felt his blood rush. He set his jaw.

"Did you think you'd just come back here and no one would recognize you?" O'Brien turned and walked to the door, where he stopped and turned and looked back, locked eyes with him. Daniel's chest rose and fell. "There's no need for you to die here, kid."

*

When O'Brien left, Daniel stormed out of the smithy and went straight to the train station to catch the 8:17 train into Monongahela. He leaned his shoulder against the pillar, exhausted and filthy, waiting in the cold while the miners drank in the warm tavern across the street, and he ached with want for a glass of whiskey. He cared about nothing and no one else now. Not the sheriff, not his father, not anyone. He was beyond hope, hatred, and revenge. He knew he would drink heavily and heedlessly into the night. But he made himself wait until he got off the train and walked to Belladonna's Saloon to drink the first drink.

Three whores called out to him as he crossed the dark parlor, lewdly gesturing and laughing, one flicking her tongue between the V of her fingers, another pulling down her dress to expose her cleavage. But she was there again, too, watching him from across the room by the stairs, Katherine. When the first girl caught Katherine's gaze, she nudged the other two girls and they quieted and left him alone.

When she walked up to Daniel, his throat thickened and he had to swallow hard. "Sorry, kid," she said, "these dirty coal-town whores don't know a gentleman when they see one." She caressed the skin on the back of his neck, flesh touching flesh, his eyes closing. He opened his eyes and she smiled at him, her dark hair falling over her bare shoulders, his eyes wandering down her long neck. His days were long since poisoned by lonesomeness and longing, and despite the cold distances surrounding him, he remembered the hot water she had heated for him in the galvanized tub and the way the water fell on his naked back, how her soft fingers traced the ramulose scars, scars that ran deeper than the flesh and the body, and they were healed under that ephemeral caress, and the water was clean and warm as she washed his back, and for a moment he felt something ineffable, and he remembered the feeling when flesh touches flesh.

"Where's your friends?" she asked.

"They're not here tonight," he said. "I'm alone."

"You should get another drink," she said. "And take it up to my room where no one will bother you."

"All right," he said. He called the bartender over and asked for a whiskey. As soon as he poured it, Daniel downed the first shot, swallowing in one gulp. "I think I'll have another," he said. The bartender poured the second shot and as he turned to walk away, Daniel tossed it back and asked for yet another.

"Do want me to just leave you the bottle?"

"That'll work," Daniel said.

"I'd be on the floor if I was you," she said.

"I'll be all right."

He followed her up the stairs, holding the wooden balustrade with its intermittent missing spindles with one hand and his bottle with the other. While they walked to her room, he heard everywhere the drunken moans of debauchery. They walked past a man standing against the wall in the dark hallway, his belt unhitched, his eyes shut and mouth hanging slack, one of the girls, her breasts showing out of her grime-stained blouse, laughing and jerking him off.

It was dark inside, the small room smelling strongly of her lavender perfume. She lit a single candle on the nightstand and in the soft light he saw the clean wine-dark bed linens.

"How much?" he asked.

"This one's on the house," she said.

She began to undress in front of him in the candlelight, his face scarlet, and he watched her slip out of the black negligee. The wide scar of a caesarian section that had been crudely stitched by an alcoholic doctor, the slit of her navel in her flat belly. Then she blew out the candle and in the darkness he pulled off his shirt and his boots. He unhitched his belt with fumbling hands and stepped out of his greasy, soiled denims and slipped under the crimson covers with her, his hands still trembling despite his drunkenness. She leaned over and kissed him hard on the mouth. He put his hand on her waist feeling the soft skin. Her warm hand wandered down his tense stomach and down, taking him in her hand and stroking him. She put her hands on his face and pulled him close and when he kissed her she bit his bottom lip so hard he bled and jerked away and touched his lip and felt the slick blood on his fingertips.

"Come on," she said. "Fuck me."

She took it like a dagger. Biting her lips and whimpering like a puppy. Her hair pooled around her head on the pillow and he was on top of her. She hooked her ankles inside his thighs and her hands dug into his buttocks. He clutched her soft throat. He pulled out and turned her over on the bed and spat in his fingers for lubrication. Then he snatched a fistful of her hair and she arched her back. He slowed and

76

slowed and then finally pulled out again and lay down on the bed panting and glistening with sweat.

"What's the matter?" she said. "Don't you want to get off?"

"It's not going to happen," he said.

They lay together in uncomfortable silence for what seemed like a long time, both of them breathless, and then he got out of the bed and began to step unsteadily into his jeans.

"You don't have to go," she said. "Not right away."

"I should get going."

"Going where?"

"I don't know."

"Don't drink so much next time."

*

When Daniel finally left the room and descended the burgundy stairs, he felt foul and alone, sick to the stomach at the thought of his shameful lust. He knew he was going to get drunk now. There was no decision about it. He felt the inescapable need for a drink. But when he saw the sheriff at a table late in the abandoned saloon, grinning with a cigar between his teeth, shuffling a deck of cards while a pale crimson-lipped whore whispered and giggled in his ear, he nearly fell down the last three stairs. His face went pale and he stood in catatonia at the bottom of the staircase. Beneath the scar across his neck, the sheriff wore a blood red tie in a Windsor knot. He took the cigar out of his mouth and gave a toss of his chin.

"Hey kid, get over here."

Daniel steadied himself on the spindleshorn balustrade, feeling faint and lightheaded suddenly, his sight dimming, darkening. He took a few uncertain steps forward and thought he might collapse on the floor at any moment.

"You look like you got your money's worth," the sheriff said.

"You ain't kidding."

"Jesus Christ, take it easy kid. Give him a hand, Rose."

The girl, drunk herself, stood up unsteadily, wavered, and stumbled a few steps on twiggy legs, taking him by the arm. He sat and gripped his skull. Rose took a slant and circuitous route around the table, steadying herself on the backs of the chairs as she passed.

"What'd they do to you up there?"

"I'm all right," he said. "I just had one hell of a lightheaded sensation come over me."

"Have a fucking seat," the sheriff said, gesturing with his hand at the empty chair.

"No thanks, Mr. Carver. It's late."

"You can sleep when you're dead."

"I should go."

"Listen kid, have a fucking seat. Don't make me ask again."

Daniel lowered himself uneasily into the ladder back chair at the poker table. Rose took her seat next to the sheriff again and began stroking the back of his neck with her hand. "Who'd you have seeing to your johnson upstairs?"

"I forget her name."

"You just came to fuck and run," the sheriff said. "I truly respect that…Whiskey drinker?"

"Of course."

"What's your brand?"

"All of them."

The sheriff grinned and nodded. "Hey, Bobby, bring us over a bottle of Jameson." When the bartender brought the bottle, the sheriff gave him five dollars. The sheriff poured three shots. They raised them and drank. "I see you're not above a little whiskey and whoring," the sheriff said, turning to Daniel. "And I know you're a fucking poker player."

"I've been known to sit down at a game or two," Daniel said. "But it's late."

"Come on—live a little."

"All right," Daniel said. "Why the hell not?"

The sheriff was in the process of pouring another round of shots for them when he glimpsed up and saw Katherine descending the staircase, her black silk nightgown shimmering in the half-dark lampglow. "Here comes some fucking trouble," he said.

She paused on the staircase and locked eyes with Daniel briefly, but then continued on, seeming to pay no attention to the table as she made her way to the bar. But the sheriff caught her by the wrist as she passed. She winced. "You got something for me, honey?" he said.

Without answering, scowling a little, she produced a wad of bills tucked in the cleft between her breasts and held it out for him. He released her arm, took the money, and shoved the bills in his pocket without counting it. "I take it you two have been getting reacquainted since your head injury."

"Just business, Jack," she said.

"Everything's business," he said. "Remember that." Then turning to Daniel, he inquired, "You want a couple of whores under the table while we play?"

"Kind of you to offer, but I'll pass."

"I just thought a young buck like you'd want to turn around and go again," the sheriff said as he shuffled the old grimy deck of cards. "I only hope that if these dolls were to get under the table on my end, your forgoing a wet prick while we play isn't evidence of disapproval?"

"If it distracts you, I benefit from the odds."

"Nothing distracts me."

Rose, obligingly, and Katherine, noticeably reluctant, disappeared under the table. The bartender brought the poker chips and they anted up and the sheriff dealt the cards. Daniel waited until he got all five of his cards, then picked them up and read his hand. He held nothing, a ten high card. The sheriff tilted his head back, a gaze blank and pitiless. Daniel looked down at his cards.

The sheriff tossed his chips to the center of the table.

"You're aggressive, aren't you?" Daniel slid his cards forward. "Fold."

The sheriff took the pot and collected the cards. "So how's Elsinore suit you?"

79

"I feel right at home."

The sheriff riffled the deck, his thumbs facing inward, the cards interleaving. "Where'd you say you were from again?"

Daniel leaned forward and cut the deck. "Here, there."

"That's lacking some as an answer."

"I've always been a man of few words as they say."

"That's what worries me."

"If you had to pin me down, I'd say I lived most of my life working iron out in the anthracite coal fields."

"You running from something, kid?"

"Yeah, myself."

"That's a futile fucking endeavor, ain't it?"

Daniel raised his eyebrows and sipped his whiskey.

The sheriff dealt the cards and they each picked up their hands and studied them. Daniel held a pair of aces. He raised the pot a dollar, tossing in his chips. The sheriff stared him down, and then leaned back and cocked his head at an angle. "Hey," he said. "What's the rush, honey?" He looked back up at his cards and shook his head. Finally, the sheriff called. He kept two cards and dealt himself three new ones.

Daniel kept the aces and drew three new cards. He picked up a pair of eights. He raised the sheriff another dollar. The sheriff called. He laid down three jacks. Daniel's face fell when he saw the cards. "Aces and eights," he said, flinging his cards to the center of the table. The sheriff reached in with both hands and scooped the pot towards his end of the table. Daniel saw the opportunity as the sheriff shuffled the deck. He feigned scratching his thigh and reached under the table, feeling for the knife tucked in his boot, the artery in his neck pumping visibly.

"You're a dead man," the sheriff said as he riffled the interleaving cards.

Daniel sank back down in his chair, and brought both hands up to the tabletop where they fumbled shakily with his rapidly shrinking stack of chips. "What the fuck are you talking about?"

"Aces and eights," the sheriff said, collecting the cards. "That's a dead man's hand. Wild Bill Hickok held that hand when he was killed by the coward Jack McCall. Shot him right in the back of the head." The sheriff raised his eyebrows, dealing the next hand. "You're not a coward are you, Daniel?"

"I'm not going to shoot you in the back of the head, if that's what you're asking."

"Well that's good to know." The sheriff dealt the next hand of cards. "You haven't ever killed a man, have you?"

"Killed a man?"

"That was the fucking question."

"No, I haven't," Daniel said. "Do I look like a killer?"

"Sometimes looks are deceiving."

"What about you? You seemed to enjoy cracking my skull. You ever kill a man?"

"Sure, I've killed men," the sheriff said. "As for enjoyment, I can't deny that I take a little pleasure in my work... Hell, all a man really wants in life, whether he knows it or not, is a skull to bash. I've been cutting throats since I was a kid. Killed men just about everywhere I've ever been. I put a bullet in a Union cocksucker's ear right here in Elsinore." The sheriff's cold pale eyes studied Daniel with calculated detachment. "What do you think of that?"

Daniel felt a cool drop of sweat roll down from his armpit, down his ribs. "I guess they all had it coming, right?"

"Yeah," the sheriff said. "And don't we all?"

"How come no one ever arrested you?"

The sheriff leaned forward over the poker table. "Kid," he said, "there ain't fucking no one gonna try to arrest me. They wouldn't live to see the courtroom. You see, kid, the thing with me is I just don't give a damn about anyone else. That part of my brain just doesn't fucking work. Most people look at a miner and see a man trying to make a living for his family. I look at a miner and I just see a machine. A meat machine. What I'm asking you is this: What's so special about the meat?"

"I don't see things like that," Daniel said. "I don't know if I could do it."

"Murder?"

"Yeah."

"Why not? Tell me how you see things. Explain them to me."

"Don't get me wrong," Daniel said. "I hate most people. I have no qualms about beating a man within an inch of his life. I can't think of a single person who hasn't either left me or let me down. But a part of me says it's that last inch I can't take. A part of me says I don't have the right to take it."

"And what is *it*?"

"Everything that person's ever been. Everything they're ever going to be."

"Most people aren't ever going to be much of anything."

"That's true, but it ain't up to me to decide who will and who won't. That's up to God—a part of me thinks that anyhow."

"What's the other part of you think?"

"The other part of me thinks, yeah. I can do it. Sooner or later, I will do it. Because when you start accusing me, you start making me fear for my life, you better be feeling lucky, because I'll put a knife in your gut just like anyone else who crosses me."

The sheriff raised Daniel and grinned. "I'm feeling fucking lucky."

Daniel looked over his new cards, four to a flush. He looked at the sheriff challengingly. "Did you feel lucky when you were getting your throat cut?"

"No," he said. The sheriff studied his hand, exhaling deeply. "No I didn't. But I'm still alive, aren't I? And the cocksucker who did this to me, he's six feet under and looking up."

Daniel threw away one card and drew another. He missed the flush. "Who did that to you?"

"They still saying some Mexican gave me this? Rumors, I mean. What'd you hear?"

"I heard lots of things."

82

"You want to know who gave me this?" The sheriff drew his finger across the pale scar across his throat. He took the bottle and filled their glasses. "My fucking old man."

The sheriff was deciding whether or not to call, and he raised his glass and drank. Daniel tried to read his inscrutable glare. The sheriff turned a two dollar chip over in his fingers. Then there was a change in his tone of voice when he spoke again, something painfully truthful, like it was an entirely different man who was talking now, a younger more vulnerable version of himself.

"He wasn't right in the head after he came home from the war. Got all shot up to hell in Gettysburg. Well, I wasn't but twelve-years-old when one night he got good and drunk and started raising all kinds of hell, trashing the house, breaking furniture like a bull. I was in bed listening to this. Glass breaking, him screaming at no one. Then it got real quiet, but I wasn't sleeping. Thought he'd passed out. And then I saw him standing in that doorway. Just a fucking miserable shadow of a man…" The sheriff looked away and took a drink. "…but I didn't beg. And I didn't fucking cry no matter how bad it hurt. Because I knew I was going to kill him when he was done. He must've known I was thinking it too, because he took a fistful of my hair while he was still behind me and cut my throat. And even then he didn't fucking quit. My face pressed into the pillow and everything was wet with my blood and I can remember how it smelled and I was just waiting to fucking die. I just kept wondering why it was taking so long and I couldn't believe how much blood I had inside me."

Daniel stared at him, stunned. For a moment he felt an undeniable connection to Carver and forgot the bad blood that lay poisonously unspoken between them, just below the surface.

"But I didn't die." The sheriff pointed at Daniel as if emphasizing a point in a valuable lesson. His voice was back. Gravelly, low, deadly. "Hatred gave me strength when there was nothing else left."

"You killed your father after that?"

"Yeah," the sheriff said, throwing the two dollar chip into the center of the table. "He was the first."

"Shit," Daniel said frankly. "That's hard."

"Play your cards, kid."

"I'm going all in," Daniel said. Daniel held his cards with his left hand and slid his right down his thigh, lifting his right leg slightly, slowly reaching for the knife he kept in his boot

"That's the fucking spirit." The sheriff smiled and stared him down awhile before he laid down his hand: three aces.

Daniel felt his heart hammering against his ribcage, his palms slick with warm sweat, his raging blood crying out for vengeance, but his face calm. He clutched the knife handle and began slowly pulling it out of the sheath. Daniel stared at him without saying a word for what seemed like a full minute until the sheriff brought his fist down on the card table and roared: "Play your damn hand already!"

Daniel jerked his hand away from the knife and put it up on the table, fumbling with his cards. His boot toe accidently caressed Rose's backside. A high-pitched whine, muffled with a mouthful issued from under the table. The sheriff tilted his head to see under the table. Daniel flung his cards across the green felt. "You just get the best hand every fucking time," he said. "Don't you? How many aces are in that fucking deck?"

"What are you implying?"

"Not that the world's fair and honest."

"Poker table's a dangerous place for a man who thinks justice should and will prevail." Daniel grabbed his whiskey glass and drank it in one reckless and agitated gulp. The sheriff collected the chips and gathered the cards. "You want to deal?"

"I'm flat fucking broke."

"Then start making more fucking money."

"I don't care about money."

"Oh, I think you do." The sheriff shuffled the cards. "And I think you like the tail that comes with it. You got a dick don't you?"

"Why don't you go to hell?"

"But you want more than that. You want the fucking power. You're sick of a being a miserable nobody all your life. You're sick of having

84

no power in a world where a man will step on your face just as soon as look at you. I see myself in you. I used to be you… Nothing. No one. I started this mine with nothing. Now I'm everything. I govern completely. And I can fucking guarantee you, if you're working for me, you won't have any more trouble with anyone in this town."

"What trouble have I got with anyone?"

"Seems to me like you got trouble with just about everyone you meet."

"What do you need me for? You got deputies."

"Sure, I got two deputies, and they're both about as worthless as tits on a boar. But you're different. You feel too much though. Your conscience makes you a coward. I can change that. I can teach you everything—how to kill without passion, without judgment. You could run this fucking town when I'm gone. All you have to do is ask."

"You got me all wrong," Daniel said. "I ain't nothing like you. I don't want to be like you."

"Maybe you got yourself all wrong." The sheriff tossed a silver dollar across the table. "If you ever want to reconsider, you know where to find me. I think you could be a valuable fucking asset to the coal and iron police."

"A dollar," Daniel said, picking up the coin. "What the fuck am I supposed to do with this? After you took everything from me?"

"All I ever took from you was ten dollars, kid."

Daniel pinched the chip between his fingers, his teeth grinding, the emotions welling up in him, nearly throwing it back in the sheriff's face, until finally he flung it across the floor. He couldn't control himself any longer. He knew that if he didn't leave right now there were very good odds he might end the night face down in a pool of his own blood. So he stormed out without another word.

The sheriff sat alone at the table and sank back into the ladder back chair and tilted his head back. Then he took up his cigar, rolling it against a match flame. He leaned back in his chair and smoked. "I'm beginning to think that little shit doesn't like me," he said to himself. Before long, Rose emerged from under the table, wiping her mouth against the back of her hand. Then Katherine came up and tossed her hair back with a flick of her hand.

"You girls see anything unusual from your point of view?"

"I was concentrating on you, honey," Rose said, wiping her chin and licking her fingers.

"All right, honey," he said. "Go on, clean yourself up."

Katherine followed Rose, but the sheriff caught her again by the wrist. "Did I say you could leave?" he asked. "I got something for you to take care of."

"Again? Already?"

"Something else."

*

Staggering alone in the dark snowy street, sick to his stomach, Daniel fought back fierce tears of his drunken, worthless kind as he made his way to the train station on his way home to Elsinore. If an unfortunate stranger had happened to cross his path and by chance look at him the wrong way, Daniel felt like he would have stabbed him in the gut without compunction. He stumbled off the train and then fell down the last three steps from the landing. He landed in the mud and lay there for a while without the will or desire to get up. But he did soon get on his feet again, and staggered back towards his room above the tavern. There he had a half-empty bottle and continued to drink. Soon there was a knock at his door. He stumbled to it, fumbled with the knob, and opened the door. It was Katherine.

He held the bottle by the neck and raised it to his lips, tilting his head back to take a long drink, the brown whiskey sloshing around in the bottle, his throat pumping it down. The suction of his lips made a hollow popping sound when he withdrew the bottle. He wiped the back of his hand across his mouth, the liquor burning his cracked lips. He slammed the bottle down on the table, rattling the dishware on the table. She shuddered. He was looking at her drunkenly. She didn't recognize his eyes.

"You followed me here."

"Why you drinking so much, Daniel?"

"Is that what you came here to ask me?"

"No," she said. "I came because I wanted to apologize for what Jack said to you. The way he acts. He goes too far sometimes. He's not as bad as you think. There's another side to him that you don't know."

"He goes too far sometimes..." He took another drink and choked violently on the whiskey fire in his throat, spitting carelessly on the floor. Then he drank again, finishing what was left of the whiskey, exhaling a temporarily satisfied sigh. He studied the empty bottle. "Dead," he muttered. He started to stand, wobbled on his feet, sat back down. And then got up again.

"You're not going to hurt yourself, are you?"

"I'm not going to hurt myself."

"I know what you're going through," she said.

He looked up at her, suddenly hot-blooded and malicious. Without warning, he hurled the bottle at her, missing her head by a few inches. It exploded on the wall, the shards of glass raining down, glittering in a mosaic on the floor. He lunged at her and grabbed her by the hair.

She cried out.

"What do you know about what I'm going through?" he screamed. He yanked her hair back and saw her looking up at him through her wet brown eyes. He jerked her head back again, wild in his anthracite eyes, his face hardening. "What do you know about it?"

"I don't know," she screamed, hot tears spurting from her eyes. "I don't know."

"You think you have me figured out? You have nothing figured out!"

"Please! You're hurting me!"

"Why'd he send you here?"

"No one sent me!"

"Tell me why!"

"He doesn't know I'm here! I swear!"

Out of nowhere seemingly he pulled his knife, the blade flashed, and held it just under her chin, his knuckles whitening so tight was his grip on the handle. "Lie to me one more time and I'll cut your fucking head off."

For a moment she said nothing. "Then do it," she finally said through clenched teeth, her fingernails pressing into his forearm until they drew blood.

He threw her down to the floor, his deep rage unleashed, uncontrollable. Turning on the closest object, he stabbed the knife into the tabletop repeatedly, wildly, then flipped over the table, the dishes sailing off the top, breaking on the floor. She was crawling away, pulling herself across the floor. He turned on the wall, punching it repeatedly, his knuckles now bloody. He began sobbing uncontrollably, pressing his forehead against the wall. He slid down and fell to his knees.

Later, when he awoke in the darkness, he was gasping for air. He couldn't breathe. He found himself lying on the floor amidst shards of broken glass, his elbows and forearms cut up and painted with dried blood. He thought someone must have beaten him up. He looked about at the furniture destroyed in his drunken rage, the splintered wood, the shards of glass, and he remembered nothing.

Six

The next morning, Daniel walked to work, his eyes weary and bloodshot, his face bearded, the flashes of what he could remember from the night before repeating in his mind without respite, half-expecting to catch hell from Badger for being late once again. But the forge was closed and Badger had inscribed in chalk on his slate that hung from the door: Sick—gone home. Daniel threw open the doors to the shop. The mounds of coal in the forge were untouched, the air hung cold and smokeless. He found Badger's old burnt apron hanging in its place on an old rusty nail. Daniel wiped his running nose on the sleeve of his shirt and poked around. Finally, he called out toward the back room. He went back out into the cold, hoping to find the old blacksmith hobbling up the hill, cursing anyone and anything he encountered. His eyes scanned the landscape. But all he found were the regular colliery laborers going about their routines. Retreating indoors, the wind unbearably frigid, he pulled shut the double doors and suddenly felt very alone in the palpable silence.

He began vigorously searching for one of his bottles he kept hidden around the smithy. Badger would tolerate none of his drinking on the job and would pour them out whenever he found them. Daniel found a green bottle under an oilcloth in the corner, and he held it up to the firelight to measure its contents. Not having any urgent task at hand, over the next hour he got drunk, grew drowsy and sank into a deep sleep.

The sound of the deputy's boots on the hard dirt floor was what woke him. He looked through one bloodshot eye and then opened the other. He sat up straight and ran his fingers through his greasy hair.

"You sleep on the job pretty regularly around here?"

Daniel yawned and got on his feet. "When the time's right," he said with a guarded tone.

"Shit. I got the wrong job."

"You want mine?" Daniel staggered over to the forge and stirred the coals and worked the bellows a few times. The flames licked high and the black smoke rose weightlessly and disappeared in the flue. "It don't pay shit though."

"Where's old Badger at?"

"I don't know. I was just about to ask you the same thing."

"You mean he never came in this morning?"

"Nope."

"That ain't like him at all."

"I know."

"Must have come down with the influenza," said the deputy. "I ain't here for Badger though. I got a few questions I need to ask you."

"Go ahead."

"What was you doing last night after you left work?"

"Playing cards."

"Uh huh," the deputy said. "You much of a drinking man?"

"Something like that," Daniel said.

"Was you drunk?"

"I wasn't *not* drunk…"

"Uh huh…" Spearman poked his tongue around in his cheek. "Do you tend to get a little violent when you drink?"

"Only when I got a reason to get violent."

"The reason I ask is because they're saying like you beat up on that whore last night."

Daniel pinched his brow. "What the hell are you talking about? Who said that? I didn't hurt her."

"I'm just saying that's not what I heard. The sheriff said she was all shook up and in tears late last night. Had a cut under her chin. Looked like someone might have held a knife to her and tried to force himself on her." The deputy paused and stroked his chin, eying Daniel for a moment. "You know we don't treat our women like that around here."

"Well, according to me," Daniel said, "Jack Carver's a lying sack of shit."

"You ain't helping your case talking like that."

"What kind of trouble am I in?"

The deputy shrugged. "It ain't up to me what you're in. You got yourself into this. But I got orders to take you to jail till we get this all sorted out."

"I told you I didn't even see her last night."

"Well, trouble is we got witnesses saying otherwise." The deputy took the handcuffs from off his belt. "Now you ain't going to take a swing at me, are you?"

"If you think you're putting those cuffs on me, you're damn right I'm gonna take a swing at you."

"And if I don't?"

"I'll walk out of here without giving you any trouble."

*

At the sheriff's office, there was a small holding cell with two cots. A black miner was laid out on one of the cots with his hands folded over his chest, his eyes closed. Daniel stood waiting while the guard unlocked the door, the keys jingling on a large ring. At the sound of the keys, the black miner opened his eyes and raised his head slightly to look in their direction. He set his head back down and closed his eyes. The door swung open with a squeak and the guard tossed his chin, gesturing for Daniel to go inside.

"Go on in," he said. "This is your new home for the next few days."

Daniel shuffled in and the door slammed shut, the iron clanking behind him. He looked down at the cracks splintering across the floor. He held out his hand and tried to keep it steady but it began to shake and he regarded it as if he were watching a storm gather. His cellmate sat up on his cot and watched Daniel.

"What's wrong with your hand?"

"Nothing." Daniel let his hand drop and he rubbed his knees. He looked at his cellmate and then looked away.

"Shit, son, you look like you need a doctor."

"I don't need a doctor. I need a drink."

"Well, you can forget about that," he said. "What they bring you in here for?"

Daniel looked at him and then looked away. "Hell if I know."

He slept a dreamless sleep and awoke after some hours to the sound of the guard tapping the iron bars with his nightstick. Daniel's shirt clung to his chest, damp and dark with sweat. His eyes were red and his face was hot, his hair sticking to his sweaty forehead. He felt like he was coming down with the flu, his stomach terribly nauseous.

"Get up, asshole. Time to eat."

His cellmate was already seated on his cot, spooning the gruel hungrily into his mouth.

"I'm not hungry," Daniel said.

"Well you're gonna eat. I don't care if I got to come in there and shove it down your goddamn throat."

He staggered to his feet and wobbled and accepted a bowl of soupy gruel the color of rancid milk, the consistency of lumpy gravy. Daniel took one look at it and felt his gut twitch and he swallowed back the taste of his own puke. He set the bowl on the floor and lay back down, taking quick shallow breaths, his mind in a feverish nightmare.

"Pearce ain't fucking around, man. You better eat that shit."

"You eat it."

"You don't want it?"

"Please. Get it the fuck away from me."

His cellmate shot a glance across the room and scampered over to the bowl and poured the contents into his own and returned to his side of the cell where he shoveled it into his mouth, the spoon clinking in the ceramic bowl.

When he opened his eyes he saw strange colors. He was confused and didn't know where he was. He held his hand above his chest and watched it tremble and he let it fall onto his chest. His whole body shivered and he clutched his arms around himself and turned on his side, facing the iron bars and the blank wall beyond. He was cold and sweating, squirming and writhing on the stiff cot. In the lamplight, shadows quivered on the walls. The sheriff's grave visage came forth from those shadows. He saw a wall moving and he heard a bedlamite's gibbering voice as if far off down a hallway. When he opened his hallucinatory eyes again, he saw a wolf-spider the size of a large dog crawling down the wall and he cried out, shrieking and wailing. He saw a grotesque face with one eye missing, and it spoke out of the darkness: "God bless ye and may ye die of the dysentery." He came to briefly on the floor later, his cellmate kneeling beside him and the taste of leather in his mouth and felt his own spittle all over his beard. His cellmate took his folded belt from Daniel's mouth. "It's gonna be all right," he said. "You're gonna be just fine, brother."

He sweated and shook until dawn, and when he woke, he felt as if there was no blood in his body and the lining of his stomach had been scraped out with broken glass. His eyes rolled about in his head. He tried to sit up and then collapsed back down on the rigid cot. The black miner came to him, holding a tin cup of water.

"Take it easy, brother," he said. "Drink some of this."

He held the tin cup down and Daniel turned his head.

"Don't be a fool. Drink it."

Daniel propped himself up on his elbows and raised his head to sip the water, the rim of the cup touching his cracked dry lips. After a few sips, he eased himself back down and he rolled over on his side.

"I think I pissed myself," he muttered.

"That's okay, man. Sick as you were. You couldn't help it."

"I never was sick like that in my life."

"I never seen anyone sick like that in my life."

Pearce stood before the iron bars, holding a tray with their lunch. "Well," he said, "sleeping beauty's finally awake. Thought you was gonna die on us."

"I'm not dead yet," Daniel said.

"You better eat something today."

"I'll see what I can do."

He and the black sat opposite one another on their cots, spooning the watery beef soup into their mouths. Daniel felt his strength coming back to him as he ate for the first time in days, his color returning in his cheeks, but his lanky body still that of an emaciated alcoholic. He draped a moth-riddled blanket over his shoulders and rested his elbows and his knees and raked his bony fingers through his greasy hair. "Shit," he said.

"What's your name?" the miner asked.

"Daniel," he said. "What's yours?"

"Samuel. What are you in here for anyhow?"

Daniel looked up from the soup bowl in his lap and wiped his mouth on the back of his hand. "They think I was beating on someone."

"Well who?" Samuel asked.

"They think I was beating on some whore from Monongahela."

"Did you?"

"I don't know what happened," Daniel said. "I know I didn't hit anyone. I think maybe I pulled her hair or something. I don't remember."

"You know you ain't supposed to hit women, don't you?"

"I was fucking drunk. I wasn't thinking about what I'm supposed to be doing. I was just doing."

"I'm guessing that's a regular thing for you?"

"What?"

"Being drunk," Samuel said.

"Is that a fucking problem with you?"

"What's a young man like you drinking so much for anyhow?"

Daniel's face soured at the question. "Why is everyone always fucking asking me that? I guess you're just in jail for minding your own damn business, huh? You didn't do a goddamn thing."

"No, I didn't. I didn't do a damn thing. I came here looking for work like everybody else," then raising his voice so as to be heard by the deputies, "but these white boys ain't never seen a nigger up close, so they got their brains all fuddled and figured me for some kind of Union organizer... And here I am, till they see fit to let me go."

Daniel began to laugh. "Boy did you pick the wrong town at the wrong fucking time."

94

"Hey man. You'd a swallowed your own tongue if it weren't for me. I'd say I have pretty damn good timing."

"I spend my life trying to drink myself to death, and when it's about to happen, you don't let me die. Am I supposed to thank you or something?"

"I used to be a lot like you, man. Thought I knew everything. Well, let me tell you: things will start better for you quick if you'd just lay off the bottle. It's the devil's own."

"Well, that's a load of bullshit if I ever heard one."

"So that's it? You just gonna drink yourself to death when you get out a here?"

"We're all born with a death sentence. If I don't die from drinking, I'll die from something else," he said. "And if I don't die now, I'll die later. What difference does it make how I die? What difference does it make when? Today was bad, tomorrow's gonna be worse. That's the only thing I can count on anymore. It doesn't make any difference what I do." Daniel collapsed back onto his cot. He lay with his arms crossed behind his head, staring up at the ceiling. Then he rolled on his side and looked out the iron bars.

It was quiet for about ten minutes. Neither said anything to the other. Then Samuel broke the silence. "The difference," he said, "is the pain and suffering you'll cause for everyone around you."

*

When Daniel awoke the following morning, the sheriff was there talking to the deputies. He came over to the cell and put his hand around one of the bars. He pushed the brim of his hat back with his other hand. Daniel sat up on the cot, blinking and squinting tiredly. "You lost some weight, son," said the sheriff. He turned to look over his shoulder. "Hey, Pearce, you been feeding this one?"

"Hell, he was skin and bones when he came in. Then he wasn't eating."

"He been giving you any trouble?"

"He's been all right," Pearce admitted.

95

The sheriff turned back to look at Daniel, a kind of pathos in his eyes. "You all right, son?"

"Yeah, I'm all right," Daniel said.

"Now, you ain't gonna get drunk if I let you out a here, are you?"

"I might have a drink. I won't get drunk."

"You're damn right you won't get drunk," he said. "And you're gonna stay away from that whore. You got it? You really shook her up."

"Yeah I got it."

"Second chances are rare, you understand?"

"I understand."

The sheriff gave a wag of his finger towards the cell door, and Pearce went over to it with his keychain. The keys jingled and then the lock clicked and the bars swung open. He staggered out of the cell. Pearce slammed the door shut behind him, the metal clanking, the lock clicking, and then he gave a little tug on the bars to make sure it was locked. When Daniel looked back, Samuel was smiling at him.

"You keep your nose clean out there, all right, man?"

The sheriff put his hand on Daniel's shoulder, leading him towards the door.

Outside, the sheriff fished a pack of cigarettes out of his shirt pocket and shook out two cigarettes, offering one to Daniel. He accepted it, and the sheriff lit their cigarettes with a match. They stood there smoking.

"When I was your age, I was involved in a number of similar altercations with the law."

"How'd you put a stop to it?"

"I became the fucking law."

Daniel snorted a laugh. "Yeah, I guess you did."

"I hope you feel like working today," Carver said.

Daniel shrugged. "I don't feel like sitting in there. I'll tell you that."

"You think you can manage the shop by yourself?"

"What do you mean by myself?"

96

"You mean no one told you yet?"

"Told me what?"

"Badger's dead."

"What happened to him?"

"He was a lunger. Doc says he died in his sleep." The sheriff leaned forward and spat into the slush and melting snow. "You looked up to him, didn't you?"

"He was all right."

"Yeah," the sheriff agreed, taking the last drag on his cigarette and then throwing it away into the snow. "Old Badger would speak his mind and that was that. He didn't give a damn who you were. Hell, he even had words with me from time to time. If you want to know the truth, I've only known one other man who had guts like that."

"Who's that?" Daniel asked.

"It was a long time ago." The sheriff smiled and shook his head, looking at Daniel. "You wouldn't know him."

Daniel looked at his cigarette and it was burned down to his fingertips. He threw the smoking butt out into the snow. "No," Daniel said. "I guess I wouldn't."

Daniel started to walk away.

The sheriff called to him. "You know, I can't just let you go that easy."

He stopped and turned his head over his shoulder. "What do you mean?"

"I mean you're working for me now."

"I thought I already was."

"Not like this…"

"Like what?"

"Come here."

Daniel turned and walked back to him. The sheriff pulled a folded sheet of paper out of his breast pocket. He gave it to Daniel. "There's a name on that paper. It's someone I can't trust anymore. I need you to make him disappear."

Daniel didn't open the paper. He tried to give it back to the sheriff. "I'm not interested."

"And I'm not asking," the sheriff said. "I'm telling you you're gonna do it. Or I'm gonna give someone a piece of paper with your name on it."

Daniel sneered and shook his head in disgust. "They always want something from you…"

"Open it up," the sheriff said. He shook two more cigarettes out of his pack.

Daniel unfolded the piece of paper. He looked at Carver in disbelief. "Bullshit."

The sheriff gave a facial shrug, and handed Daniel another cigarette. "Like I said: I don't trust him anymore. You do this, maybe I'll know if I can trust you."

The sheriff struck a match and lit their cigarettes. Daniel held the piece of paper to the burning end of his cigarette and it caught fire. He held it as it burned down to his fingers, and the flakes of ash were whisked away on the wind and gone was the name he had written: Charlie O'Brien.

*

The darkness dropped and he didn't remember leaving the tavern. He was lying nearly dead-drowned-drunk in his own piss puddle, pleading with whatever capricious deity would hear him for redress. A calico cat perched on the fence boards watched him with languid indifference. The mud puddles in the alley had hardened with frost and his damp clothes had grown stiff. His pale blue lips muttered slurred words in a drunken madness. He saw a figure standing over him. The cat hissed and leapt into the darkness.

"Ain't you a pitiful sight?"

"Not you," Daniel muttered. "Anyone but you."

"I thought you told me you weren't going to drink tonight."

"Everyone that's nice to me and doesn't fucking want nothing from me ends up fucking dead…"

"That's life kid. Now get up—if you go to sleep out here, you ain't gonna wake up."

"Leave me alone," Daniel said.

"Let me help you up. You look like you took about a dozen shots of whiskey beyond the prudent."

"Well, I fucking left Katherine alone, didn't I?"

"That was only part of the deal," the sheriff said. "I can't have you not working this week because you're mourning like you're Badger's fucking widow."

"The deal's off and fuck you."

"What, do you think if you get drunk enough Badger won't be dead?

"All I remember's me telling you to leave me the fuck alone because I'm done trying because people are fucked up, and I can't don't even give a god damn..." His slurred diatribe stopped abruptly, and he rolled over on his side, vomiting copious amounts of soupy bile on the sheriff's boots.

"Why you little fucking rat..." The sheriff lifted one of his boots and looked at it with disgust and put it back down. "I'd snap your pencil neck right here if you didn't remind me of myself when I was your age, you little cocksucker."

"Ain't no fucking cocksucker," Daniel slurred. Then with clear articulation, opening his bloodshot eyes. "I didn't mean to puke on your boots."

He looked at Daniel and snatched him up by his collar and hauled him up, but Daniel was entirely legless with drink and collapsed right back to the ground. So the sheriff put Daniel's arm over his shoulder and dragged him back across the thoroughfare. "You fucking stink like cat piss or worse, you know that?"

"Piss on you," Daniel slurred half in and half out of consciousness.

"You fucking cuss a lot when you're drinking, you know that?"

"I like to fucking cuss."

"So do I," the sheriff said. "I wouldn't fucking trust a man who didn't."

Daniel fell again. When the sheriff grabbed him by the arm, Daniel had the sensation of waking from a blood-soaked nightmare. He wrenched his arm away from the sheriff's grip as if he had been touched by hot steel, his eyes cold and dark and reckless. "You stay the hell away from me," he hissed. "You don't touch me again, you son of a bitch."

Daniel staggered away, only making it a few slantwise steps before he walked into the tavern wall and was on the ground again, crawling pathetically, the sheriff walking slowly behind him, grinning in the moonlight.

*

Mary Beth tossed and turned in her bed. She dreamed of fire nearly every night. Her mother had died in a house fire when she was six. Somehow, a coal-oil lamp had been left burning too close to the open window, and while they slept, the summer breeze had blown the curtains over the glass chimney. No one ever talked about it anymore. They had tried to forget it in a way, but the past has a way of coming back with a vengeance. That was thirteen years ago—and she never really recovered from the trauma. She had suffered the same dreams when she was a child, for months after the incident, but they went away when Burke suggested the laudanum. Now, something had changed, the opiates weren't enough anymore, and she started having them again.

The fire bursts spontaneously from nothing, crawls up the curtains in a fury of sparks and awful brightness, and the flames lick at the ceiling, which is stained with a black ring from smoke. She feels the heavy heat grow more and more intense, sweat drops rolling from her forehead, small beads forming on the skin above her upper lip. The smoke thickens. She happens to glance at the vanity set in her room, but she never sees her own reflection in the mirror—or if it is her, then it is some distorted and blurred version of herself that she cannot quite recognize. She looks at her hands. They bubble with blisters. She hears a pounding at the door and then the glass of the vanity mirror shatters. This is how the dream always ends.

When he heard the screams, O'Brien would always burst into her room. It had happened almost every night, the same scene repeated. As usual, he found her contorted and twitching in the sweat-drenched bed linens, her mouth wide open, gasping for air. He would rouse her from sleep like this, only this time he stopped when he saw that she was bleeding badly from the nose. Her pillow was covered. Then she gripped him by the arms and her eyes were wide open. He held her until she was done shaking. She came around slowly, confused and groggy.

"I feel it."

"No you don't."

"The fire."

"There's no fire."

"Look at my arm..."

"There's nothing there."

"Don't you see the blisters?" she sobbed.

"There's nothing." He held her in his arms. "There's nothing there."

"It burns something awful."

*

Marianna, PA.
February 12, 1889

Dear Mr. Carver,

I have a good deal more acquaintances than when I first arrived here. On my way to the boarding house, I met two miners sharing a mason jar of moonshine. I could see they were well on their way to becoming drunk. I introduced myself, and they offered me a sip of their strong-smelling spirit. When I refused, they made a crude joke about the temperance movement at my expense. So I reconsidered their offer and drank with them until they were comfortable enough around me--and drunk enough--to speak frankly. I grumbled about the work as they expected me to and told them the bosses must detest me or else they would not give me such miserable work. After a good deal of conversation, they showed me their Union cards and invited me to attend their next meeting in the basement of St. Anne's church. As for myself, I am as well as I have ever been in my life. I am gaining in flesh. The emissary's life agrees with me and I enjoy myself first rate, though drinking strange moonshine is a bad idea and does not have a good effect on the bowels.

Your humble and obedient servant,

Logan O'Brien

*

When Michael left the tavern on his way to the boarding house, he met a stranger, a rawboned black man with a canvas sac full of clothes sagging at his feet, leaning against a wooden porch post, rolling a cigarette. He wore an old moth-eaten coat that was a little too large for him. The stranger studied Michael's face and nodded.

"You got a pinch of tobacco?" the stranger asked.

"Sure." Michael said, offering his pouch of Prince Albert.

"I just got in from Pittsburgh."

"That a fact?"

"Where can a man find a place to sleep around here?"

"We got a boarding house up on the hill. Was just on my way there."

"They let niggers sleep there?"

"We're all the same color when we come out of the pit, aren't we?"

"Well, all right… I'll follow you."

He held out his hand to shake. "I'm Michael."

"Samuel."

"You looking for work or you just passing through?"

"Oh, I'm here to work all right." As they got to walking, Samuel ripped open a flap concealed within his coat and produced a letter certifying him as an organizer for the UMWA.

Michael shoved the paper away. "Jesus Christ. Put that away. You're as good as dead if they see you with that around here."

"Boy that sheriff of yours really puts the fear of God in you boys."

"Yeah, well, have you met the man?"

"I just got out of his jail cell."

"And you're still here? You got some brass, I'll give you that."

"Someone's got to show a little brass around here if you want to get the big bad Elsinore Coal Company to negotiate a contract."

"I'm all for that. You just got a keep a low profile, bud."

"This ain't my first rodeo. I've been organizing all up and down this railroad. The Union's getting strong all the way down to Marianna and readying for a strike. Are you boys ready to stand up to that sheriff of yours once and for all?"

"What do you need?"

They had reached the boarding house and they stopped at the steps in front of the porch. Samuel stroked the whiskers on his beard. "You got some boys you can trust?"

*

The main gangway resounded with the shouts of the mule drivers. Silvery smoke drifted through the air after a blast in one of the chambers. Far down the tunnel, a dozen little orange points of light flickered and flashed. The miners walked deep into the abandoned corridors of the mine and bribed a door boy with tobacco to whistle if he should see a boss coming in their direction. They huddled in an empty chamber, the walls dank and dripping, the low roof ominously pressing their shoulders. They opened their lunch buckets and just beyond the light of their headlamps the rats went up on their hind legs like squirrels. Some of the men took off their coats and spread them on the floor to sit on, while others squatted on their haunches over puddles of acidic water.

They were all jeopardizing their jobs by associating with a Union organizer, risking their chances of working at any mine in Pennsylvania if they would be blacklisted. The grimy miners scratched their stubbly chins, regarding the one black miner among them suspiciously. They were equally wary of Daniel, a stranger to most of them, rumored to be half-crazy, often seen muttering when no one else was around.

"This everyone?" Samuel asked, a little disappointed with the turnout.

"What's the blacksmith doing here?" Burnside asked.

"He's with me," Michael said.

"I don't like him," Burnside said. "And I sure as hell don't trust him."

"He's good people... you can trust him."

"He looks like a fucking scab if I ever saw one."

"That's Davie Byrnes's son you're talking about," Blizzard warned.

"Bullshit. Davie Byrnes's son is dead."

Daniel smiled with one side of his mouth. "Maybe I am dead. Maybe I'm haunting Elsinore."

"I don't know who that is, and I don't trust him," Burnside persisted.

"Well, that's exactly what the company wants," Samuel interrupted.

"And just who the hell are *you* anyhow?"

"I'm an organizer for the United Mine Workers of America."

The miners looked askance at one another. Others looked down at their boots, a little embarrassed for the organizer who had the hubris to come to Elsinore.

"The company keeps you divided," Samuel went on, "and fighting against one another so you can't stand up to them. And if we ever want to do that we're going to have to learn that we're all on the same side. Now, I know you're all a little worried there aren't more of us here, but this is the first time anyone's ever stood up to the Elsinore Coal Company."

"This isn't the first time," Liam O'Loughlin, one of the camp elders, said. "We've had your kind here before."

"Well, boys, you haven't had me here before... I don't need to bother telling you about the risk you're taking by talking to me. But it's a risk worth taking. If we're gonna make anything happen, we need to stick together. We need to look out for one another."

"You're a fool," Burnside snapped. "These men won't stick together once the company brings in the Baldwin-Felts to start raising hell."

"And so what if they do?" Blizzard growled. "We'll fight fire with fire. I say it'd be a damn good thing if we raised a little hell of our own in this valley. I've never killed a man, and I hope I never have to. But I'd kill a dozen of those mine guards as I would a dozen rats."

"Look here," Samuel said. "One man alone can't do much, can't take a stand against the operators. But if we stick together, and get some more men to stand with us, we got a Union. And I'll tell you what. These operators are scared of the Union. They'll spend a thousand dollars to hire thugs to break a strike, but they won't pay you the money you earned while you're down here risking your lives with a mountain pressing down on your backs."

"How much are the dues?" Ekvie asked.

"Seventy-five cents."

"That's a lot of money," O'Loughlin complained.

"Hell, Liam, you got more money tucked away than anyone here tonight, you cheap son of a bitch," Blizzard said.

"How do you think we pay for tents and food when it comes times to strike?" Samuel asked.

"How do I know you ain't just pocketing my money?" O'Loughlin continued cynically. "I know all about you agitators."

"Take a look at the sheriff's house when you go home," Samuel countered. "How much of your money does *he* pocket? This is the United fucking Mineworkers of America, and we'll be organized in spite of all opposition. Anyone who wants to join needs to step up here, take a pledge, pay your dues, and sign a membership card. Anyone who wants to leave can leave now. But if you join us, you'll have ten thousand other miners standing beside you. The Union is solidly grouped up and down the Monongahela and Youghiogheny river valleys, all the way to Pittsburgh."

O'Loughlin grunted and waved his hand in the air. No one knew what it meant. Glances and shrugs were exchanged. Finally, he said, "Where do I sign?"

Then and there they all took their pledges and signed their Union cards. Samuel circulated among them propaganda literature he had smuggled into the camp and warned them that they would have to be careful until the Union had a strong foothold in the camp. Until then, the miners at Elsinore would have to operate in secrecy. But most of all, he stressed the cardinal necessity of encouraging other workers to stand with them and join the Union.

Afterwards, they went back to their chambers to load coal until they finished the shift. As Samuel thanked the men for coming, Michael pulled him aside. "They're scared shitless."

"They always are when they first sign up," Samuel reassured him. "They'll come around."

Michael rubbed his chin. "You got any sort of protection?"

"What do you mean?"

"I mean with the way things are going, you'd be a fool not to carry a gun."

Samuel reached his hand inside his coat pocket, producing a small Derringer pistol for Michael to see it and then slipping it back into his pocket. "Ain't no fool," he said.

"You might want to get a bigger gun."

Seven

In the boarding room bed, which was spinning rapidly, as were the walls and the entire room in which he lay, Daniel focused his gaze on a dead bug, or maybe merely the molted shell of a bug, that clung to the fissured ceiling, a black spot like a drunkard's north star around which all other points revolved. The boarders slept four to a bed. But Daniel rarely slept more than an hour or two. He always insisted on taking one of the ends of the bed so that he could reach the bottle he kept on the floor. He drank sporadically throughout the night, and he needed a good deal of whiskey just to keep his hands from trembling in the morning. Right now it was still dark and no one else was awake. Someone was snoring. Michael lay beside Daniel in bed, murmuring in his sleep. Occasionally, he would throw an arm or leg across Daniel, sometimes even spilling a splash of his whiskey in the process, and Daniel would curse him under his breath and remove the arm.

"Mmmuuhh," Michael moaned. "Mmmhh—Mary Beth," he mumbled. "Lively little gal…" When Daniel looked over at him, he saw Michael's hips rising and falling. He was slowly but surely humping a mass of knotted up bed linens. "Look at all this money, Mary Beth… all this damn money..."

Daniel screwed up his face, rolled over, away from the nocturnal fornicator beside him, and reached down for his bottle. Before long he heard the sound of the other miners grumbling indistinctly in the dark, cumbersomely tugging at their coveralls, pulling their suspenders over their shoulders, fishing their socks out of squeaky drawers, stifling yawns, farting and burping, lacing up their gumboots. The smell of the mine, the smell of coal dust, had saturated into the half-dozen overalls left hanging out to dry on large hooks. He groaned with a slight headache and a persistently sour stomach. He dropped his sockfeet to the cold creaking hardwood floor and slid out of the creaking iron bed. There were brass miners' tags scattered on the floor. He slipped into his jumpers and pulled on his boots. He was the last to leave the room, alone, and for the first thoughtless minutes of the day he sat slumped in exhaustion in the plank-back chair, nodding off until a hard thud at the window startled him. He sat up straight, tightening in the throatcords.

For a moment he thought someone had thrown a snowball at the window, hurrying him along through his slothful morning routine. But there was no snow on the window and, looking outside into the abandoned street, he saw no one. He raised the window, letting in a draft of biting cold air and inspected the ground below the window. Barely visible in the snowy darkness was a dead barn swallow, a few stray feathers, the delicate creature twitching. For the first time, he thought about leaving the camp. He thought of the railroad tracks and how he could disappear as suddenly as he had one day appeared.

*

Later that week, Daniel labored back to the smithy, hunched forward like a pauperized mendicant, worn out and sweaty, a fifty pound sack of coal slung over his shoulder. His face and beard were begrimed with soot from forging daylong, sharpening miners' picks and augers. To break up the stale reek of monotony, someone had brought him a gate hinge to mend. But now he was all but done for the day and his final task was to replenish his coal supply. This was his third and final trip from the breaker.

Inside the dark, dusty smithy, he dropped the sack of coal beside the rough shapes of iron rusting in the corner amidst old cobwebs and miscellanies of junk. He took his coat from off its iron hook and slung it over his shoulder. All he wanted was a drink, and he couldn't deny himself any longer. He went out the door, disgusted with himself, and slammed it shut behind him. As soon as he looked up, he saw Michael talking to O'Brien by the engine house. O'Brien looked towards Daniel, and Michael turned to look over his shoulder, and when he saw Daniel he started walking towards him quickly.

"Hey, Cowboy," he said. "Where you going?"

"Going down the tavern. Been a real miserable shit of a day."

"Thought you said you were cutting back?"

"That was then," Daniel said. "This is now."

"I knew you wouldn't last long."

Daniel grumbled indistinctly.

"What?"

"I don't really want to drink."

"Then don't drink."

"It ain't that easy though. I can't stop thinking about it. It's like there's this ringing in my ears, and I can't focus on anything I'm doing or anything anyone's saying to me because that's all I hear. But I know if I take a drink, it'll go away. It'll get quiet again."

"Well come on with me then. This will get your mind off it." Michael looked around cautiously, his voice dropping to a whisper. "Union's picking up steam faster than anyone expected, and we're holding a meeting up in Beazell's barn."

"I'm not interested."

"Hold on a sec. Why don't you come?"

"It doesn't concern me."

"It concerns every last one of us. Even if you're not the one working in the pit, you're still I' screwed by the company six ways from Sunday, bustin' your ass so Jack Carver can live high and mighty. When the strike starts, you'll either be with us or against us."

Daniel shook his head and gazed across the valley to the company houses and the patchwork of slate roofs. From each chimney came a black plume of coal-smoke. He could see the horseback mine-guards making their evening rounds through the patch. You never knew when you were being watched, but you always felt like it.

"What were you doing talking to O'Brien?"

"What's that supposed to mean?"

Daniel kicked at the dirt with his boot toe. He sensed something deeply evasive about Michael. When he looked up again, the horsemen were gone and he couldn't find them as he scanned the hillside. "How is it you're marrying the boss's daughter?"

"That's between me and her. Ain't got nothing to do with this."

"How's that gonna play out when the strike starts?"

"Let me worry about that when the time comes. Ain't none of your business anyhow."

Daniel stepped closer, leaning in to whisper in Michael's ear. "I know you're not telling me something…"

All of a sudden, O'Brien was standing behind them. Michael jumped and laughed uneasily. "Jesus Christ, Charlie. What are you sneaking up on us like that for?"

"Why are all those boys going up to Beazell's?"

"Wouldn't you like to know?" Michael said.

"Don't play games. Not with me."

"Calm down, Charlie. It's old man Beazell's birthday. He's got a keg of beer in the barn."

"Half those hunkies don't even know Beazell."

"I guess they're just going for the free booze. And hell. Beazell's so old he doesn't know who he knows and who he doesn't know."

O'Brien crossed his arms. "How old is he now anyhow?"

"I think he's turning eighty-two, if I'm not mistaken."

"Hmm."

"You want to come with us?"

"You're a good kid, McKeeta." O'Brien looked at Daniel and gestured at him with his chin. "I don't like seeing you with him. I wouldn't want my daughter around him."

"Hey, he's all right, Charlie."

"I thought I warned you about this place," O'Brien said to Daniel. "You're lucky Carver hasn't already…"

Daniel shoved him hard. O'Brien's crossed arms flailed out and he stumbled backwards. "That's twice you threatened me. Don't fucking do it again."

Suddenly, Michael stepped between them and pushed Daniel back. "Hey, that's enough. That's enough."

Daniel leaned and spat into the dirt, wild about the eyes and laden with violence.

O'Brien pointed at him. "I told you once. Get the hell out of Monongahela."

Michael steered Daniel in the direction of the barn. "Just walk away," he said.

It was almost dark as they walked uphill along the road to the barn. The air chilled and a violent wind tore through the trees and the topmost branches scratched and clawed at each other. It began spitting rain, cold on his arms and the back of his neck. West of the valley and beyond the hills, the great brain-shaped clouds pulsed silently with amethyst lightning flashes.

"Here comes that rain."

"Looks like we're in for it," Daniel said.

Among the last to join the meeting, they were stunned to see so many attendants. Standing among the wooden posts in the kerosene lamplight, a surfeit of miners stood shoulder to shoulder, milling about in conversation. The barn smelled of hay and dust and cattle. Beneath their feet, through the cracks in the floorboards, the vague shadows of beasts lumbered about. Michael went to the front of the crowd and shook hands with Samuel, who was waiting to address everyone. Daniel stayed behind at the back of the crowd, detached and still fuming from the confrontation with O'Brien. By and by, the mingling ceased and the meeting proper began.

Blizzard hollered, "Everyone shut the hell up so we can get this meeting started!"

The miners quieted down.

Samuel looked them over. Finally he spoke.

"Boys, you don't need me to tell you what you're risking by being here tonight and joining the Union. You stand to be blacklisted, fired, thrown out of your homes, intimidated by thugs, cheated out of your wages. The list goes on and on. You all know what's at stake. But you all came." He nodded his head approvingly. "Now the Union numbers have swelled rapidly these past few weeks at Elsinore, and the time for action has come. I'd like to put the motion on the floor to begin a strike. That way the company has no choice but to start negotiating a Union contract. All up and down the Monongahela and Youghiogheny, miners are making a stand. We're standing together at Marianna.

111

We're standing together at Ellsworth. We're standing together at Beallsville and Catsburg and Cokeburg. By God, this is the United Mineworkers of America and we'll stand together in Elsinore.

"Now all in favor, say, 'Aye!'"

"Aye!" a chorus of miners shouted.

"All against, say, 'Nay.'"

A few miners muttered, "Nay."

"The ayes carry it," Samuel said. He paused for he was interrupted by their applause until he raised a hand to quiet them. "We're having a picket line tomorrow and by God it's going to be a big picket line! We're gonna need every man, woman, and child in the camp."

A discussion on the details of the strike ensued. He explained how the Union would supply them with foodstuffs and canvas tents. He warned them that the company would hire Baldwin-Felts agents and bring in scab workers to keep the mine open. He told them it would take months of struggle and blood would no doubt be spilled. But he also told them that together they could do it. He told them they needed to do it, because the fight was not only for their own sake, but for their children and their children's children.

All the while, the thunder pealed and the wind sang through the cracks in the wall boards and the rain pelted the tin roof. At one point during the speech, the barn door flung open, swinging wildly on its hinges, slamming against the wall, revealing the violence and chaos of the storm outside. The thunder rumbled steadily. With each boom, the men jumped. Each flash of lightning illuminated the slats in the wallboards. Daniel noticed a shadow moving outside along the wall. At first he wasn't sure, and then he knew for certain that a man was prowling outside the meeting. Then he lost the lurking figure in the darkness until—he must have tripped—Daniel heard him stumble over a bucket. A few heads at the back of the crowd turned at this sound, but quickly it was lost in the sound of the storm and they turned back to listen to the speech.

Daniel slipped away from the back of the crowd. No one noticed his leaving. Catlike, he climbed down the ladder to the lower level of the barn. In the darkness below, he drew his knife. The steel blade flashed in the lightning. He climbed over the fence. The huddled cows regarded him with frank indifference as he moved slowly past them. Then he went out into the pasture and the pouring rain soaked his clothes in no time at all. His boots sank in the mud. He kept himself pressed along the edge of the barn, the knife in his right hand. He poked his head around the corner, but he saw no one.

There was a small hill that led up to the second level of the barn. He carefully climbed through the barbed wire fence and crept up the hill, edging along the barn wall. He could hear Samuel booming to the miners in stentorian bellows. He stopped at the end of the wall and listened. The wind howled. Things that love night love not such nights. His rain-soaked clothes stuck to his skin and his hair lay lank across his forehead, the raindrops sliding down his face, his heart hammering in his ribcage. Forked lightning splintered down from the clouds and pulsed rapidly, illuminating the landscape, the hills and the trees shaded pale blue. He saw the enormous tipple and, on the opposite hill, the rows of company houses in the patch. Thunder roared violently and the very ground he stood on shuddered.

Daniel readied himself, his shallow breathing quickening, his whole body trembling with fear, the knife clenched tightly in his right hand, guided only by his hardhearted will for revenge, not to be deterred or assuaged. Then he heard him lurking around the corner. Daniel swiveled around the corner to meet him and the two bodies collided. Their foreheads banged together and Daniel swung the knife up, stabbing it deep into his gut. His hands clutched Daniel's shoulders. It was then and only then that Daniel looked into a face he had not expected to see—Charles O'Brien's.

Their eyes met.

Daniel pulled out the knife, feeling the hot blood seep out onto his hand. O'Brien crumpled forward, cupping his hands at the bleeding wound. He looked like a bowing actor on the stage, his performance concluded.

"What'd you do to me?"

"You rat fucking prick!"

O'Brien groaned dreadfully.

"Does he know who I am?"

The blood spilled over O'Brien's bottom lip and down his chin. "McKeeta!" he yelled. "Help!"

Daniel lunged forward and thrust the knife into O'Brien's thigh once in and out quickly. Black arterial blood spurted from the wound. He fell to his hands and knees and crawled toward the barn. Daniel followed him a few paces and stood astride, and he snatched a handful of wet hair and passed the blade across his throat, as if he were merely doing what had already been decided for him. When he let go of the hair, O'Brien fell prostrate in the wet grass and mud and was dead.

Daniel stood panting and trembling in the cold rain over the lifeless body. The lightning flashed and he saw the black blood on his hands and knife blade. He looked around. There was no one to be seen anywhere. He heard Samuel still addressing the crowd inside the barn and the miners applauding. Daniel looked at the body again. He covered his mouth with his left hand. Suddenly, his whole body was shuddering, his knees quaking, and he broke out in a cold sweat.

"What did I do?" he said aloud.

He pawed at his wet face with his hand, unknowingly anointing his face with smears of blood. He bent down and pulled up his pant leg and sheathed the knife in his boot. Then he turned the body on its back and grabbed the legs and dragged him through the wet grass. He lugged him downhill to the barbed wire fence, then stopped, and stepped through the barbed wires and midway the wire cut the back of his neck, a sudden sharp burning pain. He stood and touched his hand to the back of his neck and saw the blood on his palm. He reached through and pulled the legs from the other side, all the while glancing in the direction of the barn. As he pulled the body under, the clothes snagged on the barbed wire. He leaned back and hauled harder and the clothing ripped. He struggled backwards, stumbling downhill. He quickly regained himself and was covered in mud as he took up the legs and heaved downhill, lightning flashes illuminating him at his frantic toil in the darkness.

Daniel pulled the body all the way down to the flat ground and came again to the perimeter of the fence. He climbed through and pulled the body under the fence. When he got the body past the fence, he saw now that the face was slashed from the barbed wire and a piece of skin was missing on the cheek. He felt the weight of the legs in his hands and realized again that this was a dead body, that he had killed him. He let go of the legs suddenly as if his hands had been burnt. He felt his stomach curdling, then he bent over and gagged. He wiped his mouth on the back of his hand and resumed dragging the corpse. He pulled it just a little further and abandoned it at the railroad embankment.

The pouring rain had washed off some of the blood on his hands. He scurried over the tracks to the creek, squatted on his haunches, and washed his hands and face in the cold, numbing water. Suddenly, he heard the voices of miners on the hill leaving the meeting. He ducked slightly and broke into a loping run on the railroad tracks. He ran until he came to the company store. Then he slowed to a brisk walk.

Before he even knew what he was doing, he found himself running up the tavern steps. He rushed through the door and shut it behind him. The bartender was wiping down the bar. "I'm closed," he said. Then he looked up. "My God, son, you look like you've been eaten by a bear and shit off a cliff."

"How much you want for a bottle a whiskey?"

"I don't sell bottles."

"How much, goddamn it?"

"Give me two dollars."

Daniel rushed over to the bar and slapped down the bills, smeared with dark blood. The bartender fetched a new bottle from the shelf and handed it over to him. He clutched it about the neck.

"That's one hell of a storm out there," the bartender said.

Daniel bit the cork and pulled it out with his teeth and spat it across the floor. He threw his head back and rifled a drink down his throat, then took another long pull, his throat burning with fire. Lightning flashed and thunder roared, shaking the very foundation of the building, the windows rattling in their frames, as though the world entire was on this night to suffer the wrath of an angry God.

*

Daniel came striding up the front steps out of Belladonna's Saloon, trying to get out of the heavy rain under the covered portico. It was late and the light was out in the vestibule, but he pounded on the front door a few times anyhow. After a few moments, the door opened a crack and he saw Bobby, the brothel bartender, peering out bleary-eyed. He was wearing a black ten-button vest with a bow tie and white shirt. "We're closed," he said.

"I'm not here for that," Daniel told him.

"I can't allow anyone in this late."

Daniel produced a bloodstained wad of cash from his coat pocket and peeled out a ten dollar bill and held it up. The door closed and the chain rattled on the other side of the door. Bobby opened the door and took the ten dollar bill and then he stepped aside. When he came through, Bobby shut the door and chained the lock. Daniel stood there in the foyer, smelling like rain, his hair dripping wet, his clothes soaked utterly. He hung his coat heavy with dampness on the rack. He could hear at least one bedframe scraping against the floorboards upstairs and the relentless fawning moans of a whore.

"She's with someone upstairs," Bobby said. "You'll have to wait."

"I need a drink," Daniel said.

"You're already drunk."

"That doesn't change the fact that I need a drink."

"Not tonight."

"Just one drink. Please."

"Fine. What the hell do I care? What do you want, whiskey?"

"Yeah. Please."

When Daniel went upstairs, he passed on the staircase a flush-faced man who didn't look at him. He did not knock on her door. He let himself in and saw her in the dark candlelight across the unmade

116

bed, stooping forward, pulling up her stockings, her breasts swaying. Surprised, she stood and covered herself with one arm across her breasts.

"I was getting ready for bed," Katherine said. "What are you doing here?"

"That's a good question. I don't know."

"I didn't think I'd see you again after last time."

"Bad habits get the best of me."

"They wouldn't be bad if they didn't get the best of you." She combed his wet hair back from his forehead with her fingers. "You look like you saw a ghost tonight."

"I need to talk to someone."

"There's blood on your clothes. What happened?"

Daniel grinned. "You should see the other guy."

"You got in another fight?"

"Something like that."

She walked around the bed and looked up into his face and she took him by the arm. "Do you want to stay here tonight?"

Daniel jerked his arm away from her. "For what? For ten dollars?"

"For nothing," she said. "For company."

"No, I'm not sleeping in those rank and filthy sheets."

"Oh, you're too good for me now?" she said.

"When were you going to tell me you were Carver's whore? Or were you just going to keep that a secret?"

"I'm not his whore," she said.

"Sure you are," Daniel said. "Sure you are. He owns this place just like he owns you and everyone else in this goddamn town."

"What did I do to you that you should burst in here and bark at me like this?"

"You did exactly what it was in your nature to do," he said with an expression of outraged righteousness. "You lied. You deceived. You flattered. You pernicious bitch."

She went to the door and opened it. "Why don't you go sleep it off, Daniel?"

117

"No," he shouted. He slammed the door shut so hard a picture frame fell off the wall and broke on the floor. He seized her wand-like wrist, hauled her over to the bed, and threw her down on the mattress. He was on top of her with her wrists pinned down to the bed and she struggled against his grip. "I'm not going anywhere until you see what you really are."

"You think I can't take it? I've been beaten by plenty worse than you."

"I couldn't do any worse than to leave you as you are. To your own conscience. The sheriff's whore, his ditch for cum. Don't you know who he is? Don't you know what he does?"

"You only see one side of him," she said. "He takes care of people. Things would only be worse without him."

"Oh, I'll bet he takes care of you," he said. "Do you slip your tongue in his ear? Do you moan and groan for him and bite your lip and whimper like the mutt that you are? You fucking flattering whore."

"I don't need to flatter him," she said.

"You're nothing but a fucking whore," he said, and his words were like whiplashes. "You deserve a life in this shithole."

He let go of her wrists and got off her, turning to the nightstand and cleaning everything off of it with one wild swat of his forearm. Then he reeled drunkenly and nearly fell. Her jewelry scattered on the floor and the glass face of the clock broke and spread shards. The candle flames went out and candlewax spilled in white drops on the floor. The room went dark. Suddenly he was calm, catching his breath. Moonlight from the window cast a pale shadowy glow in which they could just see each other.

"Why?" she asked. "Why do you hate him so much?"

"You want to know why..."

"Yes..."

"When I was seven, he killed my father." Daniel spoke with grave deliberation. "Shot him in the ear. And no one ever did anything about it—all these cowards."

118

She didn't look entirely surprised. "What happened to you after that?"

"Carver, he offered to take me in after that. Like he wanted to adopt me. But I ran away. Orphanage got me... And I became a fucking drunk and that's the story of my life. But it wouldn't have been like that if Carver hadn't done what he did. That started it all." Daniel held his face to his hands and started crying. "If he hadn't done that, if he just hadn't done that one fucking thing, I'd be a completely different person today."

"Daniel, you can't kill him," she said. "He's too dangerous. If he catches onto you, he'll kill you without thinking twice. You don't know what he's capable of. All those men he's killed. You're not going to be any different."

"He's been onto me for a long time. He's toying with me, pulling my strings like a puppet. Maybe he's still trying to take me in in some sick fucking way... But I am different. He ain't never met anyone like me." Daniel said. "And you don't know what I'm capable of. I've already killed one man today. I'll kill a hundred more if I have to."

"What are you talking about? Whose blood is this?"

"O'Brien's. Not more than two hours ago, I..."

"Oh, God, what did you do, Daniel?"

"I did what your pimp told me to do. I killed a man." His voice quavered with uncertainty. "Out in the storm. I couldn't see. I guess part of me wanted to believe it was him, Carver. But I knew it wasn't. I knew it in my bones.... We were at the fucking Union meeting. O'Brien was sneaking around outside the barn like the fucking rat that he is and I thought maybe he was the sheriff, and I was so scared, I fucking stabbed him. I didn't know what to do and then I just kept stabbing him anyhow. I lost control of myself... Anyways. I did them fucking miners a favor."

"If you stay here," she said, "they'll hang you."

"I thought about doing it myself."

"You need to leave town."

"Everyone's crooked as hell in this town, aren't they?"

"I have money to get you as far away as you can get."

"Sometimes I think the best thing would be for that dam up in the hills to break and wash this whole fucking town off the map. These people need a clean slate."

"I always wondered what it would be like to kill a man. And now I've done it and I don't even feel bad about it. What kind of monster am I?"

"If I get you the money, will you leave?"

"No," he said. "I can't leave."

"Please, Daniel. Just do this one thing for me. I have some money. I'll give you seven hundred dollars if you get on a train and go as far away as you can."

"I don't want your money."

"It's his money," she said.

"You think he'll just let you steal his money?"

"Don't worry about that," she said. "I can take care of him. He wouldn't lay a finger on me. But I can't get it tonight. You'll have to hide out somewhere. Then come back tomorrow night, and I'll have the money."

"If I leave, if I just run away, then I'm just another coward like everyone else in this town. I won't do that. That's the one thing I won't do."

"Listen to me," she said. "You have to move on. Your father's dead and there's nothing you can ever do that will change that fact. The worst thing you can do is become like the man you're trying kill."

"Why shouldn't I be like him?" Daniel said. "Maybe that's just who I am."

"You're not. And if you try to be, it'll kill you."

"Then help me kill him." Daniel pulled his vial of poison from his pocket and held it out for her to see. "He trusts you, doesn't he?"

"What is that?"

"Strychnine. Put it in his coffee."

"I can't do that. Without him, I'm..."

"You're what?"

"I'm nothing…"

"You think you're nothing because he tells you you're nothing. Can't you see that?"

"You don't understand," she said, "and I don't expect you to. A whore's thinking. He's taken care of me since I was fourteen."

"You won't help me then."

"I can't."

"Then you can go to hell with the rest of them."

*

And in his sleep he saw the knife, without seeing who held it, coming through the dark to pierce his heart. Daniel sat up gasping, a great rush of air filling his lungs, the nearly empty quart bottle of whiskey still clutched in his hand. When he opened his eyes, he was blind. Impenetrable darkness converged upon him, and he was afraid. He grabbed his chest and felt it rising and falling, his heart hammering against his ribcage. He trembled with deep cold, his clothes heavy with damp, his boots waterlogged. He touched the sharpened bones of his face. He had grown accustomed to waking up in strange places. But none such as this.

Stale musty stench of the long dead. The incessant sound of dripping water. He fished the box of matches out of his pocket and blindly scratched one and it popped and flared, releasing the sulfurous odor, a small radiant burst. He looked around blearily through bloodshot eyes, finding himself inside a mausoleum.

It was coming back to him now: he saw hazy flashes of nightmarish remembrance in his mind's eye. After leaving the brothel, he took his second bottle and stumbled drunkenly through the streets to Monongahela Cemetery, where he dropped to his knees before Badger's fresh grave in the rain and his knees sank in the mud and there he drank himself into obliteration, shaken by the fear of enduring his life, the fear of ending it. During his blackout, he must have sought shelter from the pitiless storm in the mausoleum. The match burned down to his fingertips and extinguished and again the cold burial chamber faded into the darkness.

All his body was wet, but his mouth was dry, his tongue swollen. He felt a piercing pain below the right side of his ribcage, and he let out a little groan of despair. Then he took up the bottle with his shaking hands and drank for whatever slight solace it might give him. He saw by tilting his bottle that there was no great quantity left in it, and he distinctly understood that there was no great quantity to his portion of life, that he was down to the last drops.

He put the bottle down, the glass clinking against the cold floor, and he sat with his back against the tomb, remembering the murder, his breath vaporizing quietly in the iron-dark air, so tormented and torn that he began to beat fiercely the back of his skull against the cement wall, desperate to staunch the flow of dreadful thoughts. He stopped suddenly and fumbled about his boot in the dark, producing the knife, touching gingerly the tip of the still bloodstained blade. He bit down hard on his white knuckle as he mulled over his predicament, and then he lifted the whiskey bottle and took a long pull. *I might as well be dead. Daniel Byrnes? He's nothing. Dead. Was he ever anything? For a while. But not now. Now he's nothing. Nothing, nothing, nothing! Where's the point in anything, if we all become nothing?*

He touched the knife to his throat, pressing the tip into the soft flesh.

"Here's the fucking point," he said aloud.

While pushing the knife tip into his neck slowly, deliberately, the soft flesh yielding to the tempered steel, a bead of blood trickling down his neck like a teardrop in the meekest protest against self-slaughter, he heard something else in the mausoleum. Fear clenched his heart like a fist. He withdrew the knife. Quickly, he fumbled with his small box of matches, his hands so shaky it took three strikes before he could light a match. Finally, it popped and the flame cast a weak halo of light. He saw his father's face, a grim chiseled visage. An ear gone. Blood and specks of bone and brain matted in the hair.

"Christ almighty!" Daniel screamed, his heart thumping like never before. He dropped the match and was again plunged into complete and utter darkness.

"Remember me," the ghost whispered hoarsely.

Whether those words sounded from memory or madness, he did not know. But he heeded their behest.

"I do," he said. "I will. I'll teach him how to beg—oh God, I'll do anything—I could eat his heart raw. I swear the ground itself will shudder. I'll teach him to beg for mercy with this goddamn knife. But I'll be merciless. And when they see him dead under my hand—those gutless slaves who couldn't even look him in the eye—they'll remember everything. Then I'll go. I'll go to hell with the devil's blessing."

*

Sheriff Carver stood on his front porch in the darkness, rainwater pouring over the sloped roof, his eyes scanning the grim perimeters of the camp through the downfall. Steady patter of water hitting the mud as he sipped from his cup of coffee, the warm steam swathing his face, but the coffee was not what he wanted. He had awoken with cold sweat on his flesh, trembling in those clockless hours of night. He sat down, rubbing his forehead. He raised the cup to his lips with his palsied hands and drank.

"Jesus Christ, it takes something else to fuck up a man who already had his throat cut once. That's why I am who I am. You can't scare me. I am the one you fear. I seized this camp by the throat and those hunkies don't dare draw so much as a breath without my permission. They see this fucking scar stretching from ear to ear, and they see a man that can't be killed. When I ride through the thoroughfare, they lower their eyes and slink away like dogs. Yeah, I've thrown widows out into the street, made children into orphans... But when I heard those boots thudding, those floorboards creaking—never had a nightmare like that—I felt him watching me. Byrnes. And when I looked up, I looked into those eyes."

He drew a deep breath and exhaled slowly, shuddering. He shook his head and drank again from his cup. Out in the darkness, he glimpsed a white figure moving through the dark, coming up the road. It was a girl shrouding herself under a shawl against the downpour as she ran. When she drew nearer still, he recognized the familiar cinnamon color of her hair wet in the rain: Mary Beth. He put his coffee cup down on the balustrade. When she was in earshot he called out to her.

"What's wrong, Mary Beth?"

She didn't answer him and she stopped at the foot of the porch steps, looking up at him from under the shawl.

"Get up here," he said.

After she hurried up the stairs, she draped the shawl around her shoulders and stood there dripping wet.

"I can't help you if you don't tell me what's wrong," he said.

"Something happened to my father. He didn't come home last night. I don't know where he is."

"All right, slow down. When did you see him last?"

"When he went to the mine," she said. "Yesterday morning."

"Just settle down. Let's get you inside." He put his arm around her and led her to the door. "You're shaking cold."

"I wasn't sure if you'd be awake," she said.

"I don't ever sleep." He offered her a seat at the kitchen table and she sat down. "Wait here just a minute."

When he came back to the kitchen, he had a clean folded towel in his hands. He gave it to her and she thanked him and started to dry her dark wet hair. He sat down at the table and looked at her. "So when did you notice he was missing?"

"He usually comes home not long after the colliery whistle blows, and I always have his dinner and washtub ready for him. Some days he's later than others, but I kept waiting and waiting and I started to think something was wrong. I waited up for him, but I fell asleep and when I woke up I looked around the house and he still wasn't home."

"Can you think of anywhere he might have gone?"

"No. Nowhere."

He drummed his fingers on the tabletop, figuring.

"There's something else," she said.

"What?"

124

"It's what woke me up this morning. I heard his voice. He said 'Mary Beth,' and he woke me up." She glanced up at the Sheriff with her glistening green eyes.

"You don't believe in that kind of stuff, now do you, Mary Beth?"

"I'm worried he never came back out of the mine," she said.

"They would have never blown that colliery whistle if he didn't come up to the office to sign off."

"Why wouldn't he come home then?"

"I don't know. But I want you to stay here while I find out."

She looked up at him. "You think he's dead, too, don't you?"

He stood up from the table and donned his hat. "Wherever your father is, Mary Beth, I'll find him. I guarantee you that."

*

Within two hours, the sheriff found the pale and bloody corpse in a ditch. The rain had stopped and the air was cold. There lay O'Brien below the railroad embankment. Carver halted his horse and shifted in his saddle, looking down at the body in its obscene degradation. He got down off his horse and walked around, stopping to squat on his haunches, studying the coagulated blood around the wounds.

"So he did it after all," he said to himself with a smirk. "Kid, played right into my hands."

Then to O'Brien's corpse, he said, "Like I said, Charlie, you ain't exactly irreplaceable."

He stood and hooked his thumb in his belt loop, scanning the landscape. He had sent his deputies out to search the vicinities of the colliery. He could see them off in the distance. He hailed them with a piercing whistle and a wave of his hat, and he waited there until they arrived on their horses.

"You dipshits happen to find anything interesting with your heads up your asses? I found a fucking body while you were up there doing god knows what."

"That Charlie O'Brien, boss?" Spearman asked.

"Nope. Found his fucking twin brother. Keep searching."

"He's fucken dead, ain't he?"

125

"Ain't nothing gets by you."

"What are you thinking, Jack?" Pearce asked.

"This wasn't a drunken brawl," Carver said. "And there was nothing on him worth stealing, I can tell you that much. But he made sure Charlie was graveyard dead. Stabbed him in the gut, stabbed him in the thigh, the throat. That order, too."

Pearce leaned and spat tobacco juice. "How you figure all that?"

"You ever kill a man?" Carver said.

"You know I ain't never."

"There's one hell of a storm raging inside you the first time." The sheriff tapped his finger to his temple. "Your thinking is clouded. Your hands and legs start shaking leading up to it. You're about to kill a man for Christ's sake. Or get yourself killed if you fuck up. There's a hot feeling in your face and chest. You start sweating. Hell. Your first fuck and your first kill ain't all that different. Your dick ain't hard—or hell, maybe it is—but the point is: few things are as intimate as murder. You're so scared you forget what you're doing. Ain't careful. You go in too soon. Stab him in the gut. When you look up, you see Charlie's eyes glaze over. Feel that hot breath come out. Now what do you do when you get your steel wet? No time to think. Quick thrust to the thigh, going for the artery. That's a kill. But you're not confident yet. Have to make sure you hit it. Charlie's bleeding like a pig. With all that blood pumping out, he starts getting dizzy, starts seeing black spots. Cold death creeps into his feet and crawls up his legs. But you got no stomach for the suffering, so you slit his throat. That's a kill. When Charlie tries to breathe, his lungs are sucking air through the slit in his throat. But by the time the knife's out, he's already dead and dropping to the ground."

The sheriff raised his head and turned around, gazing off towards the barn atop the hill. He turned back and wagged his finger once at the body.

"Now the torn clothes," he continued, "and the cuts on the face are from dragging the body down the hill, under the barbed wire. The killer started to panic, because he didn't have a plan, and now he

126

needed to buy himself some time. He didn't worry about hiding the body, just got it out of sight."

"You think he's on the run?" Pearce asked.

"Doesn't matter if he is or he isn't."

Pearce had his arms akimbo. "I ain't sure I follow you."

"He'll come crawling back to me."

"Something you ain't telling us, Jack?"

"He's a killer now. He'll want to kill the man he came for in the first place."

"Who's a killer, boss?" Spearman asked. He screwed up his face in confusion. "And who's he want to kill now? I thought he just killed O'Brien."

The sheriff turned to face the deputies, smiling. "The blacksmith," he said. "He wants to kill me."

"What's he want with you?"

"If I had to hazard a guess, I'd say revenge."

"What for?"

"You ain't figured that out yet?"

The deputies looked at each other, mutually confounded.

"You were there when I killed his old man," the sheriff said.

Spearman scratched the stubble on his chin, struggling to put the pieces together. "Jack, I was only there the one time when you... and that was..."

Pearce squinted. "You mean to tell me that's Davie Byrnes's kid?"

The sheriff nodded.

"Well, if he's here to kill you," Spearman said, crossing his arms, "what'd he go and kill O'Brien for?"

"Because I told him to do it. And now the jury's gonna hang him for it." The sheriff stepped up into the stirrup and saddled his horse. "Boys, we've got ourselves an outlaw."

*

Marianna, PA.
February 26, 1889

Dear Mr. Carver,

127

Patience is said to be a virtue, and I have practiced it to my utmost capacity. You will be pleased to read that I am now a card carrying member of the local Union at Marianna. I have attended two meetings. They speak of the right of revolution, and they are all agreed that the time has come to exercise it. We are expecting to vote on the strike before the week ends. But more importantly, I must tell you that an organizer is rumored to be working at Elsinore. His identity is, of course, a carefully guarded secret. It is not even evident that he is working as a miner—wouldn't it be more clever to send someone ostensibly unaffiliated with the miners?—but we are assured he is there.

As for situation here, the tensions between the miners and operators have risen steadily since my last letter. A company man distributing anti-Union propaganda was castrated and left to bleed out on the railroad tracks. Now there are armed mine guards everywhere, arresting anyone they don't like the looks of and detaining them indefinitely. Furthermore, they say the labor troubles here are the same at every other mining town in the region. Perhaps, with your permission, I will soon return to Elsinore. I should like to know that all is well at home. I cannot lie: I miss my sister terribly.

Your humble and obedient servant,

Logan O'Brien

*

The rain had stopped and the sheriff's boots sank in the thick mud. As he went up the stairs, he left a trail of muddy footprints. But Mary Beth was gone from the porch where he had left her. He went inside, called out her name. No answer. He went through the rooms, searching, until he found her in his study sitting on the floor before the fireplace. She had built a fire while he was gone. There was an open Bible on the floor, from which she had torn pages at random to light with a match and kindle the fire. She was pulling at a lock of her long red hair, separating the strands with her long bony fingers.

"Mary Beth," he said, standing in the doorway. He took off his hat and held it with both hands by the brim. "I found your father.... He was murdered. But I know who it was that killed him. Before this time next week, I promise you, he'll be hanging from the end of a noose."

He stepped into the room and put his hand on her shoulder. She looked up at him and her pupils were like pinpoints. She hugged her knees and began to rock back and forth. "Lamb of God, you take away the sins of the world. Lamb of God you take away the sins of the world. Lamb of God..."

Eight

The miners crowded together at the bottom of the hill in their worn-out denims, suspenders, mud-spattered gumboots, and coal-dirty jackets and walked uphill to the colliery in the bitter cold February dawn. But when they crested the hill, they assembled about the lamp house, the engine house, and the blacksmith's shop. No one handed out the lamps and pick axes. The coal cars weren't running and the mule drivers never went to the stables. No one went underground at all. The operations were at a standstill. The workers sat on the steps or stood smoking cigarettes.

Daniel smoked his cigarette down to a nub and stomped it out in the dirt. He read an excerpt from the Union's declaration of a regional strike.

"We say to the world: *We are Americans*! We shall exercise our inalienable rights to organize into a great industrial Union, banded together with all our fellow coal miners... Through this Union, we shall win higher wages, shorter hours, and a better standard of living. We shall win leisure for ourselves and opportunity for our children. Together we shall abolish industrial despotism. We shall make real the dreams of the pioneers who pictured America as a land where all might live in comfort and happiness."

Daniel's hat was pulled down low over his eyes, and he had his back to the wall of the engine house. He stooped forward to look around the corner towards the sheriff's office. He saw the deputy leaving horseback from the livery at the bottom of the hill.

"Where in the fuck is everybody?"

"Where's who?" Butch Blizzard was still drunk from the night before, sprawled out across the steps in front of the engine house.

"Well, fucking Michael and Samuel for starters!"

"They're all..." Blizzard paused to belch. "...all a bunch of chicken-shits. You and me Byrnes... We're the only ones who show a little cock and balls around here."

"You know, usually it's me that's drunk off my ass."

130

"Well, fuck all anyhow!" Blizzard slurred. "I got my load on today, boys."

Eventually Kelvin Ekvie and Liam O'Loughlin showed up. They said the rumor going around was that before dawn Samuel packed his suitcase, loaded his Derringer, slipped it into his back pocket, and skipped town on the next train headed towards Pittsburgh.

"That coward son of a bitch," Ekvie growled. "I knew he'd take our money and bail on us when we needed him."

"Why don't you do the talking for him, Byrnes?" Blizzard suggested and then added a hiccup.

"You're joking."

"Someone's got to do it."

Daniel looked at him. "Yeah, but it ain't me."

Blizzard hiccupped again and pointed waveringly in Daniel's general direction, but he was looking at the ground, a string of saliva stretching from his lower lip. "Your father would've wanted you to do it."

"How many times do I got to tell you, I'm not my goddamn father."

"Well you're a goddamn *spittin'* image of him."

Daniel sat on the lamp house steps and lit up another cigarette as he watched the deputy ride up the hill on his daily patrol. Palpable apprehension evident in the deputy's eyes as he approached. He was severely outnumbered by more than a hundred miners. When he reined in the tall chestnut-colored quarterhorse, she became jittery around the crowd of unfamiliar men and she turned sideways, nodding her long head, stepping nervously, and snorting in the cold air. "Oh the hell with it," Daniel said to himself, pitching his cigarette into the dirt.

"Now just what in the hell is going on here, fellas?" Spearman asked. "Why isn't that engine house up and running?"

"Just what it looks like," Daniel said. "No one's gonna be bringing up any coal unless it's Union coal. You might want to let your boss know."

"You're the one killed O'Brien," Spearman said in amazement. He put his hand on the butt end of his revolver, but didn't draw it. "I'm placing you under arrest."

A cluster of quarrelsome miners gathered behind Daniel, all of them spitting and muttering to one another and glaring at the lone deputy. Several of them flashed their pieces. "He's not going anywhere," Blizzard declared with drunken bravura.

Daniel stood with his arms crossed. The deputy's horse was surrounded now. She turned around in a complete circle as Spearman tried to keep his own composure. "All right, everyone just step the fuck back. Let's talk this through."

"All right, let's talk," Daniel said, holding up a placating hand.

"What do you want?" the deputy asked. "I'm listening."

"There's been a ten percent reduction in wages. We want those wages restored."

"I'll let Carver know."

"I'm not done," Daniel said. "It's about time these boys had their own weigh man. So they get paid fairly for how much coal they send up."

"All right," Spearman said. Encircled by the miners, the deputy's horse jigged about nervously, her eyes rolling. "Everyone just back the fuck up now! You're spooking the damn horse."

"I'm not finished," Daniel said. "We want an eight hour work day. This ten hours shit is done."

"Damn it, I'm not going to remember all this."

"Well listen up, because the mule drivers want their stables moved back to the colliery," Daniel continued. "Those boys won't walk an extra mile every morning in the snow and rain. And last, but not least, the miners want a washhouse so they don't have to walk home soaking wet in the freezing cold, stinking like the mine. But since you can't seem to remember all that, we're posting our demands on every goddamn bulletin board in the colliery, we're posting them on every door in the county, we're picketing every street in Monongahela, and we're publishing them in every newspaper in the region."

One of the miners produced a sheet of paper and handed it up to the deputy who accepted it uncertainly, as if to touch it would be akin to sticking his hand in a hornet's nest. "There's the first copy. Hot off the press. I expect you'll deliver it to your boss."

"I hope you all know I'm gonna catch a beating for this."

"We know," Daniel said. "And we don't care."

The miners released the horseback deputy, the encirclement of bodies dispersing slowly, their eyes on his back as he rode downhill. Blizzard had puked during the discussion and was sitting up now. He looked askance at Daniel. "I don't remember the washhouse being on the list."

"It wasn't," Daniel said. "I threw that in last minute. What'd you think?"

"Not bad."

"Yeah?"

"Sounded like a natural to me."

"I did. Didn't I?"

"Must be in the blood."

*

The sheriff read the *Daily Independent* while drinking his black coffee. He held his lips to the brim and blew across the coffee and then slurped the still too hot coffee. He read the headline: "Doomed Man Asks Judge to Hurry Day of Execution." Three rapid knocks on the door interrupted his reading. He rolled his eyes. He shook a cigarette out of his pack and struck a match to light it. "Yeah," he called.

"It's Donny Spearman."

"Come in, Donny."

He closed the door behind him quickly. "Jack," he said, "we got a problem with them miners again."

"What the fuck is it now, Donny?"

"They started striking. I think it's for real this time."

The sheriff peered through his eyeglasses over the *Daily Independent*. "Could you repeat those last three words you just said, Donny, because at my age I can't trust my hearing anymore."

"They started striking, Jack."

"I fucking swear I hear words I don't want to fucking hear."

"I came as soon as I could."

The sheriff put down the newspaper on his desktop and removed his eyeglasses. He stood up, turned and gazed out the window at the tipple. "Do you know how I deal with strikes, Donny?"

"I don't know, Jack. That's why I came."

"You don't know because you never saw me deal with one. The way I deal with strikes is never allowing them to start in the first place, Donny."

"That sure is the right fucking way to do it."

"Shut the fuck up."

"Sorry."

"That's the problem with these Union cocksuckers. They're like fucking fleas. By the time you find the first one you've already got an infestation... What do I do now that I'm holding this bag of shit?"

"They told me their list of demands."

"You think I give a fuck about their demands, you fucking unparalleled spectacle of imbecility! Just stop yapping for one fucking second." He looked through his reflection in the window. The dawn was long in coming, a red sun rising up over the valley hills. "All right," he said. "We'll start the evictions right away. Give em something to think about out in the cold. Then we're gonna have to wire down to West Virginia for scabs. And the fucking Baldwin-Felts will be on a train tomorrow. That's out of my hands. They'll be nothing but a pain in my ass. Christ. Why didn't you shoot a Slav or something, huh? No one gives a fuck about them. Now I have to fucking deal with this shit-storm."

"They said they didn't want any violence."

The sheriff turned around, picked up his tin coffee cup, and threw it directly at Spearman, hitting him in the forehead, the coffee spilling all over him. "So that's what you give them, you fucking drawling idiot! You give them violence!"

The sheriff composed himself and sat down at the desk. Spearman rubbed his forehead, his face contorting painfully. "Go find Pearce," he said. "Tell him we're going to have to hire some scabs from down south. We don't want any fucking Irish under any circumstances. Then I want him to get on a train to Pittsburgh to hire some guns."

"Sure thing, boss," he said. He wiped the coffee out of his eyes and then exited quietly.

The sheriff sat silently cogitating at his desk a moment, tapping his finger on the desktop. He read the headline: "Men Lose Faith. Bible League Speaker Discusses the Spread of Atheism." He read: "When men lose faith in the integrity and authority of God's word, they lose faith in God, and when they lose faith in God, they lose faith in each other, and panic and disaster inevitably befall them."

The sheriff folded the newspaper, stood up, walked across the room, bent down, and picked up his coffee cup. "You can't rely on anyone for anything these days," he muttered.

*

That evening the uneasy Union miners were playing cards with their rifles loaded and propped in the corner of the kitchen at the boarding house, not know what to expect by way of reprisal from Carver. Blizzard was sprawled out across the floor. He'd lost all his money at the card table and was now passed out and snoring. Suddenly, there was an abrupt and forceful knocking at the door. Kelvin Ekvie just about jumped out of his chair.

"Who the hell is that?"

"They started evictions already?" Blizzard slurred from the floor, awake now with his one eye drooping open.

The knocking persisted. It got markedly louder.

"They wouldn't bother knocking if it was company gun thugs," Daniel whispered. Still, he had pulled his knife before he went over to the window, not really knowing what to expect.

Blizzard pulled the old pistol he had tucked in his waist. He'd never shot it, didn't even honestly know if it worked, but he cocked it and pointed it in the general direction of the door, even though he was seeing three of them and didn't know which one was the real door. Daniel pulled the curtain aside and saw about seven or eight black miners in dirty coats and overalls standing on the porch, all of them holding either a rifle or shotgun. "What in the hell…"

The knocking continued.

"It's me. Samuel."

"Samuel?" Daniel furrowed his brow. He unlocked and opened the door. "Where the hell did you go? I thought you bailed on us."

Blizzard eased the hammer back down on his revolver.

Samuel jerked his thumb over his shoulder. "I went down the railroad line this morning to meet with some Union boys down in Marianna. Because as sure as the day you were born, the company's on the wire with them damn Baldwin-Felts by now. And this time tomorrow the camp will be swarming with company gun thugs. These boys brought enough guns and ammunition with them to let us put up one hell of a fight if push comes to shove."

"You son of a bitch!" Blizzard shouted. He got up and lurched across the room, threw his arms around Samuel and kissed him on the cheek. "You boys are fucking welcome in Elsinore! Come on in and have yourselves a goddamn swig of homebrew!"

*

Sure enough, two full days hadn't yet passed before the Baldwin-Felts detectives set out from Pittsburgh aboard barges on the Monongahela and took a train up the creek to Elsinore. Every hardware store in the county was cleaned out of revolvers and ammunition. Each detective was given five dollars for every day's work. The sheriff deputized more than thirty men as soon as they got off the train. Afterwards, he met with the leader of the Baldwin-Felts agents in his office. The sheriff poured himself a cup of coffee and then added a portion of whiskey. He offered the bottle to the agent but he held up his hand to decline. Two agents in low-crowned broad brimmed hats stood against the door. Pearce sat across the table, cleaning under his fingernails with a jackknife. Donny Spearman had his back against the wall, legs crossed, sipping a cup of coffee.

The sheriff picked up the morning edition of the *Daily Independent*. "Gentlemen, allow me to read for you a choice excerpt I came across in my perusal of the morning paper: 'The operators of the bituminous coalfields have the egregious vanity to describe themselves as its managing directors. It is imprudent, it is insulting, and it is audacious of the coal operators to speak of lawlessness when they are themselves the greatest offenders of the law. They think they superintend the earth. Never in all our experience have we met a more determined body of strikers than was found in the Monongahela valley. The strike now in progress has furnished an object lesson that it will be well for the operators in this county to take note of. The day of the slave driver is past and the once ignorant foreigner will no longer tolerate it.' And this cocksucker goes on to say, 'During the past few days, letters came pouring in from all over the state encouraging the men, showing how widespread is the righteousness of their cause and the extent of their sympathy.'"

The sheriff folded the paper. "I have no such sympathy."

"Would you like my boys to pay a visit to the man who wrote that piece of trash?"

"Please," the sheriff said. "But not yet. I would like you to deliver to him directly my rebuttal. I'll have it written by tomorrow. You'll want to make it clear—by whatever means necessary—that it would greatly behoove him to show both sides of the story, for his own edification and that of his readership as well. After all, who, if not the Elsinore Coal Company, is going to provide jobs for these low-bred hunky cocksuckers? Let him know that I'm eagerly awaiting his next piece."

"That won't be a problem. I'll send a few boys down to see him this afternoon."

"Now as for the evictions, we're going to start those right away." He handed over an envelope with a list of the names of blacklisted miners inside. "Those are the names of company employees who have abrogated their contract with the company by joining a Union. The Elsinore Coal Company has graciously allowed these miners to live on company property. It's no different than having a servant working in your house. If the servant leaves your employment, you tell him to get the fuck out of the servants' quarters. Am I right?"

"Godamned right," the detective added an affirmative nod. "There ain't a man who's white and Christian that'll argue that."

"Fucking squareheads..." The sheriff massaged his temples. "...nothing but a pain in my ass..."

"To hell with them," Pearce said. "There's always more where they came from that'll work for less."

"What you ought to do, Jack," Donny Spearman suggested, gesturing with his cup of coffee, "is bring up some niggers 'n show the hunkies what real work is."

The sheriff looked up with genuine astonishment. "My God almighty..."

Donny sank back into the wall. "Sorry, I was just thinking out loud."

"Am I going crazy or did Donny Spearman just have a fucking idea?"

"I did?"

"Niggers... why didn't I think of that?"

"I got a guy down in West Virginia who can help you out," the detective shrugged.

"I like that idea. We'll iron out the details later." He turned back to the detectives. "Now, off the record, I want everyone in this goddamn camp to know you're here and who the fuck you're working for. Officially, you're here to protect our company assets, but unofficially your job is to start killing Union cocksuckers, understood?"

"Absolutely, Mr. Carver."

"I got a list of names." He handed over a folded sheet of paper.

The detective unfolded it, nodded. "You got a spy working for you?"

"I damn sure do. Now, for starters, I think a little display of authority during the evictions would be in order. Give you a chance to cross off the first name on your list."

"The agency I represent and the men I employ have ample experience in labor disputes like this. We'll get your message across."

"I trust that you will," the sheriff said. "You'll also want to inform your men that these strikers are known to be aiding and abetting an outlaw, as it would happen, an adversary of mine, intent on my assassination. Now, I know for a fucking fact that this coward, who hasn't had the guts to face me man-to-man, is hiding out with these fucking strikers. If you were to find him at any time, I'd want him arrested and brought to me alive, and I do stress the word *alive*, but…"

"Yes, sir?"

"…if this cocksucker were to sustain any number of injuries in the process of being brought to justice, broken ribs and so on, well… who could object to that?" the sheriff said.

"What's the outlaw's name?"

"Daniel Byrnes. Scrappy little shit, ain't but nineteen-years-old. But he likes to pull a fucking cork—the kid's a drunken mess half the time. But don't let him deceive you. He carries a knife, and he's not afraid to use it, so you'll want to watch him."

"We'll take care of him for you, Mr. Carver."

"Tell your boys I got a gallon jug of moonshine I am personally donating to whoever brings him to me. Alive."

The agent stood, touched the brim of his black hat, and exited the room, his two companions following him out. Alone, the sheriff sat with his boot-feet on the desk, rolling a toothpick in his mouth-corner with his fingertips, his brow pinched pensively, eyes gazing off, contemplating his next move. He took up his paper, hoping to find something with which to distract himself. Distracted and unable to focus enough to read, he took out a blank sheet of paper and pen and ink and commenced to write:

Dear Editor:

It is abundantly clear that there is a lack of good faith on the part of the United Mine Workers of America regarding the accurate portrayal of the recent strike in Washington County. The readers of the Daily

Independent can, without my letter, know only one side of the truth. I have, therefore, to request that the Independent, in a spirit of fair play, will publish my rebuttal to the UMWA's article. I shall then be content to allow those who interest themselves in such matters to form their own opinion on the miners' strike.

A revolutionary menace is haunting Pennsylvania. The situation in the county at large has become literally intolerable. The fomenters of this anarchy, the UMWA, are an assemblage of agitators and extremists who deter thousands from working by intimidation and violence. Although UMWA President John Mitchell exhorted the miners to strike peaceably, all along the Monongahela River, strikers attack non-Union miners, terrorize their families, and lash out at private police forces and armed guards hired by mine owners. If the strikers do not presently acquiesce to the greater justice and higher moral principles of the coal operators, I fear the terrible nature of the impending catastrophe and the certainty of riots which might develop into social war. I ask that there be an immediate resumption of operations in the coal mines in some such way as will meet the crying needs of the people. Until then, I will dutifully protect—by any means necessary—the man who wants to work and his wife and children when he is at work. The rights and interests of the laboring man will be protected and cared for—not by the labor agitators, but by the Christian men to whom God in His infinite wisdom has given the control of the property interests of the country.

–I am, Sir, your most humble and obedient servant,

Sheriff J. D. Carver

*

The following day, the sheriff issued a simple dismissal notice to the newly discharged miners. It read simply: "I want my house."

Dreary, overcast skies fell on the town on the day the evictions began. The sheriff rode up and down the patch streets under a mackerel sky, overseeing his newly deputized Baldwin-Felts agents. Families gathered on their front porches, waiting to see which family would be ordered out. The agents wore coal and iron police badges pinned to their chests and carried Winchester rifles. They pounded first on the front door of the first house. When Rosa Gysegum answered the door in her apron, she had been in the midst of cooking a badly botched dish of halupki, and as the steam and stink of cabbage and vinegar wafted around her, they flashed an eviction notice signed by the superintendent, even though he was deceased and no replacement had yet been appointed, pushed Rosa aside, and barged into the house. "We might not be able to use this house again if we can't get that hunky stink out of it," the paunchy Baldwin-Felt detective joked, waving his hand back and forth in front of his nose. Within minutes, the entire Gysegum family was forced out onto the porch, where they looked on in disbelief as their furniture and all of their belongings were crudely loaded on horse-drawn wagon. It would be carried away from the company property and dumped.

At the next house, Ada Ekvie, who was home alone and six-months pregnant, cried and pleaded with the Baldwin-Felts. She was eighteen and had dimpled pink cheeks. "Please, just let us stay until I have my baby... Just let me stay until I've had my baby." She was surrounded by detectives on the porch watching her with mild and detached amusement.

A husky detective lifted up the back of her skirt with the muzzle of his rifle. But one of the younger gawky detectives stepped in and kicked the barrel away with his boot. "Christ, Ennis," he said, "have some respect for these people." He shot the other detectives a warning glance and told her to wait. "Let me see if I can work something out."

"Thank you," she sobbed. "We ain't got no place else to go."

When he approached the sheriff in the street, and explained the situation, the sheriff looked down from his saddle. "Are you out of your fucking mind?"

"She's with child, boss, and she looks just like my sister," he explained. "We can't just throw her out in the cold. It ain't right."

"I'm running a company here, not a Christian charity house. Her man violated his contract when he signed up with the Union.

Should've thought it through if he didn't want this to happen... Tell her this is what she gets for letting a goddamn mule driver knock her up. Now get her out of my house or get your ass out of my town."

The sheriff clicked his tongue and rode on down the row of ramshackle company houses.

When they came to the Glemba house, they found Eva, the Glemba brothers' sixty-seven-year-old mother, sitting on the porch with a rifle across her knees. She had her jaw set and her knobby finger on the trigger. The Baldwin-Felts detective was already mounting the steps when he saw she had the rifle pointed at his head. He stopped and put his hand on the revolver at his hip.

"This has been our home for fourteen years," she said. "You're not coming in here."

"I'm an officer of the law and I go where I damn well please."

"I raised a family in this house, and I aim to die in this house... and don't think I won't take you with me."

"Careful with that piece, grandma," he said. "That'll break your arm."

She didn't miss a beat. "Ain't half as bad as what it'll do to you," she said.

He put his hands up, took a step back down. She saw his eyes move. She tried to turn around but before she could two other detectives had climbed over the porch rails and grabbed the rifle. She shot a hole through the roof before they had it out of her hands. She fell backwards in the struggle and landed on her hip, but she didn't make a sound to show she was in agony, just puffed air furiously through her thin lips and started cussing the detectives.

When the striking miners, who had been picketing on the edge of the colliery, heard about the gunshot, they rushed into the patch to confront the Baldwin-Felts. They arrived just as the furniture of an evicted miner was being stacked in the thoroughfare. A few of the agents tried to block them, while the sheriff watched them from atop his saddle, but the great grizzly bear of a man, Butch Blizzard on another three-day drunk, bold with whiskey, all the more intimidating with his black eye patch, muscled his way through the line of agents, opening a space for the other strikers. He strode right up to the sheriff.

"What's going on here?" Blizzard said, glaring up at the sheriff.

"We're cleaning up the camp," the sheriff said. "The company needs these houses for employees who will work under my conditions, accept my wage scale, and pay their rent."

"Why, you're the dirtiest son-of-a-bitch I ever laid eyes on! These families are being evicted without due process of the law."

One of the agents grabbed his crotch and jiggled his genitalia. "I got your law right here, you motherless cunt."

"Now, now," the sheriff said blithely, "there's no need to be uncivil. Mr. Blizzard here is simply unfamiliar with the law. Rule number nine of the mine regulations states: 'any person or persons known to belong to any secret association or open combination whose aim is to control wages or stop the works or any part thereof shall be promptly and finally discharged.'" His eyes gazed off in the distance as he recited the regulation, which he knew by rote. "Persons not satisfied with their work or their wages can leave honorably by giving the required notice.'" The sheriff now turned to some of the Baldwin-Felts agents and gestured to the striking miners, "Do me a favor and arrest these men."

"On what charges?" Blizzard shouted.

"Disturbing the peace, trespassing, and seditious activities."

"Disturbing the peace!" Blizzard cried incredulously.

A scuffle broke out between the strikers and the agents as the arrests were taking place, and another gunshot was heard. One of the Glemba brothers fell on his back, clutching his chest, squirming in the mud, bleeding out. They had shot him with his own rifle. Women shrieked from the porches. The miners were trading blows with the agents, but they were outnumbered, and soon they were all in handcuffs. Even in their restraints, some of them continued struggling, kicking, cussing, and spitting. "My daddy was born on the creek, and I was born on this creek, and we have lived here for thirty years,"

Nicholas Gysegum shouted. "These damn operators can't treat us like this and get away with it! This thing ain't over with!"

As the Baldwin-Felts led away the arrested miners in handcuffs, the sheriff tossed his chin in the direction of Blizzard. "What that cocksucker needs is a bullet between the eyes."

"He only got but one," Donny Spearman said.

"Ain't nothing gets by you, Donny."

As soon as the brief disturbance was quelled, the sheriff resumed the evictions. House by house, the Baldwin-Felts agents passed like locusts through the ramshackle patch. If no one was home, or the family inside simply refused to open the door, the agents kicked it in. They whistled at the daughters and called out lewd oaths of debauchery. They dragged furniture out of the double-houses and scavenged the bedrooms, kitchens, and elsewhere to take what seemed to them pleasing or expensive. Crocks of butter, jars of preserve, books, coal-oil lamps, pillows, bed linens, gardening tools, baby shoes, boots, and women's bonnets were all dumped in the road. They smashed a looking glass and shot Bear, the Yankoskys' dog. They threw dolls in the mud and family Bibles as well. They threatened at gunpoint anyone they wished to threaten at gunpoint. The hapless families stood saturnine under cold spits of rain by the muddy guttered road with all their feeble belongings and fragile heirlooms piled up, desperately awaiting word that the Union had come through with the canvas tents the organizer promised to supply. By day's end, twenty-eight families were evicted, all the families of miners who had signed Union contracts.

*

The miners and their families picketed the streets of Monongahela the day the scabs came to town. Some of the strikers distributed pamphlets, and others carried picket signs painted red with a variety of slogans: *DON'T BE A SCAB... STOP MINING THE MINER... UNION MEANS UNITY... I'LL GO TO HELL BEFORE I BECOME A SCAB!*

144

Butch Blizzard stood on the corner of West Main and 4th Street, shouting at passersby with a megaphone: "All you people of Monongahela, we'd highly appreciate it if you came out to the Elsinore company store at six in the morning. There's gonna be a picket line tomorrow morning boys. Let's stand on our two feet and show Jack Carver that we can have a contract. Let's show the people of Washington County we stand together. The fire's burning hot now. There ain't much the company can do now. We're gonna get that contract come hell or high water. All you boys, I want you to be there in the morning. Let's show Jack Carver we stand together in Washington County. We're not letting one man run us out of town. Let's don't back off now. That's where it's happening, tomorrow morning at sunrise at the company store. Be there and support the workers at Elsinore. We're gonna stand there and sweat in the snow until we get that contract signed by Jack Carver."

Brawny, thuggish mine guards brandishing shotguns and packing brand new Smith & Wesson hand-cannons loitered about the train depot, content to chew and spit and pick their yellow teeth with jackknifes, watching the strikers at a distance with contemptuous smirks. Upon arriving, the company scabs, completely unaware of the situation at Elsinore, were surrounded by dozens of strikers. The mine guards beat them back with their blackjacks. The strikers first urged the scabs to leave Monongahela, offering to pay for their transportation back home, but most of the scabs had no home to speak of, and none of them went back. Mostly, they had come from West Virginia, but many were from North Carolina, and a few from as far away as Georgia. It didn't matter to the company if they had experience working in the mines. All that mattered to the company was that they weren't Irish. They were just fodder for the pit, necessary to keep the river of coal flowing over the tipple, herded like cattle to the vacant company houses, and given only one commandment to live by: *Stay the hell away from them Union boys*. All that mattered to the scabs was that there was a roof to sleep under and a steady pay, even if it was scrip that was only good at the company store.

*

By the end of the week, the Union's tents dotted the field along Amleth Lake like chancres on a diseased land. The canvas was stiff with frost in the morning. Each group kept to themselves for the most part: the Poles set up their tents by the edge of the woods, the Italians over by Beazell's barn, the Germans down by the frozen lake, the Hungarians and the Slovaks closer to the railroad embankment, and the Irish were right at the heart of the tent colony. Now that they were all equally exposed to the elements, they were constantly reminded of how cold it could be in March. The temperature stayed in the low thirties in the day and dropped to the twenties in the night. It got so consistently cold and colorless that most of the strikers lost the will to do anything but gripe and glower. Even though they did everything they could to blunt the sharp winter's edge, there were children who lost fingers and toes to frostbite and amateur amputations cauterized with hot iron. When they woke in a fog of ether, their tears were frozen to their face.

The fortunate families had a strip of oilcloth as a floor, while most were living on the bare frozen ground. Some dug holes three feet deep in the begrudging earth so that the women and children would be safe from a sniper's bullet. On their numb meager bodies, they wore all the clothing they had in squalid layers. Families huddled around small cast iron stoves and campfires, holding their hands over the fire heat, and then turning their backsides to warm. Everyone was hungry, miserable, and exhausted all the time. They drank heavily and fought often. Hungry families lay awake at night worrying in the darkness. They packed Mason jars full of hot water under their blankets to keep warm. They tried to sleep a few hours, only to wake shivering and numb until they rubbed the sensation back into each other's arms and legs. The miners worried the women and children would freeze if it got any colder, and were tormented by the thought that not more than a mile away the scabs were sleeping warmly at night in the company houses.

A collection had been taken among the families to bail out the arrested miners. And when they rejoined the camp, they found their

146

situation was dire. It was worse than what anyone had expected, considerably worse than what the Union assured them it would be like. Samuel was constantly placating the complainers and pleading with those who wanted to leave. Supplies for the strikers had been critically low from the start, partly because he Union's treasury had been depleted from sponsoring strikes the past two years in the anthracite region. The men did what they could in the way of hunting the local woods for deer, rabbits, squirrels, pheasants, and even crows. The gaunt leather-faced women in their shawls and babushkas, their gray hair as coarse as horsetails, would save the bones from the meat they ate and boil them to make broth from the marrow for soup. But if not for the donations from old man Beazell and the other farmers who spared whatever they could, the strike would have been quickly broken. Rumors circulated in private that the miners would soon be disbanding. Others proudly insisted to the local newspapers, "If it takes ten years to win this strike, we will be right here."

To make matters worse, they soon found they had a new problem to contend with: the Union supplies from Pittsburgh being shipped to Monongahela were being routinely intercepted by the Baldwin-Felts. First, they stopped at gunpoint the teamsters with their wagonloads on the dirt road leading into camp, and then they confiscated the goods directly at the train depot. Whatever the mine guards seized, they divvied up amongst themselves, and when it was something they had no use for, they put it up for sale on the shelves at the company store. Even when the strikers made plans to sneak their supplies into the camp late after midnight, the detectives were always two steps ahead of them. Finally, the Union put a hold on shipments altogether, since they were in effect only supplying the company, and the growing consensus among the strikers was that they had a spy among them.

Campfires burned throughout the tent colony and the gaunt ragged miners sat around the flames eating small portions of rabbit stew, firelight and shadows chiaroscuro on their unclean faces. Daniel sat with the others by the fire, the flames twisting in the wind, their eyes glowing like coals in their skulls. Beyond their world of cold, filth, and canvas, there was the sound of a fiddle and banjo, and men dancing around the fire with a mason jar of moonshine, stomping in the field, then a scattering of applause. Then the dancers caught their breath and sat cross-legged around the fire with the others, accepting and passing the bottle of whiskey while the banjo player tweaked the tuning on his banjo strings, turning the pegs, plucking a few notes, and when he was satisfied they played again.

Daniel got up and cleared his throat, then took up a log of firewood and placed it on the flames, the burnt out charcoal logs collapsing beneath it, a sudden fury of sparks released, dancing on the rising heat before they faded and disappeared in the darkness. His paranoid eyes had the look of someone who thought he was being watched from the shadows, just beyond the firelight, by any number of men who meant him harm. Lately, the people in the camp had begun to gossip about his increasingly eccentric behavior. He was frequently observed on the perimeters of the camp, by an old, moss-covered stone wall that separated the company property from old man Beazell's land, pacing and talking to himself, gesturing frantically, stroking his beard and tapping his finger against his lips. He hadn't been sleeping much, but whenever he did doze off briefly, he would always wake with such screams that he startled the others sleeping nearby. Among the strikers, he became a figure of speculation to be rivaled only by the sheriff in their awe. There were rumors that he had killed a man in Pittsburgh, that there were warrants out for his arrest in three different states. Now he was just sitting a little too close to the fire with his arms crossed on his folded knees, staring directly into the firelight.

"How you holding up there?" Samuel inquired.

"I'm worried," Daniel said in a monotone. "Something terrible's gonna happen here."

"We're all a little bit worried," Michael shrugged.

"He's right." Samuel snapped a twig and tossed it into the hissing fire. "All hell's about to break loose. This camp's like a powder keg ready to blow."

148

"Carver, he'll be coming after me now," Daniel said. He stood just beyond the firelight's range.

"We'll be ready for them when they do," Blizzard said.

"No we won't." Daniel sat down by the fire and crossed his legs. "I'm just a target for them if I stay here. Wide out in the open like this. We're sitting in a goddamn shooting gallery."

"There's hundreds of us here," Ekvie assured him. "We're not going to let anything happen to you."

"If I had a chance to leave though... Maybe that'd be for the best. Maybe things would get better. I'm bad luck wherever I go. Feels like I'm haunting this place. Maybe it is haunted."

"You wouldn't be able to live with yourself if you left us now," Samuel pointed out. "I know you wouldn't. You can't just turn your back on the Union now."

"My daddy used to talk Union like you. I see where it got him."

"He was ready to die for it and he did," Blizzard said. "When you want something so bad that you're ready to die for it, that's when you get it. He understood that. I don't think you do."

"It's like the Crucifixion," Liam O'Loughlin mused sagaciously. "You can't have nothing good without a sacrifice."

"I understand he's dead and we're still not any closer to a contract. I just know I'm outmatched. I can't do what I set out to do. I can see that now."

"Daniel, these people have been waiting for someone like you," Blizzard pleaded. "They're good people, but they're cowards. You're the only man since your father who was willing to stand up to him. You've got to hold on. Pull yourself together."

Daniel took a dangerously long drink from a mason jar of moonshine and grimaced at the burn he felt tearing through his esophagus. "Katherine. She'll... she said she'd give me money to go."

"Well, maybe you should go," Michael sipped from the jar that was being passed around. "If that's what you want to do..."

Daniel shot him a glance then looked back at the fire. "You want me to go, don't you?"

149

"You make it sound like the strike wouldn't go on without you..."

"You know what," Daniel suddenly lashed out, his mood shifting as swiftly as the direction of the wind. "You'd like that wouldn't you, if this strike ended without a contract."

"What in the hell's your problem?"

"You've been talking to Carver, haven't you?"

"You're crazy! You're a goddamn..." Michael shut his eyes, waited, then looked at Daniel and pronounced the words in a flat monotone. "You really are as crazy and as everyone says you are."

"That's right. I am crazy. I'm Daniel fucking Byrnes and I'm crazier'n hell. But I'm as right as rain about you, you backstabbing son-of-a-bitch. Who else would be telling the company when and where all the supplies are coming in? Who else would have given up the names of every single miner who signed a Union card? The sheriff knew every single one of us before the evictions started. How do you explain that?"

"I got evicted too, you know? I got kicked out of the boarding house just like everybody else, didn't I? I'm out here starving and eating rabbit fucking stew... I got my goddamn belt cinched as tight as it'll get."

"Yeah, but you're the only one of us who's been fucking a boss's daughter. You never really explained how it is you wormed your way up her skirt..."

"Hey, you shut up about her. She didn't have anything to do with this."

"I'm the only one who sees you for what you are around here, and I'm getting sick of it."

"What about you? Why should we trust you?"

Daniel threw his head back and howled laughing. "Are you saying I'm working for the company? And they call me crazy!"

"Delilah told me the sheriff offered you a job working for him..."

"Is that true?" Blizzard asked.

"Yeah, and I told him to stick it up his ass. He had me arrested the next morning."

"Maybe that was part of the deal. To make it look like we could trust you."

"I'm here to kill that murdering son of a bitch."

"Yeah, but how come you never actually do it? You just keep saying you're going to do it. What are you waiting for, the Second Coming or something?"

"I'm waiting for the right moment. I can't exactly just walk up to him and kill him you know. He needs to be caught off guard. I can't do it if he sees me coming."

"You can't do it no matter what. You won't."

Daniel stared into the fire, and the fire was like a mirror in which he saw himself deeply, a reflection of his deep heart's core from which he could not look away, though he was terrified by what black visions he saw of himself.

"I killed your father-in-law... Didn't I?"

"You killed an innocent man is what you did."

"Innocent as the devil..."

"You can't do anything right except drink yourself blind."

Daniel heard him, but he didn't listen. He wasn't sitting before the fire now. Somehow, as vivid as any dream he had ever had, he was hovering somewhere below a ceiling with cracked and flaking white plaster, peppered with bullet holes, outside of his body, floating just above a brass chandelier, and when he looked down he saw a body moving slowly.

"Why did you really come back here?"

What he saw was his own body, crawling insectlike across the floorboards in the low lamplight, crawling through his own blood. Gasping for air, but not breathing. So much blood. Who would have though he had so much blood inside of himself?

"It was all a mistake wasn't it?"

And then with greater detail, with terrible and astonishing clarity, he saw the bone-handled knife sticking out of his back, his own knife, his father's knife.

"I only wonder why he hasn't killed you yet..." Michael persisted.

And just behind him, not in a slow plodding pursuit, but standing with his boots at the edge of the blood streaking the floor, merely watching with grim delight as Daniel desperately clawed at the floorboards and pulled himself along, the sheriff, with a burning cigar in the corner of his mouth.

"Because, he respects me... He sees himself in me."

"Carver doesn't respect anyone."

"I can't explain it to you."

"You've got a pretty goddamn high opinion of yourself, don't you?"

Daniel looked away from the fire and shouted, "Don't you see? He wants me to be *him*..."

"Maybe you are just turning into a murdering son-of-a-bitch like him after all. That's the only reason I can figure why you're still alive."

"I'll tell you why I'm alive. Because he's fucking afraid of me that's why I'm still alive! He can't fucking kill me! Because he doesn't have my permission. Because I can't die until I'm goddamn ready to die. And let me tell you something, friend. You better sleep with one eye open tonight because I'm going to come into your tent when you least expect it and I'm going to cut your fucking throat open."

"Do you hear him?" Michael pointed at Daniel. "He's going batshit crazy!"

Daniel looked at Samuel and Blizzard. They seemed to be turning it over in their heads. They wouldn't look him in his manic eyes. He shook his head and stood up. "I can't believe I'm even having this conversation. I don't need this."

"You're the one who started making accusations, cowboy."

Daniel wandered off. He saw in passing, through the canvas wall of a tent glowing from a candle within, the silhouette of a miner's wife loosening her hair. He continued sad and alone in the starlit field and began to walk along the creek. The miners' dogs had hushed and the musicians had stopped playing. The night was all peace and darkness. From time to time, he looked up in perfect silence at the stars for he

152

was a lover of the night. In the star-blown sky, enormous and suspended in the coal-black night, Orion drifted across the firmament, and he saw with a terrible clarity the dark present of his life, the dark future. The misery wailing in the sound of the wind. He clasped his hands and drops of sweat formed on his pale brow.

"Father, please," he said aloud, "you're asking me to do something I can't do. He scares the fucking shit out of me every time I see him. I never know what the hell he's gonna do. I can feel his fucking knife twisting in my gut. I feel cut up and half dead already. I can feel my blood bleeding out of me. For Christ's sake, haven't I suffered enough? I don't wanna die here. I don't want to die a fucking failure at everything I've ever tried to do. To think that he's still alive, and I've done nothing about it, it makes me want to rip my goddamn teeth out. I say and I say and I say I'll do it and yet here's the thing still to do: gutless, cowardly cunt that I am. I would do the world a considerable kindness with my own self-slaughter, but if only I could take him with me... then that's what I'll do. I know in my heart of hearts I'll die before winter's end, but I refuse to die without retribution."

*

At daybreak four horseback Baldwin-Felts agents in black bowler caps and topcoats rode into the striker's camp, their breath and their horses' breath clouding in the bitter cold. One of the agents held a tin lantern aloft, shining it around the tents, the whites of their eyes cutting the dark. Each with an upright rifle or shotgun resting on his thigh, they rode their horses through the ash and smoldering embers of the fire pits, knocking over tripods and kettles. Soon several miners were awakening and hollering, "There's agents in the camp!"

Daniel woke to the shouting, scuffling, and cursing, and he pulled his boots on. He snatched from under his pillow his father's bone-handled knife and concealed it in his boot. His other knife, a small clasp knife with a four-inch blade, he tucked in his long underwear. As soon as he did this, an agent threw open his tent flap, stooped through the entrance, and shone the lamp in his face, a drawn pistol in his other hand. Against the blinding light, Daniel shaded his bloodshot eyes.

"Keep your hands where I can see them," the agent said, raising his gun, "or I'll shoot your ass full of holes." Then turning, he called out of the tent, "I got him in here!"

A second agent came into the tent with his rifle.

"Are you gentlemen looking for me?" Daniel asked innocently.

"Get out of the goddamn tent. You're under arrest for the murder of Charles O'Brien."

"Bull shit. You don't have jurisdiction here, and I'm not going anywhere."

"Get your hands on your head and start walking boy or we'll make this real difficult for you."

But he didn't move, just stood there with his fists balled, grinding his teeth.

The first agent tucked his pistol into his belt and grabbed him by the wrist. Daniel swung at him with his free hand and the agent dropped the lantern and went backpedaling into the canvas tent wall, half-collapsing the tent. Immediately, the second agent came at him with the butt end of the rifle and jabbed him in the gut, knocking the wind out of him. Daniel doubled over, sucking air. The first agent was on his feet again and got behind Daniel, holding him in a half nelson while the second agent handcuffed the wrist of Daniel's free arm and then he went berserk, for he would just as soon die as be handcuffed. He thrashed and bit and butted with his head until the third and fourth deputies came in and grappled with him. He screamed the whole time, but finally—it took all four of them—they threw him to the ground outside the tent and got the cuffs on his other hand and shackled his ankles together too, so he couldn't run.

"Where's your knife?"

They got him vertical again. "I don't have a fucking knife."

He saw Blizzard standing with his hands on his head, held at gunpoint by Baldwin-Felts agents, cursing them up and down. "Don't worry," he said, "We're gonna get you back, Byrnes."

In the midst of the struggle, the fallen lantern had set fire to the tent, which quickly became a conflagration, and strikers were scrambling with buckets and pails, trying to dowse the flames lest the fire should spread. Meanwhile, one of the agents patted Daniel down around his back and waist, never touching the area around his groin, never finding the knife he kept hidden and razor sharp. The agent patted down his pant legs and removed the knife from his boot. The agent held it up to show the others. "I thought you didn't have a fucking knife?" the agent said.

"I guess I fucking forgot that one," Daniel said.

The agent behind him swung the butt end of the rifle and knocked him in the back of the skull, dropping him to the ground. Several families came out of their tents to see what was happening. They watched the fearsome spectacle unfold as the Baldwin-Felts agent holding the knife stepped towards Daniel and kicked him in the ribs. "This is what happens to murderers in Elsinore," the agent said. He stood overtop Daniel, raised his boot, and stomped on his temple, knocking him unconscious, the side of his face pressing flatly into the mud while the ashes of the half-burnt canvas tent hissed and smoked.

Nine

Marianna, PA.
March 12, 1889

Dear Mr. Carver,

I sit down for the last time to communicate a few thoughts to you. You will please excuse this short epistle, for while I am writing I am recovering from a head injury I received while picketing the Pigeon Creek Coal Company. The camp here has since I last wrote to you drifted into utter disorder and anarchy. There is talk of martial law soon being in effect. Although the picketing miners were within the boundaries of the law and not infringing upon company property, many miners—myself included—were beaten, arrested, and jailed for several days and nights without being formally charged with any crime. During this time, I was at the mercy of men without character or dignity, who stood sentinel at the holding cell. By and by, they became brutally drunk and boasted of the nice times they had had with the wives and daughters of the striking miners. While I do not condone the principles of Unionization, the brutality of the operators and their hired guards is entirely unconscionable. I shudder to think of a similar scene unfolding at Elsinore. Above all, I fear for my sister's safety. Perhaps my eyes are now open for the first time. You may subject me to harsher treatment than I have already received, but I cannot remain in this county any longer. I shall return to Elsinore perhaps before this letter has reached you.

Sincerely,

Logan O'Brien

P.S. Since I have not heard from you, I trust I shall find my father and sister are well.

*

Carver received O'Brien's last letter the same day he showed up in town again at the train station. He met him at their house with the

156

company doctor. Below wisps of hook-shaped cirrus clouds, a hawk floated in slow circles over the patch. Only a few families had not been evicted, those who had eschewed the Union and remained unequivocally loyal to the company. In the days after the evictions, the patch was a still, silent ghost town. But the dying winter twilight saw three men emerge on the front porch of the O'Brien house, Logan accompanied by the sheriff and the company doctor.

"Where is he?"

"I have him locked up," the sheriff said.

"Locked up?"

"I understand you're upset, Logan."

"I'm more than upset."

"Let's say he disappears. We don't even have him on the books. No papers. No family, no friends. No one will come looking for him. No one will ever even remember he was here. He's a ghost."

"I want to see him hanged."

"You will," said the sheriff.

Logan lowered his head and wiped his red eyes. "What can you do for my sister?"

"There's not much I can do," Burke admitted. "What ails her is beyond my limited skills. I'd see that she gets plenty of bed rest. Avoid things that will agitate her. No visitors. And see that she gets her laudanum regularly. Give her a dose, two tablespoons, three times a day. That seems to keep her calm."

"She'll recover with time?"

"I hope all will be well," Burke said. "We must be patient."

Mary Beth emerged behind the men, barefoot and tiptoeing on her bony white feet, sneaking out the door, wearing her thin gray cotton nightdress. She was rake-thin. "I dreamed that the mines were all blazing with fire," she said.

They all turned, startled by her appearance.

"Mary Beth," Burke said. "You shouldn't be outside. You're not well."

"They say a little fever burns out the bad humors and can be good for a person from time to time," she said. "I was never well."

"You need your rest. Your brother will take you back up to bed."

"I won't go to bed with my brother. No matter how badly he wants to take me there."

"Here, your medicine will help you sleep."

"If you have poison for me, I'll drink it."

"It's your medicine to calm your nerves. You've taken it for years."

She positioned herself before the windowpane and, standing before it, studied her own reflection which she seemed to account as a stranger. "I see thee as one dead in the bottom of a tomb," she said dreamily. "Thou look'st pale." She seemed to stare deeper into her ghostlike reflection. "I played many parts—none of them were myself... O, woe is me, to have seen what I have seen, see what I see."

She turned swiftly and pushed her way through the men watching her and she stood at the top of the porch steps and sang, looking towards the No. 7 colliery and the last rays of sunlight over the hills. And she sang in a shrill soprano:

Mickey Pick-Slate, early and late,
That was this poor little breaker boy's fate;
A poor simple woman at the breaker still waits,
To take home her Mickey Pick-Slate.

The men were speechless. They tried to restrain her, but she was as nimble and spry as a forest creature, prancing about with her bare feet soiled. Burke disappeared into the house and came back out holding the brown glass bottle and a tablespoon, but she slipped past him and ran down the steps into the grass. As she sang, she plucked a dead withered flower from the garden and adorned her hair with it. And as she frolicked in circles, she sang:

Here's a story, a little bit gory,
A little bit happy, a little bit sad,

158

Of Lily the Pink and her medicinal compound,
And how it slowly drove her mad.
We'll drink a drink
To Lily the Pink the pink the pink.

Her blank expression broke in an instant, and she looked as if her understanding of the world had shattered into pieces like fine china dropped to the floor. She went through a mercurial range of emotions: at first deeply mournful, weeping loudly, spurting hot tears, her white skin hot and reddened, then suddenly saucer-eyed with terror, then high-pitched hysteric laughter. She tore at her clothing and pulled her nightdress over her head, and she was all but naked save for her white undergarments. Logan approached her slowly, snatched his arms around her, and held her closely. She smelled of wet wool and her own urine. She struggled and squirmed against him and began to shriek, cursing God and the world. She struggled so hard they tumbled over and Logan held her, kissing her hair and the hot reddened skin of her face as she cried fierce tears warm against his cheek. With time, she calmed or simply burned herself out. Logan helped her up. He held her, his arm wrapped around her, and they walked slowly back to the house.

"He's just an old coal miner, Lord," she said. "That's all he's ever been."

*

At the sheriff's office, Daniel sat on the floor in the shadows with his back against the cell wall, his head hanging down, quiet, emotionless. Flakes of dried mud cracked around the corners of his eyes, clumps of mud matted in his hair, his body wasted to nothing but muscle and bone. He touched his tender wrists and the red marks and cuts from the handcuffs. The backs of his hands were numb, and he felt a tingling sensation when he pressed on the tendons. Daniel looked up at the empty cot where Samuel had slept when he was last in jail, and he wondered if Samuel was out there in the canvas tents with the strikers or still living in the patch with the scabs.

159

By and by, the sheriff came through the door and stomped the snow off his boots and hung his coat on the coat rack. He was holding his jug of moonshine. He set it on the desk in front of Pearce. "Here's that fucking 'shine for whoever collared him."

"They were asking about it."

"Has he said anything yet?" the sheriff asked.

"Not a word," Pearce said. "Just sitting there like a stone."

The sheriff approached the cell. Daniel sat scrunched in a ball, his arms folded atop his bent knees, his forehead resting on his forearms. The sheriff cocked his head to the side, musing. "You got yourself tangled up in one hell of a mess, didn't you?"

Daniel raised his head a moment and then lowered it again.

"I can always tell when someone's a killer," the sheriff said. "I can see it in their eyes." The sheriff took his gloves off. "That's why I thought I could teach you to be me. But then I figured out who you were, Daniel fucking Byrnes. Now I just want to see you hanged by a judge and jury. You don't deserve to be killed by me."

"What made my father so dangerous that you had to kill him?"

"You've made a lot of mistakes in the name of someone you don't even know that fucking well."

"I would have known him."

"Well, if it helps you sleep tonight, I'll tell you this. Your father, you could've propped him up piss-drunk in front of a crowd of the most miserable, beaten down and broken miners and in fifteen minutes he'd persuade them that they could go on strike against God himself. I never understood how he could talk like that... But I can't have hunkies organizing at my mine. That's why I'm the sheriff. Not to enforce laws. As I disobey them at every turn, I clearly don't give a fuck about laws. But order. These scrounging hunkies not speaking a fucking word of English are threatening American order. They work half as hard as a nigger and want a white man's pay. So when one of them starts preaching about organizing and Unionizing in my mining camp, I silence the preacher. Your father was working to upset the natural order... But now—Christ, I must be losing it with old age—

look at this fucking circus act up on the hill I have to deal with now. A full-on goddamn United Mine Workers of America strike, which in turn causes the shareholders to bring in those swinging dicks courtesy of the Baldwin-Felts detective agency, who I don't think any of us fucking want around." The sheriff dropped his eyes to the ground, shook his head, and continued. "I will say this, though. For a son to bear a grudge like that all these years. Christ, it's madness. It's idolatry."

"Whenever someone calls me crazy," said Daniel, "and I look around at this fucked up world people call normal, that's when I know I must have done something right."

"Sounds like the noose couldn't come soon enough."

"You know," Daniel said. "If someone had raised the curtain and shown me my life before I ever lived it, I wouldn't have wanted to play the part. I've been playing a role that somehow always feels wrong."

"You've got a dark turn of mind."

"I can't choose how I think or what I believe."

"Did you just up and decide to kill me one day?" the sheriff asked. "What made you come back?"

"I was just doomed and destined to try to kill you."

The sheriff grinned. "I'll be seeing you in the morning, kid."

*

At dusk, the sky was a wash of crimson. A thick throng of strikers gathered around a miner-preacher in the field on an improvised altar of beer casks, crates, and various pieces of pilfered lumber. He was known in Elsinore simply as the Reverend and had been in the camp preaching and holding regular Sunday services almost as long as the tent colony had been there. He was rumored to appear wherever there were miners striking and was revered as a kind of working man's saint. His thick, heavy eyebrows and piercing gaze gave him the look of an Old Testament prophet. He had come into town afoot one day, with nothing but a bible and a heavy burlap sack, which no one else could lift, the contents of which remained a mystery. "I bet he's got a body in there," the men joked between themselves.

The air was damp and cold, Pennsylvania suicide weather. The strikers had the look of embattled soldiers, long entrenched, awaiting the grave benediction of a chaplain before battle, entirely ready to die for their cause. The men all wore red handkerchiefs tied to their arms so that they could identify themselves.

"Boys, I had been digging coal twenty-five years when I suddenly got the call to preach the word of God. Like the Apostle Paul on the road to Damascus, I was on my way to the pit when I had a vision and got the call. I stopped going to the company church that day. From that day forth I had no desire to hear the company ministers preach otherworldliness and tell me to be ye content with your wages. They say happiness and salvation lay in tolerating the hardships of this world: a world filled with blacklists, depressions, lockouts, strikes, murderous explosions, slatefalls, and mine-guards.

"Well, boys, I can't believe that God had anything to do with those human buzzards who preach in the company church. Let me tell you, those preachers are owned body and soul by the coal operators. Have you ever heard a preacher preaching against the mine-guards? No... Why, I'd rather be in hell with Cleopatra and John Wilkes Booth than hear such human lice profane the pulpit. The company preachers have not had to suffer. *You* have suffered. I know you have suffered.

"My God says the coal operators are false idols who want us to worship them. In the Book of *James,* the Lord says: Go now ye rich men—weep and howl, your miseries that shall come upon you. Your riches are corrupted and your garments are moth-eaten; your gold and silver is cankered and the rust of them shall be a witness against you and shall eat your flesh as if it were fire. Ye have heaped treasures together for the last day. Behold the hire of the laborers who have reaped down your fields which you kept back by fraud, and the cries of them which have reaped are entered into the ears of the Lord. Ye have lived in pleasure on earth and been wanton; ye have nourished your hearts as in a day of slaughter; ye have condemned and killed the just.

162

"Boys, my God is a Union God. The labor movement itself was a command from God Almighty. He commanded the prophets thousands of years ago to go down and redeem the Israelites that were in bondage, and he organized the men into a Union and they went to work. They got together and the prophet Moses led them out of bondage. For the first time the worker was free. I hear the beating heart of the Union in the book of *Ecclesiastes*: Two are better than one, because they have a good reward for their labor. For if they fall, the one will lift up his fellow, but woe to him who is alone when he falleth; for he hath not another to help him up. And if one prevail against him, two shall withstand him, and a threefold cord is not quickly broken.

"Boys, there are about three hundred of us here living in these tents in Elsinore. And up on yonder hill is our fallen fellow. That false idol's got him locked up in his office. But I say unto you he's more than just our fellow laborer. He's a working man's Moses who's ready to lead us out of bondage, through the wilderness and into the promised land. Are we going to abandon our brother, the only son of a dear father murdered, in his darkest hour? Or will we stand up together and fight for his freedom? Now is the hour for the coal miner to shoulder the cross! This is our war, boys! Now I lay down my Bible and take up my rifle in service of the Lord!"

"By God, that's what I call preaching!" someone shouted.

Their ranks swelled like an assembling army. Many of the strikers were drunk, hungry, and quarrelsome. Marchers shot pistols in the air. Samuel carried an American flag at the front as they beat on drums and mounted the hill to the breaker. There was a brief exchange of gunfire with no casualties before the badly outnumbered mine guards fled the company property. The strikers closed down the workshops and marched to the engine house to shut down the funicular equipment. The Slavic brakeman lowering the cars into the mine was ordered to stop. The column again moved on to the tipple, where the strikers hooked a plank to the whistle and left it blowing to announce their victory. The scabs down in the mine stayed below ground for safety until long after the marchers had left. Many who were working on top barely escaped in one piece. The unlucky ones pleaded for mercy, pitifully invoking the names and ages of their offspring, but the marchers had kindled themselves into a kind of collective rage, and so the scabs were spat upon, kicked, and bludgeoned, a few were stripped naked, and most were left unconscious.

Then, in a rabid and ravenous uproar, the marchers swarmed downhill to the company store, their picks and axes silhouetted against the fire of their torches. When Cyrus Swank saw them coming he locked everything up and tried to barricade himself inside, but they shattered all the windows with rocks and then broke down the door with an ax. They cornered Swank who had been trying to fend them off unsuccessfully with a broken broomstick, and when they had disarmed him he thrashed about trying to bite their hands while they tied him to a chair. Blizzard and the others began throwing food to the howling mob. "The company's always telling us they give us what we want," he shouted. "Now we're taking what we want!"

Someone had gotten the idea to tar and feather Swank. Evidently, a lot of them had been hoping and praying for an opportunity like this to present itself. It wasn't long before they had gathered the necessary tar and started to heat it in a galvanized tub, while others eagerly went off to gather some chickens. But the crafty rodent clerk had managed to wiggle out of his restraints while the strikers were busy bickering over who was going to get to do what, and before anyone knew what was happening, Swank was darting through the aisles, demonstrating impressive agility as he slipped through his captors' arms like a greased up pig. The last anyone ever saw of him, he was running at full tilt down the railroad tracks with piss splotches and shit streaks on his pants.

From there, having ransacked the company store, the marchers surmounted the hill into the patch, where they rallied around the sheriff's manor, an opulent brick mansion with six bedrooms, though he lived alone. It was set on a generous plot of land protected by a spiked cast iron fence, and it overlooked the rows of squalid miner's double-houses. Their glistening eyes were shining with the flames of their torches. "Burn it to the ground!" anonymous voices in the crowd yelled.

Uneasy glances were exchanged. Women goaded their men. But no one would throw the first stone to shatter its tall Palladian windows. Soon, the front door was thrown open and the strikers at the front of the column shrank away from the house, the fiery aggression in their black eyes giving way to abject trepidation. Michael turned to find the sheriff looming over the crowd, standing at the top of the stairs on his porch, a six-shot revolver in each of his hands.

"To think," he shouted over the murmuring, "that any of you cowards would have the gall to set fire to a man's house! To think that I would let you so much as come through the gate of my fence! Because you've somehow mustered the courage to come to my gate, you think that you can set foot on my land?" He lowered his gaze to glare at Blizzard. "Look at you, your barbarian hordes, a whole herd of squareheads, marching with that American flag in the hands of a nigger. You're a disgrace! You hunkies have no respect for that flag and you've got no right to carry it!"

Blizzard took a long swig on his bottle and handed it over to Michael. By now he was blackout drunk. Michael and Samuel tried to hold him back, but Blizzard stepped forward from the ranks with a swagger, threw open the gate and walked down the path towards the sheriff's porch. "You're not so bad as you think you are, Jack Carver."

"I reckon you thought I had horns," Carver said.

For a brief moment it was so quiet you could hear the crackling of torches burning. Blizzard adjusted his eye patch with his left hand and threw open his overcoat with his right, pulling his piece, but the sheriff was too fast for him.

He leveled the pistol in his left hand at Blizzard and fired without hesitation. A handful of gore spat out the back of his skull, some of it spackling the faces at the edge of the fence. The sheriff raised the smoking pistol at the mob. Blizzard fell on his back, his black eye patch still in place, a gaping hole where his other eye had been. The tide of strikers began to wash back and break apart, some of them hurrying away.

"That's what your Union'll get you." Smoke swirled out of the sheriff's gun as he gestured at Blizzard's body. "Anyone else who sets foot on my property is going to end up just like him…"

Samuel and the strikers behind him were all falling backwards over themselves trying to get away. The sheriff lowered his Schofield and walked slowly to the edge of the porch, standing at the top of the stairs. His eyes raked across the crowd scornfully.

"Did you think that with all of you cowards lumped together that I would be afraid? I don't know what it means to be afraid. Even if I did, I'd know I was safe in the hands of a thousand of you! I've been cutting throats for as long as any of you have been cutting coal. And yet I was foolish enough to think that there was one man among you. I was dead wrong. Where is he? Locked up in a cage and begging for the noose. Do you think he's come here to save you? He won't help you. He could've come here alone a long time ago—like a man would've—but instead there's a rambling herd of sqauareheads to stand in his place.

"Is there a man among you? Is there a man looking at me now, who will point his pistol at me? You have as good a chance here and now as you will ever have again." He paused for anyone to answer him, and his hard eyes scanned the crowd of onlookers, their frightened faces chiaroscuro in the torchlight. "And you tell yourselves you have strength in numbers? You only have more weakness. And here I am, one man, all alone… no deputies… no detectives… and there you all are, and not a single man among you. So go on back to cowering under your tents, out in the field… in the mud and piss and shit where you belong. Go back and pray to your God. Tell yourselves you'll turn the other cheek. Tell yourselves the meek shall inherit the earth. But just know this: there is only one reason why you didn't go to hell tonight, and that's because my hand has not struck you down."

The sheriff jammed the revolvers into their holsters, turned and walked back into his house, slamming the door behind him.

In the sheriff's office, Donny Spearman served Daniel his dinner. "Eat it," he said. "It might could be your last." Daniel looked down at the tray of food in his lap and the water-spotted silverware, took up the fork and knife, and started cutting into a thin gray pork chop. This meat, which he didn't care for to begin with, was cooked as dry as jerky. The little potato was almost raw. The stale bread had mold on the crust. And as for drink, there was none. There was a pitcher on the deputy's table and he called out for a cup of water.

"Your turn," Spearman said. "I fed him."

"Oh, for fuck's sake," Pearce said. "The hell with him."

"Just give him a glass of water."

Pearce shook his head and sighed heavily and poured a tin cup full from the pitcher. He approached the cell and extended the cup, but when Daniel reached out to accept it Pearce pulled it back and smirked. Then he made a wretched snorting sound as he cleared his throat and gathered all the mucous in his nose and he spat a yellow clot into the water and held out the cup. Daniel glared at him.

"What? Don't you want it now?" Pearce smiled and set the tin cup on the floor where Daniel could reach it. He returned to his desk and picked up the bone-handled knife. He sat with his boots propped on the desk and began paring a green apple with the knife. He looked at Daniel. "This is a nice damn knife. I'm gonna keep this."

Spearman shook his head, got up and poured a clean cup of water for Daniel and brought it over to the cell. "Get up," he said. "I got your water."

"Don't give that murdering cocksucker nothing," said Pearce. "Let his ass rot in there."

"It's just a cup of water, for Christ's sake. He ain't causing any trouble."

"He already caused enough trouble. Just look at this clusterfuck we got on our hands up at Beazell's."

Daniel got on his feet and took the cup and drank thirstily. He handed the empty cup back to the guard.

Pearce chewed his apple and eyed Daniel with scowling contempt. "You ain't getting nothing else, so don't ask. You hear?"

Daniel held up his middle finger and started to eat.

Pearce read the *Daily Independent* at his desk, his boots propped up on the desktop while Spearman cleaned and oiled his revolver. Daniel peeled the moldy crust from off his bread and flung it in the corner for the rodents that jointly occupied his cell. Occasionally, he heard the flipping of the newspaper pages, and he stole quick surreptitious glances at his guards. He felt the small clasp knife still tucked under his long underwear. Pearce folded his newspaper and looked in on Daniel just as he was sopping up the last of the watery gravy with the stale bread. Daniel carried the tray over to the cell door, and held out the tray before him through the slot. Pearce took the tray without a word.

Daniel lay looking up at the ceiling, gently touching his split, swollen bottom lip with his index finger, the red slit of blood there again. Spearman was sound asleep in his chair, and it was probably getting close to ten o'clock, but Pearce was still reading the *Daily Independent*, his feet propped on the desk. A green quart liquor bottle lit with a saturated rag whirled through the window, exploding through the glass, spraying fire on the floor and wall on the far side of the deputy station and part of the holding cell. At the sound of shattering glass, Pearce toppled backwards in his chair, and the commotion startled Spearman so badly that he jumped up out of his chair. Daniel sat up on his cot.

There was indistinguishable shouting and torchlight coming through the broken window and part of the sheriff's office was on fire. The deputies peered out the windows. The striking miners had galvanized into a mob and the column was moving through the camp setting fire to certain company buildings. Pearce marched over to the gun rack on the wall and grabbed hold of a Remington double barrel twelve-gauge. He loaded it and filled his shirt pockets with shells. He strode over to the door, his left hand clasping the knob as he stood with his shoulder to the door. He looked at Spearman and nodded towards Daniel.

"You stay with him and see to the fire."

"Where are you going?" Spearman asked, glancing out the window.

"Fire off a few shots at those cocksuckers."

The door swung open and Pearce went out onto the little porch, raising the shotgun aloft and firing a warning shot. Then he bellowed out for them to disperse, the mob pelting him with rocks and refuse, chanting: "Free Daniel Byrnes!"

With the deputy's back turned to him, Daniel pulled the knife up out of his pants and unclasped it. He reached his left hand through the iron bars, the knife clutched in his right. He covered Spearman's mouth and hauled him back again so that his skull banged hard against the iron bars, then held the blade below the deputy's chin. He could hear the rabid roaring of the hostile mob outside. "This can go down one of two ways," Daniel said. "You make a sound, I'll cut your throat. You give me the keys and gun, I'll let you go. What's it gonna be?"

Daniel took his hand away from his mouth and snatched a fistful of the deputy's curly hair, pressing the sharp blade down against the soft stubbly neck-flesh, the deputy's carotid artery pulsing violently.

"I'll give you the fucking keys," Spearman whimpered.

"And the fucking gun," Daniel said.

"And the fucking gun," he agreed.

When Daniel had the gun in his hand, he told Spearman to open the cell door. As soon as he was out of the cell, he pistol-whipped Spearman across the forehead, knocking him unconscious. Just then, Pearce appeared in the doorway, not yet seeing Daniel, bent forward and looking down, plugging a new shell into the shotgun barrel. Suddenly he looked up, his fumbling hands dropping the second shell, his eyes darting from Spearman slumped on the floor to Daniel who held the pistol directly at him.

"Drop it," Daniel said.

169

Pearce obeyed and held his hands up. "Don't fucking shoot me," he said.

"Go on outside," Daniel said, tossing his chin towards the doorway.

The mob of strikers seized Pearce and beat him bloody and tore his badge off his chest. Others surged into the office and dragged the half-conscious Spearman out and did the same to him. Daniel put the Colt revolver in his coat pocket and grabbed his father's knife from the deputy's desk. He made for the door, but he turned back and grabbed the sheriff's jug of moonshine before he hurried out into the winter darkness.

The miners cheered when he emerged from the sheriff's office. He looked over them in awe. Hundreds of men, women, and children. They brandished crude agrarian tools and smoking torches, kerosene soaked rags on the ends swallowed up in flames. Even their women wielded broomsticks and bread rollers. Some of the men had brought their dogs, which yapped and barked nervously.

Daniel picked up the torn and bloodied coat of one of the deputies, held it aloft, and screamed, "This is the first time I ever saw a goddamned deputy's coat decorated to suit me." He put on the coat to the applause of the roaring.

"What should we do with these filthy sons-a-bitches?" someone shouted.

"String them up where the sheriff can see them," he said.

They threw two ropes over the low-hanging branches of a wind-crippled oak tree by the creek and lynched the two deputies.

Michael did not appear happy to see Daniel. He did not celebrate as the other strikers did. But Daniel went over to him to make his amends. "About the other night…"

"Yeah?"

"I said some things… that I probably shouldn't have said."

"That's puttin' it mildly."

"Well, I shouldn't have doubted you. You been looking out for me all along."

Michael cracked his knuckles. "I suspect you'll be leavin' town now…"

Daniel was taken aback. "Are you saying I should run away? *Now?* After all this?"

"Why not?"

"Cowards run away."

"Yeah," Michael said. "The smart ones do." He reached for the jug dangling from Daniel's hooked finger, but Daniel stopped him.

"I'm saving this." Then he turned to the crowd of strikers. "Just look out there," Daniel mused, with an expansive sweep of his hand. "Everyone out there. They're all here because of me. These men are ready to fight for *me.*"

"You sure it ain't your father they're really here for?" Michael said bitterly.

"Well, I'm doing what he never could."

"Oh, for God's sake," Michael said. "You're just going to get yourself killed, like I said from the start."

"What needs doing is mine to do, not yours."

"I never said I wanted to help you."

"Then just stay out of my way."

But just then, something caught the attention of one of the miners. Not far away, on the bottom street of the patch, someone saw the smoke curling high into the night sky. He saw the glowing fire, the flames licking high into the darkness.

"The superintendent's house is burning!"

"Did we do that?" Daniel asked.

"Mary Beth," Michael muttered to himself, fearing the worst. He shoved the American flag into the arms of the man beside him, and he began pushing his way through the crowd. "Let me through, let me through!" Soon, they were all following him and the mob moved in the direction of the fire. And as the crowd cleared away, Daniel stood alone before the sheriff's house, silently watching the kerosene lamplight glowing in the window.

By the time Michael reached the house, it was swallowed up in flames, a tremendous conflagration. Michael ran up the stairs and kicked at the door until it gave way and a wall of black smoke poured out of the threshold. He was crying her name aloud. Daniel came running through the crowd and tried to stop him from entering, but Michael pushed him away and rushed into the burning house. Within seconds he staggered out, his face blackened, choking from the thick smoke.

"There's nothing you can do."

Michael said nothing.

"This is all because of me," Daniel said.

Daniel tried to help him away from the fire, but Michael viciously swung at him. He seethed, his eyes narrowing. "You stay the hell away from me," he hissed. "It always has to be about you, doesn't it?"

Daniel stepped back. He didn't say anything, just set his jaw, his fists clenching, eyes narrowing. Though he would've cut Daniel's throat if he'd had the chance, Michael knew better than to fight him, and he walked away intent on getting drunk. Soon the scabs came out into the lane to see the flourishing fire, many of them holding their awestruck children who sucked their thumbs and pointed at the burning house, their fathers dressed in long underwear, their mothers in nightgowns. Nonetheless, the strikers turned their pent up aggression on them. The fighting broke out instantaneously. Hearing the bedlam outside, more scabs rushed out of the company houses. Everywhere strikers and scabs were trading blows as the fire-gutted shell of the O'Brien house collapsed piecemeal. Soon the mine guards swarmed into the pandemonium, and they were clubbing scabs and strikers alike in the firelight. Heads bloodied, noses smashed, men staggering about half-consciously. Mere anarchy, loosed under the murky moonlit sky.

*

In the morning, as the red sun rose like a slash of blood behind the barren trees on the horizon, the sheriff rode past the gutted, smoldering ruin of the O'Brien house. As he went down through the patch to survey the damage, he spotted a circling turkey vulture, and he rode towards it. Its wingspan was a full five feet wide. It lighted on the uppermost branches of a wind-crippled oak tree by his office. The tree was full of them, roosting vultures, their lumpy crimson heads swiveling about. The deputies' bodies hung from the low-hanging limbs, a hangman's knot tied around each of their necks. Two vultures fought over something on the ground, spreading their wings, pecking at it. The swaying of Pearce's body was like the pendulum of some grotesque grandfather clock, the timekeeper of a darker era. His swollen tongue protruded fatly from his mouth, and a red cord dangled from the socket where his eye had been. Around Pearce's neck the strikers had hung a crude sign, scrawled in red paint, which read: "Gone to hell. More to go."

After that night, the mood among the sheriff's posse turned considerably uglier. It wasn't safe to set foot outside of the tent colony anymore, not that it ever was to begin with, but now strikers were beginning to turn up dead with staggering regularity. Paranoia reached a fever pitch. Nubile young girls—whether they were with the strikers or the scabs didn't matter so much as if they were vulnerable—were raped on an almost nightly basis by drunken mine guards who crooned and guffawed all night in the streets. Breaker boys who ventured out of the tent colony returned bloodied and beaten. Not a single day without an exchange of gunfire. Not a night of blessed sleep when a sniper's bullets didn't wake everybody up. Folks stopped greeting one another with *hello* and *how are you*, and instead they started solemnly asking, "Anybody been shot yet today?"

First, they found George Chapman beneath the covered bridge with his neck broken. He had been dumping his chamber pot by the creek when the detectives snuck up behind him. A sniper's bullet shattered Agnes Quinn's hipbone the next night while she lay in bed awake praying the rosary to take her mind off the insomnia. She didn't die, but she never walked right after that. Henry McGough got shot in the back three times right in town one afternoon. Plenty of people saw it happen, but no one would come forward to identify the shooter. That same day, they smashed Seamus Callaghan's head in with a brick by the old artesian spring. Everyone knew a gunfight like no one had ever seen was brewing. The banished miners sat on the edges of their cots, cleaning and oiling their rifles, their anxious breath clouding in the gray morning cold. It was clear by now that Elsinore was nothing if not a battleground.

Ten

The old gravedigger sat on the cold hard ground, scowling at the world from under his white eyebrows, his dirty boots hanging in the open grave. He had one pale blue vulture's eye and held a pint bottle of whiskey in his hands, his fingerless wool gloves soiled and gray. He had been born to grunt and sweat under a weary life. The bare limbs of the birch tree swayed in the raw wind gusting through the rolling valley hills. They had to use picks to break the cold hard earth for the grave. The young towheaded apprentice below stepped on the shovel, scooping the clumped clay and flinging the earth up to where it landed atop a little heap. The old gravedigger tilted the bottle to his cracked lips and took a long pull.

His apprentice halted his task and looked up. "Is it Mary Beth O'Brien it's for?"

"A piece of her anyhow."

"What's that supposed to mean?"

"What does it matter?" the gravedigger said. "They'll be here soon. Keep digging."

"Oh, Christ. I just saw her on Saturday."

The old gravedigger tilted the bottle back to get at the dregs and then regarded it with detached amusement. "Dead," he muttered. He looked down at his apprentice. "You know, she went mad when her father died. Or so the whisper goes."

"She was always sweet to me."

"There was some doubt cast over whether she could be given a proper Christian burial."

"How come?"

"She deliberately set fire to the house, so they say."

"Says who?"

"Says the doctor who was there when it happened. Locked herself in a room when they tried to give her her medicine and she threw a coal-oil lamp against the door."

"What's that got to do with a proper Christian burial?"

"If she deliberately set fire to the house while she was in it, then by proxy she set fire to herself, which makes her a suicide, which makes her—in the eyes of the church—unfit for a Christian burial."

"Well, if Mary Beth O'Brien wasn't a Christian then there isn't a Christian in all of Christendom."

"That may well be so."

"And it's all because of what happened to her father."

"She was too soft for this hard world."

"I wish to Christ I'd find the bastard that murdered Charlie," the apprentice said. "You bet I'd teach him a lesson or two."

"Well before you do, go find me another bottle."

"I thought you said they'd be here soon."

"You'd better hurry then."

The towheaded apprentice clambered out of the grave and held out his palm for the coins. The old gravedigger counted out each coin, one-by-one, surrendering them begrudgingly. Then the apprentice started off down the sloping path, cursing the old man under his breath.

The old gravedigger eased himself down and hoed with his spade, chopping at the hard clay. Snatches of old tunes he whistled were lost in the wind. Somewhere a crow cried out in naked tree limbs. He was still whistling when he looked up and saw Daniel dressed in a ragged suit of solemn black standing there, gazing down at him with anthracite eyes.

"Our lives are brief indeed," Daniel said.

"Are you with the family?" the gravedigger asked.

"I'm not with anyone," he said.

"I thought you were here for the burial."

Daniel's eyes scanned the cemetery, the slate tablets with cryptic epitaphs, the abundance of freshly dug graves with the cold earth yet raw and broken. "You must always have death in the back of your mind?"

"I have enough trouble focusing on what's in front of my mind let alone what's in the back."

Daniel laughed mildly. "Do you ever wonder what it's like?"

"Death?"

"Death, yes."

"I only wonder why it hasn't happened yet," the gravedigger said. "Most of the people I've ever known are right here in this graveyard. I am one of God's forgotten children."

Daniel nodded slowly. "The gospel says, 'An hour is coming when all who are in tombs shall hear his voice.' Do you believe that?"

"I would like to believe, and yet..."

"And yet?"

"...I cannot."

Daniel gazed out at the graveyard and the ghost-gray sky. "Sometimes I think about doing it, you know. Taking the easy way out."

"But it's not so easy," the gravedigger said.

"They say it's a mortal sin."

"They say," the gravedigger murmured, shaking his head, smiling with one side of his mouth and returning to his work with the spade. "I say there are no sins anymore."

"What if this is hell?" Daniel asked aloud.

Then the gravedigger steadied himself on his spade. "Even on my better days, I can only say, with some degree of certainty, that this could not be heaven."

Daniel smiled weakly at the gravedigger. "I'm keeping you from your work. I should be going."

"It's quite all right, sir. My clients are never in a hurry."

"I'll see you again."

Daniel took one hand out of his pocket and held it up before he departed. The gravedigger responded with a doleful nod. He took up the spade again and chopped at the clay. Before long he raised himself up out of the grave with some difficulty and sat resting as before. His mud-clumped boots dangled into the open grave. The raw wind stirred his grizzled hair. He waited. His pale eyes scanned the landscape and he watched the dead straw-colored grass lashing in the wind. Soon he saw his apprentice trudging scant of breath up the winding path through the rows of sunken slate tablets. He handed the half pint of whiskey to the gravedigger and then dropped down into the grave and took up the shovel again.

"This isn't what I wanted."

"That was all he had left," the apprentice said.

The old gravedigger uncorked the bottle and sniffed the whiskey. "This isn't what I wanted at all."

"Am I almost done with the digging?"

"Almost," the gravedigger said. "Did you see anyone coming?"

"Not yet."

"They'll be here soon," he said. "Keep digging."

*

The funeral procession ascended the hill slowly, the two dozen mourners trailing the rough-sawed casket they bore aloft. The women wore black-spotted veils and dabbed at their eyes with handkerchiefs. In the distance, the haunting banshee wail of a train came and went. Near the end of the procession, Michael walked as lonely as a raincloud, and the mourners sang a hymn in unison:

Were you there when they nailed him to the tree?
Oh, sometimes it causes me to tremble, tremble.

With deliquescent eyes, his hair black and glistening with oil, Logan O'Brien helped carry his sister, plucked ere her prime, to Monongahela Cemetery where only a day ago he had buried his father. An impish child dressed in foul rags led the unsighted preacher by the arm until they arrived at the gravesite. With soiled hands and broken fingernails, the blind preacher held his leather-bound Bible open and close to his heart. He bowed his head as though he were reading, but there were no words to be seen by those sightless eyes. When he recited, he would occasionally raise his head so that you could see only the whites of his eyes.

"A reading from Psalm thirty-eight," he began. "A Psalm of David to bring remembrance. I am troubled. I am bowed down greatly. I go mourning all the day long. I am feeble and sore broken. I have roared by reason of the disquietness of my heart. But mine enemies are lively, and they are strong, and they that hate me wrongfully are multiplied. Forsake me not, O Lord. O my God. Be not far from me."

From behind the birch trees in the drizzling rain, Daniel watched the pale sightless eyes of the preacher, who seemed to be looking directly at him, the white eyes piercing through him.

"From Psalm thirty-seven," he said solemnly, "a Psalm of David. Fret not thyself because of evildoers, neither be thou envious against the workers of iniquity. For they shall soon be cut down like the grass, and wither as the green herb. And he shall bring forth thy righteousness as the light, and thy judgment as the noonday. Rest in the Lord, and wait patiently on him. For the meek shall inherit the earth and shall delight themselves in the abundance of peace."

Slowly, the preacher closed the book as he closed his eyes.

"Mary Beth will lie beside a dear father murdered, whose wrongful death proved poisonous to her troubled mind. And although we remember her as a loving daughter, who cared for the sick, the poorly, and the injured among us, no remedy or medicament would mend the hysteria of her own wounded mind. Thus the sins of one man destroy much good."

The preacher raised his head and opened his eyes, revealing the milky white cataracts. "Let us sing 'Amazing Grace' as gentle Mary Beth is laid to rest."

And so they began to sing:

Amazing grace, how sweet the sound,
That saved a wretch like me,
I once was lost, but now am found,
Was blind, but now I see.

The mourners, with tearful eyes, sang softly and at a slow, adagio tempo while the pallbearers lowered the casket on ropes into the open grave. It touched down roughly, as the mourners sang on. The men began shoveling the loose dirt and clumpy rust-colored clay into the open grave, upon her resting mortal clay.

Michael wept. Keeping his distance behind the cluster of birch trees, he clasped his hand over his mouth. His whole body began to shudder. On his reddened face, tears mingled with the cold rain. "Oh, God, I can't stand it," he sobbed. "Oh, God, I can't stand it anymore."

*

The sheriff stood on his porch, his eyes hardening, staring at the encampment of strikers in the distant field under a crimson sky. *They're like human lice*, he thought. He worked a wad of tobacco in his cheek, calculating his next move. When he saw the lone figure clad in black funeral garb ascending the hill towards his house, his hand gripped the holstered revolver at his side. And as this man approached, when the sheriff saw his face, his hand relaxed. He leaned and spat tobacco juice into the muddy grass. His head tilted back with curiosity. "You look lost, son," the sheriff said.

"Yeah," Michael said, "I am."

"Strike wearing you down?"

Michael dug his hands in his pockets. He looked away, gazing off into the distance. "I never thought it'd last this long."

"Sorry to hear about Mary Beth," the sheriff said. "She was a good girl."

"You didn't come to the funeral."

"I tend to forgo sacred ground," the sheriff said. "Makes me queasy."

Michael sniffed, looking away. A chicken-hawk circled overhead in the crimson sky.

"How's our friend holding up in light of recent events?"

"Byrnes? He's still hell-bent on killing you. Maybe more than ever."

The sheriff grinned. "Good. I hope he's finally found the balls to make his move."

"He said something about Katherine giving him money to leave town the other night."

"Please," the sheriff said, extending his arm towards the front door. Logan was standing inside, just beyond the threshold, loading bullets into a small black revolver. "Won't you come inside? We have so much to discuss."

*

The next morning at the railroad embankment, shrouded in the predawn darkness, the sheriff's posse saw to their arms, blowing clean the cylinders, loading and clicking them into place, their fingers slick with gun oil. The sheriff pulled his Schofield and shut one eye and peered down the long barrel to the sight bead. Satisfied, he holstered it. From his vantage point, with a pair of field-glasses, the sheriff scanned over the colony, scattered about the land in a field of dead orchard grass. An encampment of close to a hundred evicted families. Gray smoke slowly rose out of the smoldering ash of their fire pits, a brittle calm throughout the camp.

"How many you figure are out there?" a Baldwin-Felts agent asked.

"Maybe as many as three hundred," said the sheriff.

"Do they have enough guns to put up any sort of a fight?"

"Not a chance."

"How do you want us to go about doing this?"

"Wake em up with some hot lead. Then burn the camp."

"This'll be better than a hog killing," a detective said.

"I betcha any money I kill a half dozen hunkies before we're done," said another.

"Just watch out for Byrnes," the sheriff said. "No one touches him but me, you understand?"

"Yes sir, Mr. Carver."

"This is going to be one hell of a good day for the undertaker," the sheriff said.

They waited until just before break of day, when Frenchy Dupuis emerged from his canvas tent at the front of the colony and set about poking at the embers in the blackened fire pit with a broken stick. Lying on their bellies on the ballast of gravel and stone between the railroad crossties, the agents watched him in silence, working wads of tobacco in their cheeks, their rifles trained on his chest. He fed some kindling into the mound of white ash and pulsing embers. Then he spotted a strange-looking stone in the dirt, a flint arrowhead, and he bent to pick it up. He spat on the chiseled piece and polished it with his thumb. He was dropping it in his shirt pocket when the first gunshot ripped apart the quiet and the bullet tore hot and burning through his thigh. The leg gave out from under him and he dropped. Then bullets kicked up clouds of dust in the dirt all around him and he scrambled for cover in the pit dug under his tent.

Soon gunshots were general within the colony, flames flashing out of muzzles, rifles cracking, revolvers popping, echoing throughout the valley. Tethered dogs woke in the cold and joined together in a cacophonic chorus of barking and yapping. Bullet holes peppered the broadsides of the canvas tents. When another striker emerged from a tent holding a revolver, he shouted: "You go to hell." A rain of gunshots followed. A bullet caught him in the face before his revolver was unloaded. They continued shooting him even as he lay dead.

In his tent, Daniel woke from blessed sleep to the crack of gunshots. When he opened his eyes, he was looking straight into Michael's eyes. He felt the knife blade, his own father's knife, scraping against the whiskers on his throat. Momentarily, his anthracite eyes flashed, then narrowed into dark slits, but if he felt fear, his face showed no sign of it. Nothing about him trembled. Michael was straddling him on the cot, lips twisted with disgust. His thumb pressed against the back of the bone-handled knife. "Hey, cowboy," he said.

"You go on and get it over with," Daniel said flatly.

"God damn you," Michael growled.

Daniel set his jaw, his teeth grinding. There were gunshots firing all around them. "I said do it."

Michael's face was all knotted up, teeth bared like a mutt, sucking quick shallow breaths through his teeth.

"You don't have the guts to do it. You're a coward like the rest of them." His voice remarkably calm. "I know it was you who sold me out to Carver. What was the deal he gave you? Mary Beth?"

"Shut up! You shut up now!" Michael screamed, putting more pressure on the knife so that a cut began to split open above his Adam's apple. Daniel's head pressed down into the pillow.

"You know you're on the wrong side of this thing."

"Bullshit," Michael snapped at him. "It's too late. You killed O'Brien. You killed Mary Beth!"

"Mary Be—"

"Don't you even *say* her name…" Michael leaned forward, more weight behind the knife. Daniel swallowed and his Adam's apple rose against the sharp edge of the blade, a trickle of blood rolling down the side of his throat.

"She killed herself and you damn well know it."

"Because of you! Because of what you did!"

"I did what I had to do because no one else would."

"You crazy son of a bitch. You think your father sees what you do. You think he cares."

"I know he does." Daniel said. "And your father sees you, too."

Just then there was a pounding of hoof beats so close to the tent it sounded like the rider was going to trample their tent and a rifle blasted within a few feet of them. The horse screamed. The rider cried out a curse. Whether it was he or the horse that was shot, you couldn't tell, but it sounded as though the rider had been thrown from the horse and in the chaos, with a surge of strength, Daniel pushed Michael off. But he had already swiped the razor-sharp blade across his throat. Instantly, Daniel was up on his feet, with a shallow wound on his throat that bled badly. They grappled for control of the knife, went down together, hitting the hard dirt, and Daniel landed on top of him.

He had gotten the knife free and had turned it around so the tip was just above Michael's heart. His face had gone all red, the veins bulging and thumping across his forehead.

"Wait, wait, wait…" Michael begged. "Wait."

*

On the edge of the colony, a squad of strikers, many of them clad only in their long underwear and vests and boots, armed with rifles, had flanked the agents on the tracks and were returning heavy fire. "Take cover if you can and lay the lead to them," Samuel shouted. He scrambled across a wide open patch of the field, heard bullets bouncing and spitting up dirt, and joined them, a row of strikers dug in by the Slovaks' tents, behind an old mossy stone fence, barely two feet tall. His fast shallow breathing clouded in the biting cold air. He laid on his back, right up next to Nick Gysegum.

"Anyone got any buckshot?" Samuel shouted over the bedlam.

Gysegum shook his head. Byron Burnside, three bodies down the line, pitched him a couple shells, one at a time, dropping them right in his lap. Samuel plugged them into the shotgun, locked the barrel.

Kelvin Ekvie was on the other side of Gysegum. He craned his neck to look above Gysegum. "Where's Byrnes?"

"Ain't seen him."

"McKeeta?"

Samuel just looked at him and shook his head. "He's dead."

Ekvie rose up, swung his rifle over the stone wall, and fired a single shot. "Damn," he said, wrinkling the corner of his eyes, and then quickly ducking back down. "It's jammed."

A shell casing was stuck in the chamber. No matter how he jerked the bolt, the shell would not eject. Ekvie pulled a jackknife out of his pocket and tried to pry it out, but the blade slipped over the gunmetal, and he winced as he jabbed himself badly in the pad of his other thumb. "Son of a bitch," he muttered. He pulled the hand away and sucked his bleeding thumb.

"Gimme that." Gysegum seized the rifle, sat up a little to get a better grip on the bolt action. Almost instantly, a bullet ricocheted off the stone in front of him and took off a piece of his ear. He shook like he'd been struck by lightning. His hat even spun off his head, and the rifle dropped out of his hands, glancing off a stone, falling on the other side of the wall. Gysegum fell to the ground with his hand cupped to his bleeding ear. Samuel was shouting in his face, asking him if he was all right, but Gysegum just shook his head because both ears were ringing so bad he couldn't hear a word anyone was saying.

Kelvin Ekvie started panicking. "I just need to get back and see Ada," he kept repeating. "She's eight months pregnant and I don't want our baby growing up without a daddy... I don't want our baby growing up without a daddy... she's eight months pregnant... and..." He was starting to get up, when Burnside grabbed him by the collar and yanked him back down behind the wall.

"Are you trying to get your ass shot?" he barked.

But Ekvie would not be shaken out of it. He jumped up again and took off sprinting towards the tents. He hadn't gotten very far when he actually got shot in the ass, hobbled a few steps, and dropped down on one knee. The bullets were kicking up dirt all around him. Burnside took off running towards him, holding his rifle in one hand, holding his hat down with the other. He stooped down, threw Ekvie's arm over his shoulder, and they scrambled for cover, Ekvie crying and Burnside cussing the whole way.

*

Daniel pressed a white handkerchief to his throat to staunch the bleeding as he poked around the tent. His arms were stained blood up to the elbows like a butcher. He hooked his finger in the jug handle of the sheriff's moonshine, raised it up, cradling it from the bottom with his other hand, pulled the cork out with his teeth, and took a long pull. Then he found his vial of strychnine, pulled the stopper and poured the whole vial into the moonshine. Then he pushed the cork back into the jug with his thumb and shook vigorously. The powder disappeared in the clear liquid. He stepped over Michael, the bone-handled knife sticking out of his chest still.

185

Darting out of the tent, a hellish symphony of gunshots deafened him, ricocheting bullets singing out, and the hot flashes of gunfire coruscating in the predawn darkness. He jumped back as a horse and rider surged over the spot where he had just stood, nearly losing the glass jug in the process, but he regained himself and ran. The stink of rising plumes of smoke filled the air. A man carried in his arms the dead body of his little boy, shot in the forehead. Traumatized women who spoke no English shouted at Daniel, flailing their arms, trying to ask which way to go. He pointed toward the woods across the field and beckoned them to leave everything and run for their lives. One of the strikers loped past, his shirtsleeve soaked with crimson blood. More people fled and many were bleeding, others limping, carrying children in their arms. Still others wandered about in confusion, crying the names of missing kin.

By now, an exodus of the wounded and bereaved had begun. They fled across a field of orchard grass towards the hills and woodland. Young girls hanging onto their mother's skirt and boys running alongside them. Ada Ekvie's shoe came off, and as she stooped to put it back on, straining to reach with her swollen belly, a bullet hit her in the wrist. Daniel tucked his revolver in his waist so he had a free hand, yanked her by the other wrist and they were running again. The detectives on the railroad fired at their heels, bullets spitting up clouds of dirt and dust all around them. Spatters of blood in the straw-colored grass. He looked into the eyes of the upturned, tortured faces, cheeks sprayed with blood. A place for weeping and gnashing of teeth. Everywhere in the field lay the mangled masses of gory flesh, wounded strikers on their bellies, dragging themselves along the ground, the heavy dews of blood soaking the grass.

*

After about an hour of heavy shooting, the strikers had all but run out of ammunition, and the concentrated firing coming from the railroad embankment proved insurmountable. The outnumbered strikers abandoned their position at the stone wall and fell back to the tent colony. The agents swarmed after them through the camp, some mounted on horses and others afoot. A miner dropped his rifle and raised his arms and was shot dead. They slashed the canvas tents and shot at point blank range the strikers who were concealed within. Clothes, bedding, jewelry, tools, utensils, and anything that appealed to their fancy were all conveyed away. They were deliberately setting fire to the tents, dousing the canvas with red cans of Standard oil as they passed from one tent to another. Wounded men and women hiding in the woods looked on in awe of the blazing fires, the flames sawing in the cold morning wind. Black columns of smoke slanted across the gray sky. More than half of the colony was already aflame. Soon, the smoke had all but swallowed up and obscured the camp, an evil fog drifting across the Golgothan landscape, a thunder and fury of wild-eyed horses and galloping and dust. A horse trotted out of the smoke with an empty saddle.

The strikers abandoned the camp altogether and came in clusters out of the smoke and fled towards the woods. In the culvert, men were trying to staunch their own bleeding chests, sitting with their backs sloped against the hard clay embankment, others were unconscious in contorted shapes. An old woman was frantically counting the beads on a rosary, her lips moving silently. When he looked out into the field, Daniel couldn't believe his eyes: Samuel emerged running at full tilt across the field with his hands manacled to a Winchester rifle. This man, a stranger, a Union organizer, who had perhaps saved his life, had sprinted a little more than half the distance to the woods when the sheriff's horse came pounding out of the smoke. The sheriff fired one shot at a cluster of strikers. One of them twisted in a nightmarish pirouette and fell dead. Then Daniel saw Samuel running diagonally from him through the field. The sheriff yanked back the reins. The horse skidded. He tugged left and the horse turned on a dime and raced off again. He held the reins in his right hand and his revolver in his left, hunched low, the black horse's muscular neck pumping up and down as he galloped against the infernal sky of dawn, the heavy hoofbeats pounding the dirt.

"Oh my God," Daniel whispered.

He got up off his belly and crouched down on one knee, raising the revolver in his hands, aiming carefully when simultaneously he saw the pink mist and heard the shot. Samuel tumbled forward into the tall grass, screaming, clutching his thigh, blood spilling over his fingers. The sheriff was still racing towards him when Daniel all but unloaded his gun, firing four shots as fast as he could. The black horse screamed and dropped to her knees. The sheriff pitched headlong out of his saddle, rolled, then lay still.

"The sheriff," a wounded miner whispered from the culvert. "Is he dead?"

"I don't know yet."

Daniel lay on his belly, waiting, peering over dirt and rocks. Within the minute, the sheriff got up on his feet with some difficulty and looked around blearily. His left arm dangled limp at his side. He stooped down and found his revolver in the grass, then staggered over to the dying horse. It lay on its side, not moving at all except for its eyes rolling about and its slimy nostrils widening and contracting. The sheriff looked down and spoke to it, then raised the gun and fired one bullet into its skull.

"You come on out now," the sheriff called out in the direction of the woods. "You come on out and end this."

Daniel lay still in the culvert with an arm stretched out before him, his revolver clutched in his trembling hand. He cocked the hammer back with his thumb and shut one eye, drawing a shaky bead on the sheriff's chest, touching his finger to the trigger, feeling the firing mechanisms tighten, thinking about the one and only bullet left, the one shot.

Beside him lay a miner, slumped in the culvert, his shoulder dislocated, a broken collarbone, crushed ribs, and half of his face ripped open. "Do it," the miner whispered hoarsely from the culvert. "Shoot him."

"I can't do it," Daniel said. "Not like this."

The sheriff called out to him. "You think I don't know what you're up to? You think I wasn't always one step ahead of you? I got something I want you to see."

The detectives came through the smoke, dragging Katherine, beaten and bloodied, through the shreds of ripped clothing, blanket, and sack trodden into the ground. They threw her on the ground in front of the sheriff. The detectives smiled at him. All around them lay the mutilated and dying, muttering in a collective delirium. The sheriff snatched her hair and pulled her to her feet. He pulled his bowie knife and held it under her chin.

"You're not getting out of this town alive, kid," the sheriff yelled out towards the woods. "You know where to find me. If you're not there by tonight, I'll snap her pretty little neck."

*

Hours later, the families wandered through the absolute wreckage of their former lives, their tent colony reduced to smoldering cinder and ash, calling out the names of their kin. The whole valley was full of smoke. Wild dogs, mangy and skeletal, gathered at the corpse of a mine-guard, lapping up the blood from his wounds. Men wandered about with glazed eyes, half-hypnotized by the scene. "It's just like the day of judgment I saw as a little boy in Bible histories," Liam O'Loughlin muttered.

An old woman stood crying into her dirty shawl. In a pit dug out beneath one of the tents, she had found a mother dead with all seven of her children. The blackened corpses huddled together, the arms of the mother and eldest daughter still clasped together, the smaller bodies piled atop one another. Soon others were gathering around the old woman. Someone made the sign of the cross, others followed, and O'Loughlin began to pray: "God is our refuge and strength, a very present help in trouble. Therefore will not we fear though the earth be removed, and though the mountains be carried into the midst of the sea."

*

Daniel walked the tracks alone, shivering under a clear star-spattered firmament, his heart heavy with sin, carrying only the purloined jug of the sheriff's moonshine from which he did not drink. As he gazed upward at Orion and Taurus, the sheer enormity of the universe evoked in him a kind of nameless misery, and the moon disappeared behind the clouds. Behind him, over the naked treetops, the fires burned with a feverish glow.

By the time he reached the town, no soul walked the abandoned streets save himself. A scavenging bony dog barked at him and then slunk off down the trash-strewn alleyway. When he came to the brothel, the upper windows were all dark, but he could see a candlelight radiant in the transom window over the door. He rapped his knuckle lightly on the door and then pulled his coat lapels closer and hugged himself, his teeth chattering in the cold. He knocked again and listened. But no one came to the door. He tried the handle. It was unlocked and he let himself in.

Daniel saw Katherine's body on the davenport, a dried rivulet of blood running from her nose, her two knees touching, her long legs spreading out with her left foot turned inward. Slumped back lifelessly. Her two hands lay on either side of her. Dun-colored palms facing up. Her head hung down, chin resting on her chest, the black hair fallen all about her face. He knew she was dead, but he couldn't stop himself from going over to her and saying her name aloud.

Daniel heard the distinct sound of a knife stabbing into wood repeatedly: *thuck, thuck, thuck*. He turned. The sheriff had his hand palm down flat on the bar with his fingers spread wide, stabbing the blade of the bone-handled knife, still stained with Michael's blood, in the gaps between his fingers. "You ever play this game?" he asked. "The fucking hoople-heads play it in here all the time. Always seemed to me like it'd be more fun to use someone else's hand. Besides," he said. "I fucking never miss."

"Why'd you kill her?" Daniel gestured with the blood-soaked handkerchief.

The sheriff stopped his game and examined the blade on his knife. Then he sheathed it on his belt. "Believe me," the sheriff said. "I'm not proud of some of the things I've done." He produced two tumblers from under the bar, holding them up to the lamplight for inspection. He took up a white towel and polished the glass and then set it on the bar. "But no matter what I do I just can't fucking abide a woman's betrayal. Even when she's nothing but a goddamn whore. But she was my whore. And now," the sheriff sighed, "now I need a fucking drink."

He came out from behind the bar carrying the two glasses. He set them down on top of the poker table and sat down. "Come on. Sit down," he said. The sheriff locked eyes with Daniel. He held the bone-knife up, tilted it so the blade flashed in the light. "You know whose knife this is, don't you?"

"Yeah," Daniel said. He sat down at the table. "I do."

"I haven't seen this knife in thirteen years."

"I want it back."

"You shouldn't have left it sticking out of Michael's chest." The sheriff regarded the knife in his hand. "You remember that night? When I killed your old man..."

Daniel watched the sheriff as he sheathed the knife at his hip. "I tried to forget."

"Tried... But that didn't fucking work now, did it?"

"I wouldn't be here if it did."

"If we could forget the things we wanted to forget, what the hell would there be left to remember?"

"Nothing..."

"I'll drink to that." The sheriff tipped his head towards the jug cradled in Daniel's hands.

Daniel passed him the jug. He pulled the cork with his thumb and tilted the jug over the first glass, filling it with the clear moonshine, then the second glass. He pushed Daniel's glass forward and raised his in a toast. "After you," the sheriff said.

Daniel took up his glass of moonshine in his hands, held it up so that he could see it in the lamplight briefly, then tossed it back and swallowed it down. He winced with the burn. The sheriff grinned and then drank. "You're starting to look like me." He drew his finger across the scar at his neck. "Looks good on you."

"You should see the other guy," Daniel said.

The sheriff laughed heartily. He looked at the empty glass in his hand. "You know, I used to hit the bottle pretty hard," he said. "Just another thing we got in common. I tended to—how should I put this?—overreact in my drinking days."

"It's the devil's own," Daniel said.

"Yes," the sheriff said. "It certainly is."

"But that's no excuse," Daniel said, "for what you did."

"No," the sheriff said. "Nor did I say it was." The sheriff poured another round for them and they drank. "So where do we stand?"

"I'm killing you."

The sheriff smiled. "You are now?"

"It's as good as done."

"If you were going to do it," the sheriff said, "you would've done it." The sheriff poured himself two fingers of moonshine and then he reached forward, taking Daniel's glass. He poured slowly. "No," he said as he filled the glass. "You're overplaying your hand, kid. You forget you're dealing with an old pro."

"Your luck's bound to run out somewhere."

He slid Daniel's glass forward to the center of the table. "Is that so?"

Daniel just stared at him levelly.

"Drink up," he said. "And then we'll see."

"You ever get the feeling God hates you?" Daniel asked.

"I get the feeling God hates us all."

"Do you hate me?"

"I don't hate you. I'm just disappointed."

"Disappointed in what way?"

"Because I thought you had heart. I wanted you to come at me out there today. I wanted you to try to cut me up as bad as I wanted to cut you up. But now I see what you really are and what you've always been. You're nothing. You're nothing but another little cow-eyed fucking kid. And you ain't getting out of here alive."

Daniel drank down the moonshine. "I never expected to."

The sheriff smiled and sank back in his chair and dropped his arm under the table. "But I will say this: a part of me just couldn't help liking you, kid. I don't know why but I do."

Daniel pushed his empty glass towards the jug. The sheriff's fist sprang up from under the table clutching the bone-handled knife, and as fast as a striking serpent, he stabbed Daniel's left hand. Then the sheriff let go of the knife handle, leaving it so that it pinned Daniel's hand to the tabletop. Daniel cried out. His chair toppled over behind him and he swallowed his urge to scream more, sucking air through his teeth, his bloody fingers writhing on the green felt. The sheriff lifted his glass of moonshine and watched him coldly and he drank. "You see," he said. "This is why I ought to quit drinking."

Daniel's face was red, his lips writhing. He screamed with hot tears in his eyes.

"Life's all about seeing how much pain you can take." The sheriff lifted his glass and drank. "Just take the fucking pain to the grave."

Daniel clenched his teeth and he tried gripping the knife handle. The sheriff took his Schofield out of his holster and held it by the barrel like a hammer. With his left hand he wrenched Daniel's right hand away from the knife and slammed it palm down on the tabletop.

"Didn't I tell you to take it?"

The sheriff brought the butt end of the heavy revolver down on the back of Daniel's right hand. Daniel sang out, his face contorted in a rictus of agony. The sheriff's face clouded and he hammered the revolver down again. The blows crippling Daniel's hand.

"You think you can just come into my fucking joint? And take my money from my fucking whore?" The sheriff pounded the revolver down again on his hand. "Huh?" He slammed the revolver down again and Daniel was out of his mind with pain. "Open your eyes and look at her. Look what you made me do to her. Do you see how I broke her neck? I'm gonna put your fucking head in your lap just like that."

Then the sheriff let go of Daniel's wrist and he eased himself back into his chair. Daniel fell to his knees, his left arm outstretched, his hand still pinned to the tabletop. The sheriff poured himself another drink. He watched Daniel kneeling down on one knee, his right hand quivering, the green felt stained dark burgundy. He tilted his glass back and leaned forward and spat a spraying mouthful of moonshine over the wounded hand. Then he sat back and drew the back of his hand across his mouth.

"Your cocksucker friend, McKeeta… you know he sold you out, don't you? Told me about your little plan with the whore. Reptile though he may be, he was smart enough to know this strike wouldn't amount to anything. So he came to me… With friends like that, am I right kid?"

Daniel's head dropped in despair. He let out a little moan.

"But now I'll tell you something you don't know," he went on. "The world's a terrible fucking place for a man to be without an enemy. He'd have no one to blame but himself. I mean, without me, what the fuck would you do? Who would you blame…? To be honest, kid, I applaud you for not putting a bullet in your own skull. First time I saw you, I said to myself: now there's a suicide if I ever saw one."

The sheriff reached out and gripped the bone-handle and wrenched the knife up out of the tabletop. The steel painted red and dripping dark gouts of blood. Daniel fell to the floor quivering in pain, his face drained and pale, holding up the bloody hand in shock, an oozing slit in the center of his palm. He rolled on his belly and began to drag himself across the floor, away from the sheriff, a demented monkey-crawl on his elbows, slowly pushing himself along with his legs. The sheriff's chair scraped against the floorboards when he stood up wielding the bloody knife. He walked a few paces behind Daniel, grinning with delight.

"It's judgment day, kid. And you can't imagine the fucking restraint I've had to demonstrate." The sheriff stomped on Daniel's bleeding hand and twisted his boot heel and then knelt and raised the knife and brought it down, stabbing him in the back between the ribs, piercing his left lung. He left the bone-handle protruding out of his back. Then he stood up and walked away.

Daniel lay on the floor bleeding and coughing and struggling to breathe. The sheriff went over to the jug and filled his glass. Then with a triumphant smirk, he took the cigar out of his shirt pocket and bit the end. He struck a match and rolled the cigar atop the flame. "Who the fuck did you think you were up against?" he asked.

Daniel shifted his waist this way and that as he inched along the floor, leaving a trail of blood, slowly crawling closer to the davenport, the knife sticking out his back. He was at Katherine's limp white feet, and with his broken hand he reached up and clutched her dress.

"You're just making a fool of yourself, son," the sheriff said.

Daniel tugged the dress again and the body slid down and dropped to the floor, half slumped on top of Daniel. Her Derringer dropped out of her dress and fell on the floor. He fumbled under her for a moment and was reaching for the chrome pistol, his arm outstretched when the sheriff came walking over and stepped on his hand and twisted his heel. Daniel cried out again and the sheriff eased off. Then suddenly the sheriff reeled back a step, regained himself, his eyes widening.

The cigar fell out of his mouth.

He leaned forward and spat. His face had gone pale. Daniel watched the poisoned moonshine working, smiling dementedly with his face flecked with blood. Yet he felt the same poison working in his own veins.

"You were right," Daniel said with difficulty. "I am a suicide."

The sheriff staggered a step to the side and reached out to steady himself on a chair, but his hand sliced through the air. He drew his revolver and tried aiming it at Daniel, but his hand was unsteady. He shot a hole in the vermillion Davenport cushion and a white tuft of cotton spat out. Then the Schofield slipped out of his hand and hit the floor with a heavy thud. He staggered one, two steps, and then collapsed onto one of the tabletops and slid off it and slumped to the floor.

Daniel sat looking at the sheriff's body laid out flat on his back. Wincing and gritting his teeth, with strength of sheer desperate will, he managed to stand up, holding himself steady with one hand on the armrest of the davenport. He stooped forward and felt the knife handle in his back. He stumbled over to the table, fighting for every inch, determined to endure his suffering beyond all conceivable limits. He clutched the poisoned jug about the neck and carried it over to the sheriff who was still alive, if only barely. His eyes moved about and he was making small puffs with his lips. Daniel knelt beside him. He grabbed him by the jaw and forced his mouth open and he poured the contents of the jug on his face and down his throat.

"Look at me..."

The sheriff gagged and a convulsion swept through his body and he went still. His drowsy ice-blue eyes glazed over. Daniel threw the empty jug across the floor.

After a long time, he managed to stand up. He was coughing up blood. He held himself against the bar and spat. Then he managed a few more staggering steps before he slipped and fell in his own blood. He pulled himself up on a chair and sat sideways in it. He was lightheaded and confused. His eyes were fixed on the door and then he looked back at the sheriff's body on the floor. All he wanted now was to go out into the night to meet the stars once more.

He was barely conscious when Logan O'Brien came quietly through the front door dressed all in black. He held a revolver in his hand. Daniel saw him in the corner of his eye and he looked up, a hint of a smile at his mouth-corners.

"Like a fucking rat," Daniel muttered.

Logan raised the pistol and fired one shot, a small pop echoing in the dark river valley. Daniel's head jerked to the side. He saw the white-hot flash of God as a wine-dark mist spat out the side of his skull. He fell out of the chair and lay on the floor. Logan held the pistol trained on the body. Face down. A leg jerking. Soon, the wind stirred and the open front door of the brothel swung gently on its hinges, the doorknob tapping against the wall boards. Murky clouds drifted across the night sky and cold spits of rain began to fall, the light sprinkle releasing the earthy smell of the street.

Logan tucked the revolver in his belt, walked down the steps and looked back inside. He had the sheriff's badge in his hand. The door was still open, but he turned away and fled down the abandoned street, his footfalls clapping farther and farther off in the distance until there was only silence.

Epilogue

The old gravedigger chose a plot close to the river, beneath the shade of a tall scarlet oak. He hacked at the hard earth in the spits of cold rain. The edge of the rusty spade struck sparks from the sandstone as the gray wash of sky darkened over a land saturated with bruise-colored shadow. The miners would be coming to bury him tomorrow. The gravedigger's skinny, towhead apprentice sat on the edge of the open grave with a wide grin, his boots dangling over. He leaned forward, as if about to utter a secret.

"It's for the kid who killed Jack Carver, isn't it?"

"You always want to know who it's for."

"They say he only slept an hour each night. They say he talked to ghosts..."

"Did they tell you I'll be digging one of these holes for you next?"

"I heard he could throw a knife straight into your heart from thirty yards away."

"And his piss flowed uphill, didn't it?"

"The sheriff shot him full of holes and he just kept coming. He wouldn't die."

"Well, he's dead now, isn't he?"

Neither of them had noticed the dark brown horse and rider crossing the dead land in the distance. There was an uneasy silence between them as he approached. The old gravedigger steadied himself on his spade and straightened his back. The horse snorted. The rider's eyes peered out from under the broad brim of his hat. A glint from the star on his breast. He leaned in his saddle and spat.

"Whose grave is this?"

The apprentice was about to speak but the old gravedigger cut him off: "A corpse's..."

The rider's leather gloves crinkled as he gripped the reins tighter. "Why don't you give me a straight answer."

"You want a name?"

"What else?"

"I never ask for their names."

"It's for the kid who killed Jack Carver," the apprentice chirped. "Daniel Byrnes. That's who it's for."

"Well, he's dead all right," the rider agreed. He leaned and spat tobacco juice into the grave. He looked across the landscape, then back at the gravedigger. "He passed in considerable pain."

"How do you know?" the towhead asked.

"Because I was there." The rider raked his heels and the horse began to walk. "He sure as hell doesn't deserve a damn Christian burial."

"None of us do," the gravedigger said as he resumed digging.

*

The strike dragged on into May. But a few days after the battle, the governor declared martial law and dispatched the State Militia to the Monongahela valley. The cavalry and infantry set up a base camp outside of town along the railroad tracks. They would control Washington County for the next two months. The gun fighting diminished between the strikers and detectives. Uneasy young men in frayed and ragtag uniforms patrolled the streets and indulged newly discovered appetites for cruelty. But the rumors of a contract were everywhere. In a fog of hearsay, hushed in gatherings around campfires, whispered in huddles around midnight tavern tables, people were hearing that the company was ready to sit down and negotiate.

The night before the company finally agreed to sit down and negotiate a contract, a semi-conscious striker was found castrated on the railroad tracks, a final farewell, courtesy of the Baldwin-Felts detectives before they left town. The miners were discussing measures in the way of retribution against the company. A hot-blooded plan to bring down the tipple with black powder kegs was laid out before the huddled mass of sopping wet strikers in Beazell's barn. Afterwards, Samuel took the floor and pleaded for forbearance. It was during the hardest rain anyone had ever heard. Lopsided and steadying himself on a gnarled cane, the gunshot wound on his thigh still bandaged and seeping pus, he could hardly be heard over the pellets of rain pounding the tin roof. He was worn-out and feverish. His voice, which had lost its commanding presence, was hardly more than a whisper now. The insomniac survivors with their cauterized bullet wounds and amateur bone settings hushed one another so that Samuel could be heard.

"It's taken a lot of blood to get the company to sit down and negotiate. We've been fighting for a contract. We've bled for a contract. And I've been all around the blood. I've seen enough damn blood for one lifetime. I've seen enough damn suffering. I've seen men dying at my feet for a contract. All this suffering, all these men and women and children died for a contract. Daniel Byrnes died for a contract. If it wasn't for him, I don't think we'd have anything to talk about tonight. Because the Union was like a ghost in Elsinore until he made it real enough that the company had to take us seriously. We ought to do right by him. See, our dead are just dead to the company. They're easily replaced. The company would be more upset over a dead mule than a dead striker. But our dead are not dead to us. They'll haunt us. They'll haunt us every day and every night. It's for them that we have to hold our peace tonight. They wouldn't forgive us if we didn't."

The cold and miserable rain did not stop or slow for days. During the storm, a pregnant cow roamed into the inundated streets of Monongahela where she birthed a deformed calf with no eyes. There were other unnatural occurrences. The day the Union contract was signed, the strikers butchered a hog that had no heart. Later, a number of the cavalry's horses went wild in the steady downpour and kicked at their gates until the gates broke open or the horse was hobbled and had to be shot. Stray dogs snarled and barked at nothing and ran directly into brick walls in pursuit of the nothing that they saw. And all throughout the valley, there were sightings of a strange winged creature roaming the county. It had first been seen moving through the charred remains of the tent colony at midnight, moving through the shadows like an angel, always glimpsed from a great distance but estimated to stand seven feet tall. Those who saw it were afflicted with migraines and burning bloodshot eyes for days afterwards.

200

It rained on, until the ground couldn't absorb any more water. In the evening, the sky began to glow a biblically fearsome green. It had begun. It was irrevocable. The old Van Voohris dam holding Amleth Lake above the camp failed. A wall of water rushed into the valley. Houses were knocked off their foundations; they crumpled as if squeezed by some great and invisible vengeful fist. Telegraph poles snapped. Displaced families spent the night in the trees, clinging to the branches while the black water gushed inches below their feet. Ada Ekvie's water broke during the storm as she hugged the trunk of sugar maple. Kelvin heaved her up to the highest branches that would hold her, and he clambered down so close to the floodwaters that they were splashing his knees and his boots were submerged. A breech birth prolonged her labor and the baby came out with the umbilical cord coiled around her chubby neck like a noose. She turned bluish purple and wasn't breathing. Kelvin held her upside-down by her fat ankles, slapping her behind, with Ada standing above him in the tree limbs looking down, asking what was wrong, and then in the howling storm the newborn began to wawl and cry.

By early morning, the destruction was done. The murky skies cleared for a new day. When the waters receded enough, Kelvin climbed down and reconnoitered the grim landscape. He found that the river had swelled over its banks and carved its way through the cemetery, where the raging currents unearthed caskets of the recently deceased and the long dead, devoured headstones, swept away mausoleums, and toppled the old stone archway, carrying the remains miles downstream towards Pittsburgh in a great undulating wall of black debris and frothy water. The flood left in its wake a world of rubble and mud. The dead were ubiquitous. For days, the bloated corpses and fragmented skeletons would be found in strange places. They found bodies with no heads. Broken caskets spilled putrid grave wax. By the time the strikers returned to the company houses, they found headstones in their flooded cellars. Byron Burnside had a leg on his roof. Rosa Gysegum found a jawbone on her kitchen floor. Down by the Church of Christ, a yellow ribcage dangled from a low-hanging limb like a gutted hornet's nest. Grime-streaked children pranced through the shards and ruins flaunting a human skull with gold teeth. But the body of Daniel Byrnes was never found.

Acknowledgements

To learn more about the miners' way of life at the turn of the century, I researched a number of primary and secondary sources. *From the Furrows to the Pits: Van Voohris, PA*, by Charles Gersna, was the book, given to me by my father, which initially inspired this novel. That led to an interview with a retired coal miner and Van Voohris resident, Joseph Zelinski, followed by several trips to the Carnegie Library's Pennsylvania Department. Other crucial sources included David Alan Corbin's books, *Life, Work, and Rebellion in the Coal Fields: The Southern West Virginia Miners, 1880-1922* and *Gun Thugs, Rednecks, and Radicals: A Documentary History of the West Virginia Mine Wars;* Robert Shogan's *The Battle of Blair Mountain: The Story of America's Largest Labor Uprising*; and Barry P. Minchrina's *Pennsylvania Mining Families: The Search for Dignity in the Coal Fields*.

Additionally, I owe a great deal of gratitude to my wonderful family for their continued support over the five years I spent writing this book. I would also like to thank Ellie Wymard, Michelle Stoner, James Heaney, and my faculty mentors, Niall Williams, Jane Candia Coleman, Carlo Gébler, and Joseph Bathanti, for their insight, patience, and guidance at Carlow University. Thanks to Lynne Barrett for teaching me about plot and Joe Clifford for the help, inspiration, and guidance over the years. I am especially grateful to Danielle Koupf for her many careful readings of this book. Finally, thank you to everyone else who read sections of my manuscript and helped me along the way.

Notes

pp.10-11: Byrnes's speech to the miners was strongly influenced by the rhetoric of Mother Jones, a famous union organizer. To learn about her life and work, I read Elliott J. Gorn's *Mother Jones: The Most Dangerous Woman in America*.

p. 12: A line of dialogue spoke by the sheriff was adapted from the words of George F. Baer, President of the Philadelphia & Reading Railroad, who famously said to the Anthracite Coal Commission in February 1903: "These men don't suffer. Why, hell, half of them don't even speak English."

p. 168: The excerpt read by Daniel here is inspired by the "Steel Workers' Declaration of Independence," written by Pittsburgh union organizer, Tom Shane in 1936 for the United Steelworkers of America.

pp. 181-182: The sheriff's closing remarks in his letter are influenced by, once again, George F. Baer, who in 1902 wrote: "The rights and interests of the laboring man will be protected and cared for -- not by the labor agitators, but by the Christian men of property to whom God has given control of the property rights of the country, and upon the successful management of which so much depends."

pp. 209-210: The Reverend's sermon to the strikers in this chapter was inspired by historical accounts of Union preachers in David Alan Corbin's *Life, Work, and Rebellion in the Coal Fields: The Southern West Virginia Miners, 1880-1922*.

About the Author

Robert Lee Bailey's writing and photography has appeared in numerous literary journals and online magazines. He received his B.A. in English Writing at the University of Pittsburgh and his MFA at Carlow University. He lives in Pittsburgh, Pennsylvania.

www.ingramcontent.com/pod-product-compliance
Lightning Source LLC
Chambersburg PA
CBHW022149240626
47153CB00007B/2574